ALSO BY T. M. GOEGLEIN:

Cold Fury

Flicker & Burn

T. M. GOEGLEIN

G. P. Putnam's Sons

An Imprint of Penguin Group (USA)

G. P. PUTNAM'S SONS

Published by the Penguin Group
Penguin Group (USA) LLC
375 Hudson Street
New York, NY 10014

USA | Canada | UK | Ireland | Australia
New Zealand | India | South Africa | China
penguin.com
A Penguin Random House Company

Library of Congress Cataloging-in-Publication Data
Goeglein, T. M. (Ted M.)
Embers & ash: a Cold fury novel / T. M. Goeglein.
pages cm
Summary: "Sara Jane Rispoli is on the wrong side of the Russian mob, but closer to
finding her family than ever. And she's willing to do whatever it takes to rescue them—
even if the price is her own life"—Provided by publisher.
[1. Secret societies—Fiction. 2. Missing persons—Fiction. 3. Organized crime—Fiction.
4. Violence—Fiction. 5. Chicago (Ill.)—Fiction. 6. Mystery and detective stories.].
Title. II. Title: Embers and ash.   PZ7.G5533Emb 2014   [Fic]—dc23   2013042498

Printed in the United States of America.
ISBN 978-0-399-25722-3
1 3 5 7 9 10 8 6 4 2

Design by Marikka Tamura.
Text set in Calisto MT Std.

For V.K.S., master storyteller

PROLOGUE

MY NAME IS SARA JANE RISPOLI.

I'm a sixteen-year-old girl—no, woman—which is an age that doesn't reflect how I've lived my life during the past six months.

Disappearance. Bloodshed. Lies upon lies, built like fancy layered pastries.

Terror and isolation stalk me, and violence has become a tool of survival. It helps me stay alive as I fight to locate ultimate power, hidden beneath the mysterious Troika of Outfit Influence.

I've done terrible things trying to discover that hidden place.

My worst sin has been serving as counselor-at-large for the Chicago criminal organization, the Outfit. It's my job to decide how members who break its rules are punished. There are bodies buried in landfills, sunk beneath Lake Michigan, and scattered elsewhere in charred bits and pieces that have me to thank for their deaths.

If it weren't for the Outfit, my life would be what? *Normal?*

I don't know what that word means anymore. Normal is a fantasy that belongs to some other girl.

My birthday came and went without notice.

There was no cake or ice cream. Instead, I received the gift of a tattered old notebook bursting with Outfit secrets that I use on my enemies like a flamethrower.

I also discovered cold fury, burning inside me.

It grows colder and more furious the longer this nightmare continues.

My hope is that someday soon, I'll lock eyes with the people responsible for my family's disappearance. When that happens, they will cower and beg for mercy, seeing and feeling their own worst fear.

Me.

1

THE SKY ROARED AND FLASHED AS A VIOLENT
thunderstorm clustered over Chicago.

By late afternoon, dense clouds made it as dark as midnight. Rain fell like bullets as muddy ponds rose up, engulfing
avenues, and electrical lines came down, blacking out neighborhoods. It had been an agonizing month to the day since
someone disguised as one of Juan Kone's ice cream creatures—those poor, addicted teens—disappeared into the void
with my family.

An ominous Saturday if ever there was one.

I'd just finished presiding over a sit-down and was rushing
to my hideout, the Bird Cage Club, when Doug Stuffins, my
best friend, sent me an urgent text message:

> SJ—Get back here on the double! Major break-
> through in ToOl!

He didn't have to tell me to hurry. Those four little letters did the trick. They stood for Troika of Outfit Influence (I still didn't know if it was an object or a location), beneath which ultimate power was buried. It, too, was a mystery; the notebook spoke of ultimate power and provided a key to its vault, but did not reveal what it was.

I believed in it because there was nothing else to believe in.

Ironically, a mortal enemy strengthened my faith in the existence of ultimate power and its ability to help save my family. Elzy, my former nanny and recent assailant who'd vanished, had been crazed to get the notebook from me; she was certain that a secret existed among those old pages—a secret so strong that it could conquer the Outfit.

I hoped she was right.

I hoped so hard that I stopped paying attention and drove into a trap.

In the street ahead, a fallen electrical line jumped like a cobra on fire, spitting sparks. A skinny ComEd guy in a reflective vest and helmet used a flashlight to divert traffic around it, sending me down a flooded backstreet. I obeyed, driving slowly as water seeped beneath the doors of my car. Between slapping windshield wipers, I peered at a larger, burly ComEd guy waving me to a halt. The utility van sat with its orange siren twirling in the storm. It seemed so real that I stopped, just as instructed, sitting like a complacent fool until I saw his goggles.

They were just like those worn by the other men who'd been chasing me for the past week—actually, less chasing than tracking, as if I were a deer in the woods rather than a girl in a 1965 Lincoln Continental.

My latest pursuers were invisible until the last second, sneaking up in the rolling camouflage of the city—garbage trucks, taxicabs, and other vehicles that blended in unnoticed—until I realized how fast they were approaching. I'd escaped each previous time because I'd been hyperalert, as usual, and driving really, really fast. But now I'd been distracted by Doug's text and found myself sitting stupidly, motionlessly, staring at the burly guy.

If the goggles were meant to block cold fury, they were a weak defense.

Then I saw a claw-head hammer in his hand.

He swung once, shattering the driver's window into jagged bits.

I leaped for the passenger side but the other ComEd guy, the skinny one in the reflective vest, was jerking at the door, battering the window with the flashlight. He wore the same goggles above a gaunt face decorated with a dark goatee.

I pushed into the back of the Lincoln, scrabbling at the seats, pulling them down, and rolling inside the trunk. The old car is more than just a vehicle—it's a V8-charged weapon equipped for bad situations, stocked with water, a tire iron, disposable phones, a baseball bat, and the steel briefcase holding the .45. I knew then that the power line hadn't fallen—it had been pulled down to stop me. I grasped for the briefcase, desperate for the gun inside, and cursed myself, remembering it had no bullets. I'd taken Doug to a deserted warehouse to teach him to shoot correctly, and hadn't refilled the clip.

And then my assailants were splashing toward the back of the car.

I heard them muttering, making a plan under the pelting rain.

There was nothing to do but fight.

I grabbed the baseball bat, held tight, and kicked open the trunk top.

It hit something hard—the face of the skinny guy—there was a grunt, and he fell, and then the hammer barreled toward my face.

I held the bat wide, a hand at each end, catching the powerful blow as a metal claw splintered wood. The burly guy reared back for another shot but I dodged it, swinging awkwardly, missing him but knocking the hammer from his grip. He reacted quickly, grabbing the bat. I held on to it and he pulled so hard that I flew from the car. Now he had the bat while I went headfirst into cold water, scrambling away as he crushed the spot where I'd lain seconds before.

The skinny guy with the goatee was on his back, groaning, and I was on my feet, running, when the burly one grabbed my collar and flung me toward the Lincoln.

Spinning like a top, I hit the bumper and fell to my knees, hearing the burly guy sloshing toward me. I plunged a hand inside the open trunk, fingers grazing metal, and yanked out the tire iron. With jelly for legs, I gripped the weapon and turned toward the big man, who grinned. "You're going to lose, girl," he said, sounding like, *Yoord goink to loose, girdle,* his voice riddled with a thick accent.

"Maybe," I said, "but when you see your face in the morning, I guarantee you won't feel like a winner."

He smiled again, lifted the bat, and swung. It was like an opponent in a boxing ring throwing a huge roundhouse right, except that it was a thirty-two-ounce Louisville Slugger instead of a fist. I went low, hearing it whoosh above my head, and came up behind him. He turned and alarm flashed in his eyes as I swung the tire iron. Lightning cut the sky like an electric whip and I saw it clearly—the ComEd helmet circling through the air, the guy pirouetting like a three-hundred-pound ballerina, and his skull. I don't mean his own, which was bald, and bleeding where I'd hit him, but a smaller one, with evil eyes, tattooed on his forehead. There was time for one thought as thunder boomed like a cannon—*What kind of freak tattoos a skull on his own head?!*—before I broke and ran, going headfirst into water again with Goatee holding my ankle. I brought the tire iron down and heard fingers crunch like dry twigs, the guy making kicked-dog noises as I waded down the alley. Soaked strands of hair covered my face like overcooked spaghetti and I spit rain, pushing past downspouts that were puking liquid gunk. It was like fleeing through quicksand, and I heard shouting and the whining of an engine.

I looked behind me.

The van's emergency light made orange ripples in puddles as the vehicle cut through the deluge and halted a few feet away. Skull Head climbed from behind the wheel and slung the bat over a shoulder like a caveman hunting meat. Goatee got out of the other seat and angled around me, pointing a gun with his unbroken hand, until I was surrounded.

His words were plain and cold; he was saying, "It ends now," sounding like, *Eet ainds now-uh*. I nodded slowly, dropped the tire iron, and raised my hands, signaling surrender, and then rushed him, tucking and rolling like a gymnast as he fired over me. A double *boom!* was followed by the *chik!* of a bullet biting brick and the meatier *thook!* of another piercing Skull Head's skull. He huffed once and toppled into a puddle, dead in a second. The shock of it froze Goatee until he turned his jaw into the freight train of my left hook and went down hard, the gun skidding away. I jammed a knee into his chest, pulled his face toward mine, and saw that I'd been mistaken—a goatee didn't occupy his chin. Instead, it was a dark, angular tattoo of a devil's leering face.

I blinked once, cold fury flickered and burned, and I grabbed his gaze, trying to find the mental swamp where his deepest fear lived, but—

"My own brother . . . I kill him . . . it's your fault . . . ," Goatee mumbled.

—I couldn't locate a single image, not one looping film clip; his mind was shut off to me. Vibrating heart to bone, I said, "Who the hell are you?! What do you want?!"

Goatee spit, smiled with bloody teeth, and said, "*Eh, fug you, stupid girl!*"

It had to be the goggles—they were blocking cold fury somehow—and I ripped them from his head and jammed them into my pocket. "Look at me," I said. He squeezed his eyelids, but I pried them open with my thumbs and grabbed his gaze until he was unable to look away. He whimpered once, and I saw him cowering inside a prison cell, surrounded by men tattooed with crude images of stars and skulls, barbed wire, bears, and crosses. The mob converged, holding him down so he couldn't move. One of them slapped masking tape over his mouth, sealing the screams inside his throat, while another lifted a rusty needle dripping with ink over his chin, saying, "Присоединитесь к нам или медленно умирать . . ."

I couldn't understand the language, but its rhythm—and Goatee's horror—was disturbingly familiar. Not long ago, for research, Doug made me watch a foreign movie with subtitles called *Brother*, about a young guy drawn into the gangster life, and how his rivals wanted to murder him. I learned how members were recruited in jail, sometimes against their will, and tattooed to identify their gang affiliation and rank.

For two hours, I'd listened to criminals speak the same language, and I shuddered, realizing what it was.

At that moment, the Outfit was embroiled in a street war with the Russian mob.

They were highly organized interlopers who had clawed away at the Outfit's core businesses of drugs, prostitution, gambling, and hijacking. The Boss of Bosses, Lucky, had finally had enough and declared war. The conflict was bloody, from knee-cracking to car bombings, shotgun ambushes to plain old knives dragged across a neck. The violence was bad enough, but even worse, the war was expensive. Spending time fighting meant business suffered and profits plummeted. It made perfect sense that my pursuers were trying to catch me.

Preoccupied with losing my family, I hadn't considered what a juicy hostage target I was as counselor-at-large. What I didn't know, what no one in the Outfit knew, was who was issuing orders on the Russian side. Their boss remained hidden in the shadows. The identity of their boss was invaluable information, and knowing it would make my always tenuous position with the Outfit more secure.

I looked at Goatee and said, "You belong to the Russian mob . . ."

Quivering, he said, "Mob? You mean *Mafyia*," and nodded.

"Who is your boss? The one in charge? What's his name?"

Tears and raindrops cut lines into his filthy face. "Please, please . . . ," he said, sounding like *plis, plis*. "Let me look away . . ."

"Tell me!"

"I don't know! I swear! I'm *soldier!* Only officers know boss . . . the ones with stars, *here!*" he said, pointing a shaky finger at his knuckles. "They say, bring girl, we pay *this* much! Bring girl *and* old notebook, we pay *more!*"

"Notebook?" I said, the word an icy needle to my spine. Besides Doug and me, the only other living person who knew about it was—"Oh god," I said quietly. "Elzy."

She'd once commandeered the Chicago Police Department to try to capture me. Was it possible—had she done the same with the Russian mob?

"That name, Elzy—you know it?" I said, boring my gaze into Goatee's like a blue diamond drill. He shook his head, drained of all emotion except terror. "What else did the officers tell you? What else have you heard?"

He tried not to answer, tried to squeeze his mouth shut, but it was impossible, and he said, "When they have notebook, no more need for family . . . please . . . no more . . ."

Family—it stung my ears as a charged current burrowed through my body, searching for an outlet. Goatee was struggling to look away. With my thumb and forefinger on his chin, I squeezed his face firmly in place. "Your *Mafyia* has them," I said, twitching with voltage, trying and failing to hold it in check.

"I don't *know!* I only *hear!*"

"You're lying!" I said. "Tell me *now!*" An electrical dam burst, flooding my fingertips, setting fire to the devil head on his chin. His body kicked and buckled, and I didn't want to kill him—*I didn't!*—but I'd lost all control. The bottom of his face was eaten by flame, and then his entire head, and then my fingers were ablaze. I fumbled away, shoving my hand into rainwater, hearing it sizzle as that same torturous electricity attacked my heart. I lay on the alley floor clutching my chest, gasping for air, sensing death creep through the storm; my eyelids fluttering, I was just on the other side of consciousness and the deadly specter looked and felt like Elzy.

She'd come back. No—she'd never left.

After finding my body, it would be simple for her to track down the Bird Cage Club and the notebook. The phone in my pocket with all its text messages between me and Doug, all its telling information. And then no more need for my family, and—

—inch by inch, pain receded like a slow tide.

Cool droplets of rain covered my eyelids and cheeks.

11

I was able to breathe, and rose weakly to my feet, shuddering with knowledge. Elzy had lost Poor Kevin. She'd disappeared from the Chicago Police Department.

But she'd gained control of the Russian mob.

2

I HURRIED PAST THE UTILITY VAN, ITS ORANGE light still spinning, got into the car, and made waves through the flooded streets. Ten blocks away, I pulled to the curb and cut the engine. The downpour thumped the top of the Lincoln like tiny hammers. I'd taken a last glance at Goatee, incinerated from the neck up. Skull Head was a pile of rain-soaked flesh, lying in a puddle, staring at eternity.

Two fresh deaths, one I caused, the other I committed.

You weren't born to kill, I thought, looking into my own eyes in the rearview mirror. *You do it to protect yourself. If you die, no one will save your family.*

The car was silent except for the rain outside.

Doesn't make it right, I thought, looking away from myself.

Throughout the past six months, I'd learned a hard, indelible lesson. The unspeakable acts I'd committed—the things I was forced to do, and chose to do—erased parts of who I was. My senses of sympathy and compassion were waning. Worst of all, human life had begun to seem expendable. I felt like a building whose original bricks were being removed from the foundation, one by one.

Those spaces couldn't remain empty. No one is immune to her own experiences.

My survival habits had become less conscious and more instinctive—more an ingrained part of who I was. The original Sara Jane felt like a childhood friend who'd moved to another place, never to return.

Did I even remember who she'd been?

It was if I'd taken a step away from the old me, and then another, and when I looked back she was opaque, difficult to bring into focus. But then, when I really thought about her, a singular trait she'd possessed rose to the top and surprised me—hopefulness. Despite a lack of friends and the insularity of my life, I'd once thought that every new day came with its own happy possibilities. But since my family was kidnapped, almost from the moment I became counselor-at-large, that belief—that illusion—had been torn away piece by piece. Belonging to the Outfit was as much of a balancing act on the edge of a knife as a self-imposed life sentence in prison. There was no escape. The organization needed a Rispoli as counselor and so it owned them, generation after generation.

It owned me.

My belief in a joyful future had disappeared with the old Sara Jane.

My concern now was who I'd be when this ordeal ended, however it ended.

I had once resisted going down the road before me—the one leading deeper into the Outfit, toward increased violence as I sought my family—but now I was in its ruts, part of the flow, and turning around was no longer an option.

What I wanted more than anything was to stop before I went too far.

When I was younger and broke a rule, or got too angry at my little brother, my dad would warn me that there was always a line that shouldn't be crossed. I'd never again be who I used to be, but if I could stop before crossing that line, maybe I could save a part of myself. I clung to the thought like a life raft in a raging sea.

I'd talked to Doug about those feelings, of course.

I discussed everything with my friend, who had a talent for drawing me back from the edge of emotional cliffs.

Your life is dangerous and unfair, he'd said recently, *but you can't waste one second being a victim. Stay in the moment, and do what's necessary to save your family.*

For half a year, I've been terrified that the boss of the Outfit, Lucky, would discover my excuse for their absence—that my dad is gravely ill—is a lie.

I could have admitted they'd been kidnapped, but for so long I didn't know who'd taken them or why; I had no proof it had even happened other than our ravaged home. It was more than likely the suspicious old man would've assumed that my dad had faked his disappearance, gone to the Feds, and was in the process of betraying the Outfit. In that case, my life would have been worth little. The organization would not tolerate a rat, or even the daughter of one, in its midst.

I glanced at my phone, seeing that half an hour had passed since Doug had sent the text urging me to hurry back to the

Bird Cage Club. He'd worry if I didn't reply soon, so I tapped out a message that I was safe and on my way. And then, phone in hand, I was overcome by an urge to talk to someone else.

What would I say to him?

Maybe that my odd behavior had been caused by family issues. Or that the half-truths and outright lies I'd told were due to circumstances beyond my control.

Those explanations were too weak, far too lame.

I owed him more.

I owed him the truth—about my family, and about me, as counselor-at-large.

Somewhere nearby, a siren screamed and died. The quiet phone glowed in the cloudy darkness. If I paused I wouldn't call. My fingers moved over the keypad and I waited—one ring, two rings—until Max said, "Hello?"

The boy I loved, greeting me from sunny California.

Hearing his voice, I touched a brass key inscribed with *U.N.B. 001* that hung at my neck. Max rode a cool old Triumph motorcycle and had given me a *T* pendant, which I'd once worn in place of the key, sort of like a steady ring. But my existence was one big, dangerous secret—the opposite of steady—so I kept lying to him about why he couldn't meet my family, why I was so standoffish at times, until it was obvious I was hiding something. Inevitably, my deception broke us apart. He left school (Casimir Fepinsky Preparatory—good old Fep Prep), Chicago, and me, and moved to Los Angeles with his dad. Afterward, I replaced the *T* pendant with the key, a cold, constant reminder of my search for ultimate power.

"Hello?" he said again.

My number was blocked. He didn't know who was calling him, but like every curious person, he kept listening. *It's me, Sara Jane!* I screamed in my mind. *Tell me to head west and not stop until I reach L.A.! Tell me to save the last shred of myself so I can be with you, and be happy!*

I couldn't let him tell me those things because I might do them.

I might leave Chicago behind if he told me in his reassuring voice that another existence was possible.

Except it wasn't, and I would never leave the city without my family.

Good-bye, Max, I thought, hanging up.

And then the Lincoln filled with flashing red light and the *bwaa! bwaa!* of a fire engine's horn. I twisted the keys as the car roared to life, realizing what an idiot I was, waiting to be attacked. But no—the large red truck sped past filled with goggle-free firemen, kicking up a swell of water. I exhaled, watching it go, and then stepped on the gas and headed toward the Bird Cage Club.

Back to the life that was my only choice.

3

IN CONTRAST TO THE RAIN CLOUDS BLAN-keting the Loop—Chicago's nickname for its vast downtown area, looped by elevated trains—entering the Bird Cage Club at the top of the Currency Exchange Building was like walking into an exploding star.

A large, round electrical outlet stood in the middle of the former speakeasy; in the 1920s, its huge lightbulb sent out a beacon to alert thirsty Chicagoans that illegal booze was flowing. Doug had been trying to make it work for months, and now, blinking into its intense glare, I realized he'd succeeded. "Doug!" I said, shielding my eyes. "You're burning the retinas out of my head!"

"Oh! My bad!" he said, and the room went gray. "You didn't come right back after I texted you, so I decided to work on it, and guess what? It wasn't the bulb after all! It was the wiring! I ripped out the old . . . ," he said, and then paused. "You're soaked."

I saw him clearly now—baggy jeans, T-shirt bearing one of

his favorite movie quotes ("Forget it, Jake. It's Chinatown."), and a welder's mask over his face. "Would you take that off?" I said. "I've endured enough freaky eye coverings for one day."

It clanged to the floor as he crossed the room. "The goggle guys again?"

"Two of them. In a ComEd van this time."

"You escaped, obviously. Where are they?"

"Not heaven."

"Crap. Did you . . . ?"

"Yeah, I did. One of them, at least," I said quietly. "I didn't mean to."

He spotted my burned fingers and lifted his eyebrows. "Looks like he touched a live wire named . . . um, let me guess . . . Sara Jane?"

"Something like that."

In his best therapist voice, he said, "You want to talk about it?"

"No. I think I'm okay," I said.

"Except for that hand. Listen, I can say this because we're BFFs . . . you're an idiot." He hurried away and returned with ointment and bandages. "You have to take an aspirin every day or you'll fry yourself . . . to . . . *death!* Do I really have to remind you?"

He didn't, but he did, and still I avoided taking the pills.

Watching Doug dress my wound, I realized again how much I depended on him, and as his own hand shook slightly while applying medicine to mine, I thought of how much he'd endured over the past several months. He'd beaten his addiction to Sec-C, the drug-infused soft serve ice cream, and emerged dramatically thinner. Exercise was sharpening the edges of his body. His face, with its ruddy complexion and spray of freckles, had grown angular, and even the sandy-colored bush on his head had been reshaped into a presentable haircut.

Step-by-step, my friend was taking control of his physical self.

It was his emotional self that concerned me.

Once he was clean, Doug's natural obsessiveness had come roaring back, fixated on the Troika of Outfit Influence. He was as crazed as I was to find that hidden object or location, and to unearth the ultimate power buried beneath it. If anything, his focus on saving my family—our "noble quest"—had increased. But Sec-C had been designed to burrow into other parts of his mind, the places where a person locks up the most personal thoughts about himself. He despised his appearance, with the heaviness of his body weighing him down mentally as well. For most of his life, he'd considered himself capable of little more than consuming mass quantities of Munchitos and movies. Sec-C made him feel attractive, but it went far beyond that; it made him believe he could take on the world, and win. Since those positive feelings had dissipated, his greatest fear was regression—not to Sec-C, of course, but to resuming an existence, as he'd put it, as a useless lump.

It was the PAWS talking.

He'd researched it online—Post Acute Withdrawal Syndrome—PAWS for short, which was ironic, since Harry, our little Italian greyhound, provided Doug with daily doses of sympathy and affection. The main characteristic of the syndrome, common among ex-addicts, was intense, needling self-doubt. It also came with panic attacks, minor and major, brought on by stressful situations. Trembling, sweating, loss of breath, dizziness—Doug had felt them all over the past month. The ones he hadn't experienced, and dreaded most, were hallucinations (the freeze response, where stress renders a person unable to move), and aphasia (the temporary inability to speak).

That didn't seem to be a problem now.

His mouth was going a mile a minute, asking me about the Russians, how I'd escaped, if anyone had seen me. As he finished wrapping my hand in gauze, I told him everything about Skull Head and Goatee, careful not to exclude a single detail, and then put the cherry on top.

"Elzy," he said quietly. "How did she get control of the Russian mob?"

"How did she infiltrate the cops?" I said with a shrug. "She grew up with a dad in the Outfit. Elzy knows a lot of tricks and lots of bad people."

Doug nodded, then reached into his pocket and pulled out a pack of cigarettes and a square, steel lighter. He lit one, coughed smoke, and said, "Let's think this through."

It was my turn to lift eyebrows. "You're *smoking*?"

"Can't sneak anything past you."

"Doug, what the hell? Since *when*?"

"Since recently, okay?" he answered, smoke snaking above his head. "And what the hell is that nicotine has a calming effect on people with PAWS. Besides, all great detectives . . .

Humphrey Bogart as Philip Marlowe, Jack Nicholson as J.J. Gittes . . . required a cigarette to help them think."

"You know what it makes me think? Rotten teeth, lung cancer, and addiction. Seriously, you just got one monkey off your back and now you're starting all over."

"Relax, Surgeon General. I smoke Chippewa Naturals. They're non–habit forming. Look, the package says so, right there."

"Oh, well, as long as it says so. Who would ever lie about tobacco?" I said, staring at him. "You're self-medicating, Doug. When are you going to quit?"

"When you *start* self-medicating," he replied, blowing a smoke ring. "One little aspirin, every morning."

It was a staring standoff until I said, "Let's think this Elzy thing through."

"As if it's a movie," he said. "Act one. She sends Poor Kevin and a bunch of cops to capture you and the notebook . . ."

"So she can gain control of ultimate power," I said. "She's not sure what it is, doesn't even know it's *called* ultimate power. But she knew there was *something* in the notebook that could help her take over the Outfit."

"But she fails to get her hands on it. She disappears . . ."

"In the meantime, Juan Kone kidnaps my family . . ."

"He wants a different type of power," Doug said. "Enzyme GF. The thing floating in Rispoli blood that creates ghiaccio furioso. Wants to create and sell armies of cold fury freaks to the highest bidder."

"Act two," I said. "Juan also fails, but not before someone

22

disguised as an ice cream creature snatches my family again . . ."

"Ice cream creatures. Those red eyes." Doug shuddered.

"It *had* to have been Elzy. She infiltrated both the cops and Juan's operation. Damn, she's good . . . in a terrible way," I said. "Speaking of eyes. Look what I got." I pulled Goatee's goggles from my pocket and handed them to Doug.

He ran a thumbnail over the lenses, then hurried them to the control center. It was covered with laptops and reference books on every conceivable subject to do with Chicago, all assembled to help us find my family. Riffling around, he came up with a thick, black folder.

La Ciencia de Ghiaccio Furioso—The Science of Cold Fury.

We'd taken it from Juan Kone's laboratory before torching the place.

It explains how part of my brain produces enzyme GF when I feel threatened or angry. The enzyme travels via electrical impulse, fills my eyes, and produces a powerful laser effect called cold fury. My adversary absorbs it with his gaze, triggering his deepest fears and broadcasting them back to me. I've learned to use the anger component to control it—to turn it on and off literally in the blink of an eye.

The problem is Au 79, the periodic symbol for gold.

My ancient ancestors, Egyptian assassins, believed that eating raw gold extended their lives; instead, it became part of Rispoli DNA, glittering from our eyes. Au 79 has no effect on cold fury—but cold fury affects the gold, which is a highly conductive metal.

If I get threatened, or channel my anger, my eyes flood with enzyme GF.

An electrical impulse delivers the enzyme but also charges the gold, turning me into a walking, talking lightning bolt. The more emotional I become, the more enzyme is released, the more voltage fills my body. I can release some of it (just ask Goatee) but not all. If left unregulated, I could electrocute myself from the inside out.

That's where aspirin comes in.

Its main ingredient, acetylsalicylic acid, blocks the gold from becoming electrified. After learning of it, I recalled how my grandpa and my father each took an aspirin every day. I had once asked my dad why he popped the pill. "It's good for you. Thins the blood," he'd said, then locked his eyes onto mine. "When you get a little older, you should take one every day, too. Just in case."

Good advice that I couldn't follow.

Even though it could kill me, I needed the electricity. Beyond a left hook, beyond cold fury, it was my last line of defense.

Doug looked up from the folder. "Juan Kone was a genius. Sick and twisted, but a genius. The ice cream creatures were his lab rats. He pumped them full of chemicals, trying to turn them into supersoldiers."

"Must've been a disappointment when their brains blew up like grenades."

"True, but he succeeded in another way. They produced a weird little enzyme of their own, Enzyme R, that turned their eyes red and gave them the ability to withstand cold fury. It's right here," he said, pointing at a document, "how Juan extracted creature blood and used it to make his own red contact lenses."

"Enzyme R. If Juan could make contacts—"

"Maybe someone else could use it for easy-to-wear, easy-to-remove goggles? Perfect for catching Sara Jane Rispoli," Doug said.

"Elzy wanted ultimate power, but she also wanted me. If I surrendered the notebook and joined her, with her brains and my cold fury we'd rule the Outfit together," I said. "My guess is that her basic plan hasn't changed. Instead of Poor Kevin in a mask—"

"She's got a bunch of ex-con gangsters in goggles," Doug said, following my thought. "Plus, this time she has your family. If she doesn't catch you, it's a major bargaining chip to force you to give up the notebook and go to work for her."

I nodded. "Even the street war makes sense. Elzy knows that Outfit members never really want to fight, it messes up the profit margin. I think she's pushing them to the limit, hoping they'll surrender."

"And then what?"

"She'll probably do what the Outfit does to smaller, weaker gangs. Absorb them."

"Absorb them," he said. "You think Elzy's planning a merger?"

"More like a hostile takeover. The Russians are brutal and there seem to be a lot of them. The tables have turned. In this case, the Outfit is feeling more like the smaller, weaker gang. That, plus cold fury and me, plus the notebook? Elzy would rule Chicago, just like she'd always planned."

"So where does that leave us?"

"At a very dangerous act three," I said. "Whatever ultimate power is, Elzy knows it exists. She also has to know that if I find it, I'll use it against her. If possible, locating the Troika of Outfit Influence has just become even more urgent."

"Well then, get ready to hug a small Italian greyhound," Doug said with a grin. "Because Harry found it."

4

I COULD HEAR MY HEARTBEAT.

Sitting rigidly, I clenched and unclenched my fists, trying to tamp down hope. "Are you sure, Doug?" I said. "The Troika of Outfit Influence? Please say yes."

"Maybe. Possibly," he said, whistling once.

Harry limped from my bedroom, clicking painfully across the room. He touched a nose to my bandaged fingers and whined as I rubbed his smooth head. Harry had once belonged to my brother. There was a time when the little greyhound and I had been enemies, jealous over Lou's affection, but we called a truce after my family's disappearance, bound by the common cause of saving them. He was as much a partner to me as Doug; Harry had proven to be smart and fearless—a four-legged hero, as Doug called him. He'd saved me from Poor Kevin and never left Doug's side as he sweated through Sec-C withdrawal.

"Why is he walking like that?" I said. "Is he hurt? What happened?"

"Don't worry. It's minor, and he's tough," Doug said, petting Harry's back. "Right, buddy?"

"I don't understand. You said he found it."

Doug walked behind the control center and stood before the enormous wall map of Chicago taken from Club Molasses, the old speakeasy hidden beneath my family's bakery. "I think so. As long as 'found' means this giant thing hanging right in front of our dumb-ass faces." I stared at the yellowed map with its city streets drafted in perfect lines. It showed hundreds of Chicago buildings in great detail, some now demolished, others still standing after more than a century.

When I'd first discovered the map, it was pierced with dozens of colored, lettered stickpins. I moved it to the Bird Cage Club after diagramming how they were placed, and put them back exactly as they'd been. It wasn't until I'd read and memorized the notebook, particularly chapter one— "*Nostro*—Us"—that I realized the pins represented the locations of significant Outfit front businesses. Some were long outdated, like the *F* representing the Fischetti Brothers Mortuary (extremely dead) and a *K* for Katzenbaum's Deli (bomb makers; blown up). But others were of the moment—there was a pin for Knuckles Battuta, VP of Muscle, and his front business, BabyLand. And another for Tyler Strozzini, VP of Money, and his front business, the multinational junk-food producer StroBisCo. Of course, the pin where Rispoli & Sons Fancy Pastries stood, my family's front business for three generations, was the simplest to identify.

The map seemed unchanged. I looked back at Doug as he stubbed out the cigarette and lifted up *The Weeping Mafioso,* the screenplay written by Uncle Jack, Grandpa Enzo's long-lost brother who'd appeared out of the blue a month earlier with his daughter, Annabelle, and his granddaughter, Heather. The old man, riddled with Alzheimer's disease, came back to Chicago searching for my dead grandfather, hoping for a final reunion before dementia overtook him. Heather's death accelerated the disease, leaving Uncle Jack drifting like a ship without an anchor, but before returning to L.A., he'd left the screenplay and urged me to read it.

Doug flipped to the end. "If I've said it once . . . all of life's answers can be found in the movies." He pointed at three lines of dialogue spoken by the character Renzo, and read, "'I know the secret to ultimate power . . . *potenza ultima . . .* and all I need to get my hands on it is one little brass key. It's in a vault made of brick deep beneath the streets of Chicago. Right under what the old-timers used to call the Troika of Outfit Influence.'"

"So it's a place," I said. "We've always known the vault is underground—"

"Not just underground," he said, "under the *streets* of Chicago." He put aside the screenplay and lifted the notebook. "We've gone through it endlessly looking for the Troika. It's mentioned in the screenplay but not here, not in any of the chapters. Okay, so I decided to concentrate on the other word, *influence.*"

"Yeah . . . so?"

"So," he said, "your uncle Jack transcribed the passage in the notebook about ultimate power from your great-grandfather Nunzio, right?"

"Right," I answered.

"And Jack later used that information in his screenplay, along with the term Troika of Outfit Influence, which must've come from Nunzio," he said.

"Had to. It's so specific."

"Nunzio was the original counselor-at-large, a genuine old-timer. In his day, there was one guy who controlled not only the Outfit but also the entire city . . . the only person with real, lasting influence. It was so strong that his shadow still looms over Chicago. You've said it yourself—Outfit members consider him their personal god."

A dull shiver climbed my spine. "Al Capone."

"Scarface Al. No one was more influential, not then, not now."

"It's true. I can't make it through a sit-down without someone—an enforcer, a coke dealer—wondering WWAD? What would Al do?" I said.

"Now listen to this, from chapter five, 'Sfuggire—Escape,'" Doug said, flipping pages and reading: "'Capone Doors were invented in 1921 by Giuseppe "Joe Little" Piccolino, the chief officer of weapons and devices, and were installed in and around Chicago between 1922 and 1950 . . . a boon to Capone Doors came in 1938, when the city began to dig subway tunnels in order to supplement El trains. A far-ranging and wide-reaching system of secret tunnels that already existed beneath the muddy surface of Chicago, to which Joe Little had long ago connected many Capone Doors, was engineered to access the subway system as well.'"

"Joe Little was underneath the streets of Chicago, building stuff," I said. "You think *he* built the vault?"

"It had to have been him," Doug said. "Constructing secrets for the Outfit was his job. Which made me think . . . I bet there's a Capone Door leading to the vault."

"But . . . which one?"

"No clue. Maybe they all do."

I thought about it, gnawing a thumb, saying, "We still don't know how Nunzio found out about ultimate power. Or how he got the key."

Doug nodded. "But we know the key was taped to the inside back cover of the notebook for a long time. So I took a closer look," he said, turning it toward me with a magnifying glass. I stared at the back cover, seeing a faint outline where the key had rested for decades, and inside it, letters in Great-Grandpa Nunzio's handwriting, printed so lightly they were barely visible:

B U R G L R.

I said it phonetically. "Burglar?"

"Confusing, since the notebook is a who's who of thieves, pickpockets, and safecrackers. I wouldn't have figured it out if it hadn't been for Harry," he said, rubbing the little dog's ears. "A pin fell out of the map, the green *G,* and he stepped on it. You should've heard my poor baby howl. After making sure he was okay, I put it back where it belonged. That's when I saw this." I rose from the couch and went to the map, staring at the spot where Doug pointed. Two other pins stood close to the green *G*—another *R,* this one purple, and a white *U*—indicating businesses on different corners in a neighborhood called Uptown. "So many pins, clustered in so many shapes," he said, "I never noticed how those three make a perfect little triangle."

"No . . . a troika," I murmured, staring at the intersection of a trio of streets.

"Broadway, Racine, and Lawrence Avenue, the heart of Uptown," he said. "That accounts for the *B,* one of the *R*s and the *L*. After that it was easy. The notebook is full of info about Uptown since it was the epicenter of Capone's North Side operation. Chapter one, '*Nostro*—Us,' lists every piece of real estate he owned as a front business. It includes the Green Mill Lounge on Broadway, which he used as headquarters, the Riviera Theatre on Racine, where he ran an after-hours casino, and the Bridgeview Bank, a perfect money laundry, on Lawrence Avenue."

"*G* is for Green Mill, *R* is for Riviera, but what about the bank? You said it's called Bridgeview," I said, "but its pin says *U*. It doesn't fit."

A smile creased his face. "It used to, back in the day. When it was called the Uptown National Bank."

"Uptown National Bank," I said, touching the key at my neck. "U.N.B. 001."

"The vault holding ultimate power is somewhere beneath those streets and buildings. The bank is the likely location but we won't know until we look."

"So . . . let's look," I said with muffled excitement.

"Subterranean stroll, first thing tomorrow," he said. "We're gonna need some stuff . . . boots, maybe helmets . . ."

I lunged, pulling him into a hug. "You're amazing, Doug!" I said. "You found it!"

"*We* found it!" he said, standing back and smiling at Harry. "Actually, he did."

"All three of us. Our own little troika," I said. "If I drank, this would definitely be a pop-the-champagne moment."

"I'll settle for a celebratory cigarette," he said, drawing one out and lighting it.

"You like that thing, don't you?"

"The cigarette?"

"The lighter. Shiny steel, the *click* it makes."

"I enjoy the whole experience, from click to puff," he said. "You have to admit, it makes me look cool."

"You don't need a cigarette to be cool. Doug Stuffins is awesome."

"I like where this is going," he said, "tell me more."

"Seriously. You're as smart as a little Einstein, resourceful as hell." I was silent for a moment. "Confession. As much as I need you, and I do, Doug, like crazy, I feel guilty about having dragged you into this mess. You should be living your life—"

"This *is* my life," he said abruptly. "The search for your family began as a big adventure for me, like playing a sidekick in an action flick. But . . . confession of my own . . . the weirder it got, the more I thought about quitting."

"Really? I mean, I completely understand. I just didn't know."

"I considered taking Harry with me and hiding behind a locked door with an endless supply of movies and Munchitos," he said. "Couldn't do it, though. I owed you."

"You don't owe me anything."

"Yeah, I did. You came to rely on me, if I can be so bold . . ."

"Couldn't do it without you," I said, nodding at the three pins stuck on the map.

"Backing away would have left all you alone. You gave me your trust and confidence. I owed it to you to see this thing through," he said. "But it's different now."

He twisted out the cigarette in an ashtray, staring at it, and looking back at me.

"Your family's freedom means everything, Sara Jane, but it's not the only thing. That goddamn Sec-C, this stupid syndrome . . . whatever . . . I need to prove to myself that I'm . . . worthy or capable, or something." He sighed.

"I think I understand," I said quietly.

"Sorry. I sound like the star of a twelve-step program for the clinically self-doubting. Hi, I'm Doug, and I have no idea who I am."

"You're not a sidekick, I can tell you that much," I said. "You're my partner."

He nodded once, slowly. "From start to finish."

Wherever that was, the journey would continue tomorrow, deep underground. Something about the moment demanded a handshake, and as we did, a thunderclap rumbled through the Bird Cage Club, followed by a whiny growl from Harry.

He was spooked by the noise, cautioning us that it might happen again.

An electrical boom and a warning.

It was the perfect way to end the day.

5

SLEEP. YEAH. RIGHT, I THOUGHT, STARING AT THE
ceiling of my office-bedroom.

The joy of discovery was hissing away like a slowly
deflating balloon.

Lying on my mattress, cracking my knuckles, I saw the
Troika of Outfit Influence for what it really was—the beginning of the end—but what sort of end? What if the thing
buried beneath the troika was neither ultimate nor powerful,
or worse, didn't even exist? The possibility had occurred to me
before but I'd pushed it away, desperate to pin my hope on,
well, something.

Something could very well turn out to be a big pile of
nothing.

I rolled onto my side, willing myself to sleep, but it was no
use.

A pile of books sat next to the mattress and I reached for
an Italian dictionary. What seemed like a lifetime ago, my
parents had promised me a trip to Italy if I graduated Fep

Prep with honors. But studying the language seemed like such a normal thing to do that it felt completely ridiculous, not connected to me at all. Instead, I picked up my journal, which I'm writing in now. As a condition of graduation, Fep Prep students have to record their high school career and then turn it in at the end of senior year. Of course, I had no intention of ever handing mine in; it was nearly as full of secrets as the notebook. I flipped to the entry I'd made months earlier and read:

It hadn't occurred to me until now that the key to ultimate power may actually be a key, and that it could open a vault. Now, all I have to do is find it.

I stared at the words, trying to summon the hope I'd felt when I'd written them. They'd been penned by the Sara Jane who hadn't yet endured the horror of Juan Kone, or taken a human life. Strength grows from confidence, and that's how I wanted to begin the trek underground, but disappointment loomed like Poor Kevin or an ice cream creature. What I needed was assurance that stepping through a Capone Door into darkness would lead to the light of discovery—that ultimate power was real. I lifted my phone, stared at it, thinking of Max, and then, to my surprise, someone else came to mind.

Tyler Strozzini.

He's a handsome and confident eighteen-year-old who inherited his dad's role as Outfit VP of the important Money division. After working together for six months, a level of trust has grown between us—I settle Money disputes quickly and without remorse, which makes his division run more efficiently. In turn, he became, in Outfit parlance, my Whispering

Smith. I don't know where the term originated but it refers to a member who passes on vital information to another.

Tyler whispers about who hates me, and why.

When a thug loses a dispute, I use cold fury to impose a penalty—a hefty fine, physical punishment, or worse—and he complies. But that doesn't mean he likes it, or me. No one has sought revenge, not even the families or friends of those I've ordered put to death. But, as Lucky once reminded me, cold fury or not, I was open to attack when my back was turned. Not long ago, when the room had cleared after a sit-down, except for Tyler and me, he said, "Hey . . . Eddie Hernandez, the car booster?"

"Ready Eddie," I said, remembering the ten-thousand-dollar fine I'd imposed on him a week earlier. "What about him?"

"I heard he said he'd like to stick a knife in your neck," Tyler said solemnly. He's good-looking in a movie-star way—smooth, coppery skin, jet-black hair never out of place, and broad shoulders that seem padded, which they are, with muscle. His green eyes tempered even the most disturbing news, like the tidbit he'd just delivered.

I shrugged, trying to seem cool. "You've seen me in action. Every order I hand down comes with a warning never to lay a hand on me."

"Still, you have to know who your enemies are. I just want you to be aware," he said, shrug-smiling.

"Thanks. I appreciate it."

"How long does it last, by the way?" he asked. "Ghiaccio furioso."

"Forever," I lied. The truth was that I was unsure how long the effects of cold fury endured, a gap in my knowledge that sometimes gave me worrisome pause—except, in my life, pausing to worry could get me killed. On the contrary, anything that helped keep me safer was a gift, and Tyler delivered, whispering a growing list of names and threats; he was right, it was better to know than not. Tyler never asked for anything in return, but when he mentioned that he was having trouble collecting operating tax from a low-level smash-and-grabber—a jewel thief who smashes a display case and grabs as much as he can—I helped him do it. It was a breach of protocol; like everything else, there were rules when it came to debt collection. It didn't matter to me. I wanted to repay his ongoing favor because he was the only friend I had in the Outfit.

Actually, he was a little closer than a friend.

Only a month earlier, depressed and forlorn with Max gone and my family seemingly out of reach forever, I'd agreed to travel to Rome with him for a long weekend on his private jet. But as we flew toward Italy, I stumbled upon a clue to the Troika of Outfit Influence; it shook me free of self-pity and instilled new hope that I could save my family. In a burst of frustration, I used cold fury to make Tyler turn back to Chicago. But as soon as I saw his worst fear, I was sorry I'd done it. It was just for a moment and I couldn't bear to witness the whole, awful scene—Tyler at age seventeen, watching from the ground as his parents' private jet took off, faltered in the air, exploded in a fiery blaze, and crashed. Whatever followed—whatever deep terror burrowed into his heart following the accident—felt like something that was none of my business.

He was shaken but, to my surprise, neither angry nor resentful.

With a weak smile, he told me I didn't have to use cold fury, that he would've turned the jet around for me. I apologized, explaining that I'd remembered some urgent, unfinished counselor-at-large business, but that I should've been more patient.

He asked then, had I seen his worst fear?

Part of it, I replied, hesitating, and told him only about the part up to the plane crash.

Tyler nodded slowly with something like a look of relief, admitting that he'd never discussed how he felt about his parents' untimely end with anyone and, well, could he—with me? We sat then, the two of us alone at the back of the jet as he spoke quietly about grief and loneliness, how deeply he missed his mom's light sense of humor that dismissed all bad things as temporary, and his dad's wisdom and guidance. His eyes were wet and we held hands. He tried to explain the emptiness he felt, wondering when or if it would ever fill in, and if he wanted it to. It hit so close to home that I found myself talking, too. I couldn't tell the truth about my situation, of course, so I channeled feelings of fear and loss into the lie about my dad's dire illness. I'd decided to go to Rome for a respite; instead, the cancelled trip became a mutual therapy session, and it felt good, even a little cleansing. Toward the end, Tyler uttered something so undeniable that it made my eyes wet, too.

"There's nothing as permanent as the death of the people you love most," he said quietly.

In a single sentence, he'd articulated my own worst fear.

We were at the back of the jet sitting side by side, the engines humming low and steady around us. Tyler glanced out the window and then turned to me, saying how sure he was that the VP of Muscle, Knuckles Battuta, had orchestrated his parents' plane crash.

It sent a chill through me, a family so quickly separated by murder. "Why?" I asked.

"Power. When it comes to the chain of command in the Outfit, only Lucky sits above Money and Muscle," he said. "The two positions are interdependent. Muscle needs Money to fund its army of enforcers and Money relies on Muscle to collect street tax, operating tax, and all other funds."

I nodded. "I've settled a lot of disagreements between the two sides, as you know."

"My dad," Tyler said, and faltered, taking a breath. "He was younger than Knuckles, and charming—charismatic, I guess you could say. He and Knuckles were like oil and water." Tyler was convinced that after all of the disputes between the two men over so many years, Knuckles took out his dad, hoping to exert influence over the teenaged Strozzini.

"It didn't work out that way, huh?" I said.

Tyler shook his head and leaned in closer. "I despise Knuckles and everything he stands for as the chief enforcer," he said in a confessional tone. "But you know what? Even more, I hate that I'm bound to the Outfit. After my parents died, Lucky made it clear that I had to become head of

Money, or else. My family had served too long and knew too many secrets for me to be allowed to become a civilian."

Tyler was chained to the organization, just like me.

Beyond that, we shared the reality of being different from everyone else in the Outfit. For me, it's gender. For him, it's because he's half African American. The organization practiced its own hypocritical version of multiculturalism—members could be Italian, Greek, Jewish, whatever, as long as they were male and white. Our disparity brought us together almost as much as the loss of our families. When we were done talking, emotionally spent, he asked if I wanted to watch one of his favorite movies. Huddling together, we stared at *The Shawshank Redemption,* and I understood why he liked it so much. It's all about escape.

After returning to the city, our romance, if that was what it had been, slowed and cooled—I was diverted by looking for my family, of course, and the street war had begun to rage—but the bond forged on the flight remained. I sat up on the side of the mattress now, wondering if Tyler's feelings for me, combined with his own emotional scars, outweighed his loyalty to the Outfit—could I tell him about my family and ultimate power, and trust him to somehow help me?

The answer was a definite maybe.

But it wasn't an absolute yes, which meant no, and I put down the phone.

It was just past midnight, Saturday surrendering to Sunday.

Doug and I now had twenty-four hours to locate the vault before returning to Fep Prep on Monday morning. Trying to fool myself to sleep, I shut my eyes and began counting

42

in Italian—*uno, due, tre*—but the numbers reminded me of people.

I pictured my mother as she'd been the last time I'd seen her—smooth olive skin, silken black hair, lithe, delicate hands—but couldn't help imagining a red stump where Juan Kone had sliced off her finger. Then I saw my dad, tall and lean with an easy smile, and purple scars on his wrists, track marks from where Juan had extracted gallons of blood—I'd never seen the wounds, but I knew he'd been experimented on, and tortured.

Finally, Lou walked through my mind.

He was as pale and bruised as I'd seen him at the Ferris wheel.

Lou hooked my pinkie and said, *Rispolis stick together even when we aren't together. All or nothing, remember?*

I remembered.

Nothing, neither fear nor anxiety, could stop me from looking for ultimate power.

I stood and paced the room, opening drawers, turning over loose papers, seeking—what? A sign maybe, a signal that my subterranean search wouldn't be in vain. I pushed aside the dictionary, the journal, and stared at the old notebook. I'd been through its chapters countless times, scratching out the truth about my family, using its criminal methods to survive. Through trial and error, and sometimes luck, I'd learned that its secrets weren't always so obviously placed, where just anyone could find them. I'd turned every one of its pages searching for information about ultimate power.

Or had I?

Rereading the final entry for the eighth chapter, *"Volta,"* revealed nothing new. I examined the page, hoping it was like the ones that had concealed Uncle Jack's scribblings in Buondiavolese, but no—it was a thin, single sheet. The notebook was bound in leather while the inside back cover was overlaid with a rectangle of yellowed paper glued into place. I looked at the key's outline and Nunzio's faint letters, B U R G L R, using a fingernail to dig at the cover's corner. The paper crumbled into pasty bits until a strip peeled away. Slowly, like removing a stamp from an envelope, I pulled the page free and turned it over. It was a note from Great-Grandpa Nunzio to my grandpa Enzo:

Caro Enzo,

Io sono vecchio e i miei occhi blu sono sempre così debole che non posso vedere la pagina. Presto, vostro fratello Giaccomo registrerà tutte le mie parole per me. Ma ho bisogno di scrivere questa lettera io.

Come i miei occhi si dissolve, quindi fa ghiaccio furioso. Il tuo tempo come Consigliere rapidamente si avvicina. Ho insegnato molte lezioni, ma tre richiedono ripetere.

Questa lettera è un ricordo utile ed essenziale . . .

I put it aside, lifted the Italian dictionary, and translated the entire letter until I was able to read it:

Dear Enzo,

I am old and my blue eyes are growing so weak that I can

hardly see the page. Soon, your brother Giaccomo will record all of my words for me. But I need to write this letter myself.

As my sight fades, so does cold fury. Your time as counselor quickly approaches. I've taught you many lessons, but three bear repeating.

This letter is a helpful, essential reminder.

First, we serve the Outfit because we must; refusing to do so would endanger our family. Serve it, but never trust it.

Second, without cold fury, we have no value to the Outfit. Remember—it is a beast that eats its own.

Third, if you or the family are ever in danger, from outside the Outfit or within, resort to ultimate power. I cannot say what it is in case this book falls into the wrong hands. Only that it dwells beneath the letters on the other side of this page. I am confident you will find it, but hope that you never need it.

If you do, know this—for our family, ultimate power is freedom.

I love you,

Papa

A pleasing chill tiptoed over my shoulders as I stared at the words. From the distant past, my great-grandfather not only affirmed the existence of ultimate power, he'd spoken of it in the context of saving his, and my, family. The description was far from specific but it was enough—more than enough—to reignite the hope I needed to begin the trip underneath the streets of Chicago.

Freedom, I thought with a shiver. *Ultimate power is freedom.*

I placed the notebook aside and closed my eyes.

My sleep held no dreams, but also no nightmares.

The last thing I remembered was saying thank you to Nunzio.

6

THE SUN ROSE LIKE AN ORANGE BALLOON OVER
Lake Michigan, spreading morning light through the Bird
Cage Club as I stared at the triangle of thumbtacks.

A tiny, momentous secret waiting to be discovered.

I wondered if my dad had left them pinned there, similar to
how he'd left the steel briefcase and its contents for me to find.
The .45, cash, and prepaid credit card had been placed inside
to keep me safe and moving, while the notebook's purpose
was to guide me through the dangerous maze of the Outfit.
If he'd left the pins in place, then he must've suspected that
I'd need ultimate power at some point. Knowing the peril of
being associated with the Outfit, three generations of Rispolis
had compulsively planted clues and safeguards in case something catastrophic happened to their children.

It had, and I was grateful for their paranoia.

In their lives and mine, someone (from Elzy and Uncle
Buddy to Juan Kone and now Elzy again) was always
watching, listening, or plotting. So they'd obscured facts and

information and then relied upon the love we felt for one another to keep us moving toward the truth. In that way, the past six months of my life had been spent scratching at surfaces, trying to find what was hidden beneath—and here I was again, plunging into the unknown. It was enough of a reason to stare at an aspirin in the palm of my hand that morning and then put it back into the bottle. More than hope, more than luck, finding ultimate power might require a little extra power of my own.

"Spelunking anyone?" Doug said. He stood grinning in an oversized Blackhawks jersey and camouflage pants, hair mashed from sleep, holding a pair of miner's helmets with electric lights above the brims.

"Where'd you get those?" I said.

"Snuck out last night to Trader Jack's Survivor Emporium, down on Halsted Street. That freaky joint has everything," he said. "Rubber knee-high boots, flashlights, rope, because you never know. Water, of course. What am I forgetting?"

"The .45, loaded this time," I said, "and the notebook."

"The gun, I get. There might be giant zombie rats," he said. "But the notebook? Is there a map in it I missed? In case we want to tour Chicago's prettiest sewers?"

"In case we don't make it back."

"Ri-i-ight," he said uneasily. "Hadn't thought about that. Guess we can't just leave it lying around, huh?"

"Nope. Look, Doug . . . it may be pretty dangerous down there."

"You're telling me. The notebook said Joe Little connected the tunnels to the subway. You know how deep that is? Might be poisonous or explosive gases in the air, not to mention cave-ins. Anyway, we should be fine," he said, smiling. "Excited?"

"Thrilled."

"Take your aspirin this morning?"

"Yep," I lied, using a rubber band to contain my wild hair.

"Good girl. So, where's our entry point? Which Capone Door?"

I looked at the pins on the map, with my dad and the steel briefcase in mind. "Club Molasses. Where it all started," I said, thinking of the speakeasy hidden deep below my family's bakery, Rispoli & Sons Fancy Pastries.

"Are you sure? That's way over on Taylor Street," he said. "We're right here in the Loop. There are a dozen old buildings nearby with Capone Doors."

"With hundreds of people milling around," I said. "The bakery is deserted, locked up since Uncle Jack and Annabelle left last month. Why risk being seen?"

"You're the boss," Doug said, putting on a miner's helmet and striking a pose. "How do I look?"

"Like you should be in an old music video singing about the YMCA."

He nodded, smiling. "Compliments will get you everywhere."

Fifteen minutes later we were in the Lincoln, battered but a rocket on wheels. The window Skull Head had broken out had been replaced by a thick piece of plastic duct-taped into the empty frame. It wasn't pretty, but it worked.

I wanted to get to Taylor Street quickly, and stepped on

the gas, past a slow-moving station wagon, around a pair of buzzing scooters. As we sped beneath the El tracks on Wells Street, spraying sidewalks with leftover rainwater, the *blip* of a siren sounded behind us. The light turned red and I came to a halt, looking over at a police car easing next to me. My other foot hovered over the gas pedal, ready to step on it if the cop made a threatening move, but he simply pointed and mouthed the words, *Slow down.* I nodded agreeably. When the light was green, I drove slowly ahead, just a law-abiding teenager and her pal out for a Sunday-morning spin. The cop passed by without a glance, cut in front of me, and sped on. "Holy shit." Doug exhaled. "What if he'd stopped us and looked through the car? The backpack's right there, in the backseat, with a gun inside! Not to mention all the other suspicious crap, the helmets, the rope!"

"That would've sucked," I said, shaking off the jumps.

"And you don't have a license!"

"There's lots of things I don't have. Relax," I said, turning onto Randolph Street.

"You're talking to Doug 'Ice Man' Stuffins. I'm relaxed," he said, thumbing at a line of sweat. "Besides, how can I not be? We're going, like, five miles an hour."

He was right. We'd come up behind a street-cleaning truck taking its time, weaving toward the sidewalk, back into the lane, scrubbing the pavement. Watching it slosh through the avenue, an alarm went off in my gut. "Weird," I said quietly.

"What? That the city is actually cleaning a street?"

"No. That it's happening the day after a huge storm," I said, picturing its driver in crimson goggles.

"Maybe they're saving money. Using water that's already there," he said.

"On a Sunday? Does the city even work on Sunday?"

"Gee, I don't know, Sara Jane . . . let me check my city utilities handbook," he said sarcastically, as a horn began to blare behind us. Doug looked through the back window. "Careful. That idiot is trying to pass." Seconds later, a rusty van swung out and then screeched to a halt next to us as the street cleaner wove back into the lane, blocking its path. I looked over at a stringy guy in a White Sox cap and at the side of the van, which read, A-1 HOME PLUMBING—YOU BREAK IT, WE SNAKE IT! His eyes were wild as he screamed muffled obscenities through the windshield. When the truck moved, the van roared past. A hand jutted from the truck's cab giving the stringy guy a one-finger salute.

"My turn," I said, and hurried past the street cleaning truck, too.

The driver was chewing a cigar, back at work. He wore nothing over his eyes and didn't even look our way, much less flip us off. I exhaled, relieved, and continued down Randolph. A few blocks later, traffic grew heavier, beginning to slow. I changed lanes, impatient to keep moving, and glanced in the rearview mirror.

Somehow, the rusty van was directly behind us now.

I'd been too preoccupied with cops and street cleaners.

Keeping my eyes on the mirror, I watched the stringy guy at the wheel slide something over his face. "Doug," I said, trying to remain calm, "I need the gun."

"What? Why?" he asked, brow furrowed.

"The van behind us . . ."

He turned, staring, and swallowed hard. "Is it one of them? A Russian?"

I nodded. "The gun."

"It's in the backseat, in the backpack!" he said.

"Go get it, please . . . now," I said. Without pause, he climbed over the seat and began tugging at the backpack.

"I can't . . . get it . . . open," he said, breathing heavily. "My hands . . ."

"Are you okay?!"

"Panic . . . attack. Hands are . . . shaking too badly . . ."

I was in the left lane; a gap appeared in the right and I called, "Hang on!" twisting the steering wheel, jumping ahead with the van on my bumper. I flew toward a side street and made a screaming right as Doug tumbled onto the floor of the backseat with a yelp. The side street was deserted and I treated it like a racetrack, peeling rubber. "Grab the gun, Doug!" I said, looking back at him.

"I'm trying . . . to get up," he grunted. "You're . . . going too fast . . ."

A flash caught the corner of my eye, and I turned, staring through the windshield at a woman pushing a stroller through the crosswalk. I hit the brakes, stopping inches from her as the van came to a skidding halt, nearly smashing into me. The woman, face and body frozen, now gathered herself, shooting daggers as she continued across the street. When she reached the sidewalk, the van pulled around next to me.

The stringy guy leaned across the passenger seat wearing normal sunglasses.

It was his turn to flip someone off—me—as he sped away.

"He's . . . gone," I said, leaning my head on the steering wheel, catching my breath. "The guy was just a plumber. He wasn't chasing us. He was just . . . in a hurry."

"God almighty," Doug said, giving up the struggle to right himself and lying back on the floor. "That was nerve-racking . . ."

"Can you breathe?"

"Yeah, I'm fine now. The panic, like, evaporates when the danger passes—"

Out of nowhere, the buzzing of giant mosquitoes cut off his words.

I looked up at a guy on a delivery scooter stopped in front of the car several feet ahead, facing us, and around at his partner, parked on another scooter the same distance behind. The drivers each wore T-shirts—one bearing the image of a pizza, the other a taco—helmets, and crimson goggles. The pizza guy in front straddled his scooter, leveling a short-barreled shotgun, while the taco guy jumped off his machine and hustled toward us, popping a clip into a handgun.

"Doug! Stay down, turn over, and get ready to open the door! Hard!"

He did as told without a word, the urgency in my voice moving him.

When Taco Guy reached the car, I screamed, "Now!" The Lincoln was blessed with a vintage feature called suicide doors that opened from the middle outward, like barn doors. Doug pushed against it with all of his strength, nailing Taco Guy like a linebacker, laying him out on the street. It gave Pizza

Guy pause, a precious few seconds for me to jam down the accelerator. The Lincoln leaped, and all Pizza Guy could do was raise his arms as I hit him, sending him and the shotgun up and over the car with a thump and a roll. Doug yanked the door shut and scrambled onto the backseat, gaping through the rear window, and we sped away.

"Did you kill him?!" he asked.

"I . . . don't know," I said, staring ahead, foot pressed on the gas pedal.

"He's not moving." Doug turned and sat on the seat. His eyes met mine in the rearview mirror. "We got away, Sara Jane," he said. "That's all that matters."

"Right," I said quietly, knowing he was wrong.

As bad as my enemies were, as evil as their intentions might be, my life was not an action movie, where the good guy mindlessly blows away assailant after assailant without a second thought. If anything, I was closer to a soldier at war, aware that body counts mattered. It wasn't that the corpses were piling *up* as much as piling on *top* of me, threatening to smother my better self once and for all. If the old Sara Jane had hit someone with a car, if he'd died, she would've felt it for the rest of her days. I knew that within an hour, maybe less, I'd forget all about Pizza Guy.

It scared me more than the Russians and their anonymous vehicles.

Every day, I was growing nearer to the line that shouldn't be crossed.

I wondered again who I'd be if I stepped over it, or if I'd even notice that I had.

· · ·

The rest of the trip to Taylor Street was fast and quiet.

I pulled to a stop at the curb in front of the bakery, staring at leaves and litter piled against the door, the unlit neon sign, and the brown paper covering its windows. The REMODELING—PARDON OUR DUST! sign had slipped sideways at an odd angle.

It looked like an abandoned property, forsaken by its owners.

My heart sank, feeling how vibrant the place had been before my family disappeared, and further back, when my grandparents were alive and Uncle Buddy hadn't yet shapeshifted into Uncle Judas. I looked past the bakery to the unrolled awnings of Coffinetto's Funeral Home on one side and at Lavasecco's Dry Cleaning next to it. A pair of signs were posted in the cleaner's window—a plain, sad one announcing it had gone out of business and a larger, flashier one that screamed COMING SOON . . . THE CUPCAKE BOUTIQUE! Not long ago, the idea of opening a cupcake-anything next to the venerable Rispoli & Sons Fancy Pastries would have been laughable. The block had been central to my life, a vital piece of my identity. Now it was changing and there was nothing I could do about it. Life marched on, with or without me.

"I don't want to go through the front," I said. "Seeing the place empty sucks too much." Doug said nothing, just opened the door and slid out. It's one of the best things about my friend; he knows that sometimes, silent commiseration is more important than encouraging words. After making sure neighborhood snoops weren't watching, I led him down the alley behind the bakery. Using a red key on my dad's key chain, I unlocked an electrical box and pushed the button inside. A rusty grumble was followed by a section of brick wall rolling open like a garage door. A small elevator revealed itself, done in mahogany and green leather, complete with a small crystal chandelier.

"The alley-vator, right?" Doug whispered, climbing aboard. "Cool."

I locked the electrical box and joined him. The chandelier tinkled as we descended, and then we stepped into the foyer of Club Molasses. During Prohibition, the alley-vator had been the main entrance to the speakeasy, depositing customers thirsty for booze and gambling into a luxurious anteroom where coats, hats, and guns were checked by Outfit goons. Now, ancient silken wallpaper hung in strands, powdery dust blanketed plush, worn divans, and cobwebs, long deserted by their original spinners, fell from wall sconces like clumps of gray cotton candy. Doug kicked at a flat, padlocked box and said, "This is where they checked the tommy guns, right?"

"Right," I said, leading him to a metal door with an eye slot. Long ago, an armed guard peered out from the other side demanding a password for entry. I opened it as we stepped inside, moving beneath a pyramid of wooden molasses barrels—one stacked on top of another, framing the door—and into the club. It was as cool and silent as a burial tomb. Antique slot machines stood in a corner like rows of soldiers frozen in salute. The mahogany bar stretched long and empty in front of a mirror gone cloudy with age, nearly obscuring

CLUB MOLASSES in curlicue script. Doug walked onto the dance floor where the letters CM were done in parquet.

"Just like old times." He sighed. "Poor Kevin beat my face in right here."

"And would've choked me to death, if it hadn't been for Harry." It was puzzling how the little dog had found his way to Club Molasses, but that was far down the list on mysteries yet to be solved. "Let's get moving," I said, hurrying toward the office. It was empty except for a desk, which I'd combed through several times—removing the drawers, nearly disassembling the entire thing—hoping for further clues to help find my family, to no avail. The Capone Door sat exposed on the opposite wall, formerly covered by the large map of Chicago.

"Hang on a sec," Doug said. "Can we take this back to the Bird Cage Club? Sort of like an artifact? It belongs with the map, you know?"

I turned to a framed photo of Al Capone at a baseball game with Great-Grandpa Nunzio sitting nearby, trying to avoid the camera. It bore the inscription:

To N.R.—Thanks for the cookies!—Your pal, A.C.

I'd contemplated taking it the first time I saw it, but it felt like a grave robbery. Now it seemed like just another forgotten relic of my family's criminal complicity. "Whatever." I shrugged.

"Awesome," he said, and tried to lift it from the wall, but it didn't budge. "Hm . . . it's stuck." He tried again, peering closer. "Along the edge. You can barely see them—hinges."

I stepped up, stared, and pulled at the opposite side of the frame, hearing a grudging *click* as the picture opened like a door. Inside, a dust-covered skeleton key hung from a hook, attached to a key chain in the shape of a pharaoh's head. I removed it carefully, turned it over, and saw a yellowed piece of paper stuck to the back. In looping handwriting recognizable as Nunzio's, it read:

Deposito segreto di Nunzio Rispoli, numero 9291-R.

Looking over my shoulder, Doug said, "Deposit-o segret-o?"

"Secret deposit of Nunzio Rispoli," I murmured, feeling its heft in my hand. "But not a deposit box. The key is too big. I wonder . . ."

"What?"

"About a month ago, Tyler asked me to settle a dispute between Money and a young Outfit guy. A baby-faced smash-and-grabber," I said. "Guy walks into a jewelry store, puts a gun on the owner, uses a hammer to shatter a display case, grabs all he can carry, and runs for it. Simple, but effective. Tyler figured out that his success didn't square with the cut he's required to pay the Outfit . . . the operating tax. Usually, a formal sit-down is convened with other division heads present. I expedited the process and ordered the kid to take us to his stash house."

"'Expedited the process'?" Doug said. "Fancy words for doing Tyler, that is, Mister Handsome, a favor. As counselor, aren't you supposed to treat everyone the same?"

"Yeah," I said, feeling a blush creep up my neck. "But we're, you know, friends."

"Really?" he said, lifting an eyebrow. "What kind of friends?"

"Business friends," I said. "My point is the stash house. It's an Outfit tradition. Every member has one or two hidden around Chicago. All that dirty cash, bales of pot, bags of coke, cases of guns . . . it has to be stored somewhere. All you have to do is look at self-storage places or apartment buildings lining Lake Shore Drive, and wonder what's hidden inside. Anyway, one blip of cold fury and Baby-Face took us to his stash house."

"Lots of bling?" Doug said.

"A small fortune. Tyler counted out the operating tax in gems." I looked at the key again. "I can only imagine what Nunzio squirreled away, wherever this place was."

Doug took it from my hand and stared at the Pharoah head. "This is no Troika of Outfit Influence, Sara Jane. In fact, it's no mystery at all. It's King Ramses II."

"How do you know?"

"How do you think?" He smirked. "*The Ten Command-ments,* 1956, directed by Cecil B. DeMille, with Charlton Heston as an unlikely Moses, and Yul Brynner as a perfect Ramses II. See the striped headdress and steely gaze? That's him, I'm sure of it. In fact, I used to see him and his twin every Wednesday."

"You lost me."

He shook his head ruefully. "God . . . I used to eat a *lot.* I actually planned my bingeing by the day of the week. Wednesday was two-for-one pork-chop sandwiches with unlimited fries at Fat Sammy's on Clark Street. Statues of Ramses II and his twin stand guard outside the place next door, a big old warehouse called Reebie Storage. It has all these Egyptian symbols and one of those plaques saying it was built in 1922."

"Then it's possible Reebie could've been a stash house for Outfit guys," I said.

"There's one way to find out," he said, pulling the notebook from the backpack and opening to the first chapter, "*Nostro—Us.*" It listed details, arcane and modern, about the Outfit's history, how it's organized, its known front businesses. Flipping pages, Doug said, "Let's see . . . Warehouses . . . Houses of Prostitution . . . Here it is, Stash Houses, Outfit-Approved, 1919–1932. I wonder why it ends in '32?"

"Just a guess, but that's when Capone went to jail," I said. "The Outfit was in disarray, everyone grabbing for power. No one trusted anyone."

"Those guys would've been fools to let each other know where their stashes were hidden," Doug said, trailing a finger down a page. "Here it is. Reebie Storage, 2325 North Clark Street." He looked up with a grin. "Right next to Fat Sammy's."

"You know your junk food."

"Knew it, past tense."

"So if Reebie was Nunzio's stash house . . . could his stuff still be there?"

"There's a way to find out that, too," Doug said, handing me the key.

I closed my fist around it, feeling cold metal against my

skin. "It's a mystery for another day. We've got enough on our plate as it is." He nodded, we slipped into our boots, put on our helmets, and I pushed the tiny *C* on the Capone Door. It opened with a vacuum *pop!* and I peered into darkness. Until now, it had felt like fate was perpetually against me, sitting on one side of a table with a stacked deck while I sat on the other trying to guess what cards it held. I needed one real answer that would help me save my family, and the notebook had provided it—ultimate power existed.

Turning to Doug, I said, "Ready?"

"I was born ready." He smiled. "I've always wanted to say that."

One step, and then another, as the door sealed behind us.

The Outfit had turned Chicago into its own personal monster by feeding it a steady diet of violence and lies.

We flicked on our helmet lights, descending into the belly of the beast.

7

AS WE LEFT THE SURFACE BEHIND, I THOUGHT of the Hemingway novel we were studying in Ms. Ishikawa's class, *The Sun Also Rises.*

Not down here.

We'd entered a place nearly devoid of daylight. Natural color was replaced by shades of gray, and although it was late morning, it seemed like dusk. Feeble illumination streamed through a distant sewer grate, eaten up by gloom. It's said that when people lose the ability to see, other senses grow stronger, and something like that felt true now. Sounds and smells were more intense, more present. The city's innards gurgled, hissed, and dripped while the air filled with rich earthiness one moment, human putrescence the next, the funk of chemicals after that, and then a potpourri of all three.

Our deep descent from Club Molasses ended at a rusty door.

As we moved down a stone staircase, I showed Doug the painted hands on the wall pointing the way. They'd been applied more than half a century earlier to guide fleeing Outfit members, when Joe Little created the Capone Doors and tunnels. We stood at the rusty door, feeling the rush of wind beneath it and hearing the ghoulish shriek of brakes as a train slowed to a halt on the other side. Nearly six months ago, I'd yanked open that secret entrance to a subway plat-form and leaped into a train car, narrowly eluding Uncle Buddy. Today, however, wasn't about escape; it was about discovery, and I pointed a flashlight into the shadows. Riv-eted beams rose from floor to ceiling. The wall supporting the staircase was solid brick. The other wall, before us, held only the rusty door. The rest of the musty space revealed no other way in or out.

"What now?" Doug said.

"We need a pointing hand to show us the way."

He walked in a circle shining his flashlight up and down, and stopped, toeing at the ground. "Help me," he said, and I joined him, kicking away a layer of silt until a hand indicated a square of metal with a recessed latch. Doug pulled on it and the door in the floor sprung open, revealing a dark pit. We looked at each other. "Ladies first," he said.

"Thanks a lot, pal."

"There's the top of a ladder, attached to the wall. See it?"

"Yeah, but where does it end?" I said, my flashlight beam swallowed away.

"Down there . . . somewhere."

"That's comforting." I lowered myself inside, my hands and feet finding the rungs. "See you on the other—" I said, as the ladder's ancient bolts pulled free and I fell, landing with a painful *thud*. The ladder clanged nearby, missing me by inches. I sat up on my elbows, seeing the circle of light from Doug's miner's helmet.

"Are you okay?" he said.

"Peachy." I groaned. "This hole's not deep enough to kill, only wound." I stood, brushed myself off, and looked up. "You can't jump. I got lucky but you might break something."

"No problem!" he said. I heard the *chink* of metal on metal, the rope unfurled at my feet, and Doug shimmied down beside me.

"Very slick. What did you tie it to?"

"Did *Cliffhanger* teach you nothing? I didn't tie it, I hooked it to a steel beam." He yanked the rope but nothing happened. Looking up, whipping his arm, he said, "It's all in the wrist," and then, "Look out!" We leaped backward as a pointed claw hit the spot where we'd been standing.

I stared at the claw, which was attached to the end of the rope. "A grappling hook?"

"Told you. Trader Jack's has everything."

"Way to be prepared," I said. "Were you a Boy Scout?"

"No," he said, stuffing the rope into the backpack, "but I liked the uniforms."

I surveyed our surroundings, seeing a hand pointing into a tunnel in a nearby wall. "Ready?" I said.

"Lead on," he said, as we entered the tunnel. After a few steps, he paused, saying, "Hey, how far did you drop? Ten feet?"

"Felt like it," I said.

"Hm. I guess that's deep enough."

"For what?"

He laid his hand on the cool, dirty tunnel ceiling above us. "Feel that."

I did, sensing a not-so-distant vibration. "What is it?"

"Think about where we just came from. What was whizzing past behind that rusty door?" he said. "We're right under the subway."

"Um . . . that doesn't seem safe," I said.

"You're the one who said it might be dangerous, remember?" he said. "I sure hope Joe Little knew what he was doing when he dug these tunnels."

"Don't hope," I said, moving ahead, "pray."

Darkness sucked up light like a black sponge, making the flashlights nearly useless. Traveling in single file, me in the lead, time began to evaporate, too, and I said, "How long have we been walking?"

"Either half an hour or sixteen years," Doug said. "Can't really tell. It's like being on a treadmill with my eyes closed."

"It's pretty tight in here, huh?"

"Yes, it's *still* pretty tight in here. Just like the other three times you said that."

"Sorry. I don't like enclosed spaces," I said. "Makes me tense. Feels like a tomb." It occurred to me then that if something fatal happened, if a train fell on top of us, for example, it really would be my final resting place. With my family gone and Max in L.A., no one in the daylight world would notice I was missing. It sparked a thought, and I said, "Doug, can I ask you a question?"

"Why am I so cool?" he said. "Born that way."

"How is it that you're able to stay at the Bird Cage Club?"

"With its lack of amenities? Without my own Jacuzzi and walk-in closet?"

"Seriously," I said. "I know the relationship with your mom and stepdad sucks, and that your real dad is a problem—"

"He's not a problem. He's a pothead who lives in a station wagon."

"Okay, but your mom . . . Doesn't she care that you're never home?"

"I am, rarely. I stop by to get clothes and the weekly envelope of cash she leaves for me," he said. "But the short answer is no. Shopping and vodka are very important to her. Dougie, not so much. The only thing she ever taught me was when I was thirteen, tall enough to see over the dashboard of a car. She had this old five-speed Mercedes and she instructed me in the art of clutch, gas, and brake so I could drive her around when she was blitzed."

"But what if something happened to you, like—"

"I don't know," he said. "I was never a priority. It was always, 'Stick Doug in front of the movie channel with a bag of something salty while the adults party,' or, 'Send Doug to the multiplex with enough money to see everything twice.' And I did, and I'm lucky I did, because movies gave me more than my mom ever could." We were quiet again, steam pipes hissing around us. "One other thing. It's so effed up," he said.

"What?"

"Her method of parenting was out of sight, out of mind,

right? But like every kid, I'd get into trouble now and then . . . busted for shoplifting a candy bar or something."

"Shame on you."

"I know, surprise, I'm human," he said. "And then you should've seen her. She became super-disciplinarian, raising holy hell, watching my every move. It was sick, like . . . she did so little, it made her feel like a mom. But then after a day or so, she'd get distracted by a martini or three and I'd become invisible again."

"Mother of the year," I said.

"Mother-something," he said. "Can I ask you a question?"

"Shoot."

"How could you let Max go?"

It caught me off guard, slowing my step. "Being around me was too dangerous for him. I had no choice. You know that."

"What I meant was, how were you strong enough to let go of someone who loves you?" he said. "I can't imagine having the courage to give that up."

"There was cowardice in it, too. I was scared what he'd think about me, the things I'd done. I hated letting him go." I sighed. "But then, I hate a lot about myself."

"You do what you have to do," he said quietly.

"Doesn't make it right." We fell silent, trudging ahead, until I said, "What about your hockey player?"

"The lunkhead hadn't even seen *Citizen Kane*. We were doomed from date one," he said. "Your turn again. Spill it. What kind of friend is Tyler?"

"I'm not sure. I know he likes me . . . and it feels good. I trust him, at least a little."

"Remember *The Godfather*. Trust only your *consigliere*," Doug said. "For the record, that's me."

"What I meant was, Tyler and I operate in the same world. We understand it," I said. "But it doesn't mean we like it."

"How do you know he doesn't like it?"

"I just know."

"Gut feeling?"

"We talk. We text. Okay?"

"Okeydokey," he said. "Just watch your step."

"Speaking of—is the ground getting muddy?"

"Definitely sticky . . . goopy," he said.

I felt bricks scrape my helmet, the walls press against my shoulders. "Either I'm growing," I said, "or it's getting smaller in here."

"I was worried about this," Doug said. "Settling."

"What do you mean?"

"All those books on the control center you never read? They explain how Chicago is built on mud and clay," he said, touching the wall. "Bricks are missing. The earth is seeping in. This tunnel's probably settling, sinking."

"What if it *settles* on top of us?"

Doug was quiet a moment. "Just keep moving."

The space narrowed more with each step, pushing down from the top, rising up from below. Doug was correct—the ceiling was sinking while wet dirt crumbled in from the sides, filling the floor. I stumbled, reached out to steady myself, and started a small avalanche of bricks and mortar. Overhead, a groaning noise sounded as a shower of grit rained down on our helmets. We froze, waiting for the whole thing to collapse on top of us. When it didn't, I said, "My bad."

"Do not do that again," Doug said.

"Guaranteed," I said, pushing on.

Soon it was difficult to walk upright—we were bent over like two question marks in the dark—and it was all I could do not to scream at the sense of being buried alive. The cold, wormy smell of soil enveloped us as the ceiling pressed down and the path beneath us pushed upward, and then it was so tight the only way to continue was by crawling through the muck.

Doug said what we were both thinking. "We could . . . we might get stuck. We should go back."

"To what?" I answered, spitting mud. "This is it, my last chance." When he didn't reply, I said, "Doug? Are you having a panic attack?"

"I'm too scared to panic," he said quietly.

I felt it then, a faint breeze blowing from just ahead. I squinted, seeing an actual light at the end of the tunnel—a horizontal half-moon shape, all that was left of the top of the tunnel exit. "Keep moving," I said, pulling forward on my belly, ten more feet, then five, and then using both hands to dig away a larger opening through the half-moon. When it was just wide enough, I wiggled out, sliding face-first down a steep mound of dirt to a concrete floor below. I rolled onto my back, never so happy to be reclining in filth. Doug squeezed out using his elbows, slipping down next to me, saying, "Thank *god* I lost weight!" Rising woozily, he yanked the backpack from the crevice and looked around. "Where are we?"

"Sort of like where we started," I said, nodding at a ladder bolted to the wall. Next to it, a painted hand pointed toward a high ledge. "There's another tunnel up there."

"Let's get the hell out of here."

"If the ladder holds," I said.

"We have the grappling hook. If that doesn't work, I'll sprout wings and fly our asses away from this muddy death pit," Doug said.

I pulled on the ladder but it didn't budge. We ascended to the ledge and hesitated before the tunnel entrance. The darkness was impenetrable; it was impossible to tell if the ceiling and walls were intact.

"Are we really going in there? Again?" Doug said with a shudder.

"Once, when I was first learning to box, I dropped my guard and got punched in the face so hard I saw stars," I said. "My trainer, Willy, said it was the dumbest thing he'd ever seen. Made me promise to remember one of his rules of the ring."

"What's that?" Doug said.

"'Never do the same dumb thing twice.'" With a sigh, I said, "Forgive me, Willy," and stepped inside the tunnel.

8

NOTHING CRUSHED OUR SKULLS AND WE DIDN'T have to crawl through sludge. Instead, traveling on, it was our noses that were assaulted.

"*Mamma mia,*" Doug said, sniffing the air, "do you smell that?"

"Are you kidding? How can I not?"

"It reminds me of the worst field trip I ever took," he said. "A chicken farm on a hot day. *Disgusting* is too small a word for it."

I slowed down, shining the flashlight in front of me. The tunnel ended abruptly. Moving the beam, I said, "Is that a door?"

Doug brushed cobwebs from it, showing a painted hand pointing upward and the words *To Fillmore Avenue*. "Fillmore?" Doug said. "I've studied the crap out of Chicago streets and I've never heard of that one."

"Look, no latch," I said.

Doug pushed on the door but it didn't move.

I stepped up and thumped a shoulder against it, and it budged a little. "Help me," I said, and we shoved together. It opened slightly, scraping at the ground.

"Pee-freakin'-yoo!" Doug said. "Something in there needs to change its socks!"

"Once more," I said. We threw ourselves against it and the door popped open with a thunderous crash as we stumbled inside.

"Is that . . . it's a *snake*!" Doug said, rolling around in the dark. "Help me, Sara Jane! It's a huge—"

I shined a beam toward him. "Hose. It's a hose, Doug," I said, moving the flashlight, spotting a light switch. I flipped it and lit the space. By pushing through the door, we'd knocked over a shelf that had been placed against it, scattering tools and round plastic tubs. I stared at one marked *Chromic Acid* and another, *Ammonia*. "I think we're in some type of storage area," I said.

"Look," he said, pointing around. "Three walls built from concrete blocks. But the one we came through . . . old brick." He looked closely at the door. "It was sealed off. See how it was soldered at the edges? Someone did a lousy job."

"Thank god," I said. The stench was stronger, and I looked across at another door that was decades newer than the other one. "Come on," I said. It opened easily, and we stepped onto a concrete platform that seemed to stretch forever in both directions. It was bisected by a slow-moving stream of beige goop, emanating a scent best described as slaughterhouse mixed with nursing home. Another platform, just as wide, ran along the other side of the stream. "Sewer. A big one and fairly modern, too," I said, looking at the concrete walls and buzzing fluorescent lights. "This thing is fairly new . . . built way after Capone Doors. No painted hands."

The muffled sound of traffic *guh-dunk-guh-dunk*ed from far above.

Doug tilted his head. "That's why there's no Fillmore Avenue," he said. "Walking northeast from the bakery . . . I bet we're under the Eisenhower Expressway. Fillmore probably got wiped out to make room for it."

"That's not all that got wiped out," I said, staring around the cavernous space. "The tunnel used to continue somewhere up here, but it's gone. Built over by the city."

"Now what?"

I shrugged. "No idea."

"I know you don't want to go back, but I think we have to, and find another Capone Door. I hate the idea of squeezing into that tunnel, but it's our best option," he said, reaching for the door that had closed behind us. "Okay, scratch that. It's locked."

I looked at the punch code on the door, at the stencil reading *Maintenance C-316,* and at Doug biting his lip. "So, we head north," I said, pushing the helmet back on my head, wiping at a line of sweat. "Hopefully, we'll find something that leads back to Joe Little's tunnels."

Doug shifted the backpack and sighed. "Hopefully," he said.

The platform was covered in a layer of slippery scum, with large pipes jutting from the wall, dripping into the terrible canal. We stepped over them carefully, our boots making suction noises as we walked. Now and then a big bubble of methane gas would pop lazily in the stream beside us, while cars and trucks rocketed overhead. It was as impossible to ignore the unbearable odor as it was the feeling of defeat, until I remembered something. "Last night," I said, "I found a letter from Nunzio to Enzo hidden in the notebook."

"Really? Where?"

"Under the back cover. It said all kinds of stuff but only one thing that mattered."

"What?"

I grinned at him. "'Ultimate power is freedom.'"

"Wow," he said. "What the hell does that mean?"

"You got me. But I like it," I said, as my ears perked up, hearing a familiar tune—someone whistling "Take Me Out to the Ball Game." Carefully, with a finger to my lips, I pulled Doug into a dark corner.

Footsteps echoed toward us as a wiry guy in an orange vest and hard hat appeared on the platform across the stream. A walkie-talkie crackled, asking if he was at the door yet. The guy told it to relax and asked what the code was again. The walkie-talkie told him—*four-six-three*—as he stopped at a door stenciled with *Pump 12,* punched the buttons on a lock, and swung it open. A light flicked on and I squinted through the gloom, seeing the walls inside, made of old brick. After some clanking and hissing, the guy reemerged, slammed the door, held his nose, and told whoever was on the other end of the walkie-talkie that there was something in the air down here that reminded him of the Cubs. When the footsteps faded, I said, "Come on."

"Over there?" Doug said, pointing at the stream. "Through *that*?"

"How else are we going to get to the other side?" I said. "What, you're scared to get dirty?"

"No. I'm scared of drowning in toilet paper and nightmare condoms."

"It can't be that deep," I said, stepping over a low railing and sliding in, the sludge rising to the top of my boots as my feet touched bottom. It was syrupy and warm even through rubber. I moved cautiously, terrified of the slightest splash. Doug eased in behind with the backpack on his head. I grabbed the railing on the other side, pulled myself up, and helped him climb up, too, right outside the door.

"Let us never speak of this again." He shuddered as I punched four-six-three into the lock. Inside, the fluorescent light spread a yellowish glow. The pump dominated the room like a huge steel octopus, fat in the middle, pipes twisting off in several directions, the thickest ascending into darkness. Doug touched the wall and said, "It's the same brick as in the tunnels. But this place goes nowhere. Now what?"

Something else answered, high-pitched and insistent.

I turned to a tiny pair of gleaming yellow eyes.

"Antonio?" I said.

It wasn't possible, of course. The two original sewer rats that Great-Grandpa Nunzio had trained to guard Club Molasses decades ago, Antonio and Cleopatra, were long dead. But throughout the past six months, their descendants had appeared at critical moments to do what they'd been bred to do—aid and protect a Rispoli. This one twitched its worm tail, impatient, not the least bit intimidated, and scurried up the high middle pipe. I aimed the flashlight after it, seeing footholds, and said, "Let's go."

"Whoa, time out," Doug said. "I was willing to walk through a stream of human gravy, but follow a rodent to who-knows-where? Really?"

"At least it goes up."

"At the very least." He sighed.

We climbed quickly, leaving the ground far below. The helmet lights helped but the rat made the difference. It scrambled from foothold to foothold, guiding us upward, reassuring us with encouraging squeaks until it was quiet. I peered around, seeing nothing, and then spotted the little animal directly across from me, standing in the entrance to a tunnel. I knew rats were good jumpers; it had leaped across the three feet of air floating between the pipe and the tunnel entrance, and we'd have to do the same.

Running in a frenetic circle, the rat squeaked once in fare-well and disappeared. "We have to jump over there," I said to Doug. "Can you make it?"

"Of course. I'm in great shape," he said nervously.

I took a deep breath and pushed off, landing solidly on both feet. Peering down into darkness and then at Doug hug-ging the pipe, I said, "Don't think too much."

He looked down, and then back at me. "I'm thinking too much."

"Jump!" I yelled, the word bouncing from the walls, and he did, but with his arms extended instead of feet first. He hit the ledge at his chest, fingernails digging at the brick floor, and began sliding backward. I grabbed his wrists and pulled like it was a tug-of-war, grinding my heels, yanking with all I had as he came barreling up and over, knocking me flat. While he lay on the path fidgeting and talking to god, I rose and looked at the wall across the chasm. Just like in the sewer, it was solid concrete. My guess was that once, long ago, the tunnel we occupied continued on the opposite side. I turned and looked at a pointing hand on the wall behind me with the words LOOP—½ MILE. Doug stood, foul-smelling and trembling. "Uh . . . is that your boots, or you?" I asked.

"At this point, what's the difference?" He shuddered, drawing out a cigarette and the steel lighter. "Sorry to be a cliché, but I really need a smoke."

"Doug," I said, "remember? Explosive gases?"

He glanced at the lighter, sighed, put it away, and followed me into the tunnel. We covered the half-mile in silence until he said, "Hey. Look." I turned my flashlight on a pointing hand with the words MONADNOCK BUILDING—6 FLIGHTS UP next to a passageway.

"We're beneath Jackson Street, downtown," I said. "In the Loop."

"There's another one," he said, shining on the words SHERMAN HOUSE HOTEL—VIA COAL ELEVATOR. "Never heard of the place."

"Must be gone. Knocked down and built over," I said.

Our trek took us past more passageways leading to other phantom locations—Henrici's Ristorante, The Venetian

Building, St. Hubert's Grill—until, slowly, the ever-present darkness was cut by weak illumination. It came from an entrance just ahead and we picked up our pace, hurrying toward it. Doug entered the large room first and I followed, gaping up at a cathedral-like ceiling, tall and airy, with light streaming through distant grates. There were no seeping pipes or flowing sewage, but instead, in the middle of the room, a circular bar. Empty bottles and overturned tumblers sat on it next to a rotary telephone and a ticker-tape machine, all of it caked in decades of dust.

"It's an octagon," Doug said, staring around the stop sign–shaped room, "like an intersection or crossroad." Each of the eight walls bore a sign above a tunnel entrance leading to a specific location. "Krauss Music Store, Bruno's Diner, House of Eng," he read, nodding at three of the openings. "Never heard of those places, either."

"Wrigley Field is still there, of course," I said, picking up where he left off. "That tunnel leads to the Issel Building, that one goes to St. Alphonsus Church." I turned and looked at the tunnel from which we'd emerged, its sign reading LOOP, which was now behind us. It was the seventh entrance, leaving one more. I walked across the room and stared at the words above the eighth tunnel. "Riviera Theatre," I said, turning to Doug with a grin. "You know where the Riviera Theatre is, don't you?"

"Next to the Green Mill Lounge, across from Uptown National Bank," he said. "Follow that tunnel and we'll end up beneath the Troika of Outfit Influence."

"Where ultimate power is waiting," I said quietly.

It was one of those pause-before-you-leap moments, and Doug exhaled, staring around the room. "There hasn't been anyone down here in a long time. The old telephone, that ticker-tape thingy . . . I wonder how it's survived."

"The tunnel got cut off. It was forgotten," I said, lifting the phone, hearing nothing. Knowing the Outfit as I did, I realized that the tunnels weren't used only to flee the law, or one another; they were also ideal places to conduct dirty business in private. As counselor-at-large, I could only think how perfect this room was—beyond perfect—for a sit-down. I looked at the bar's scarred surface and blew away a layer of grit, seeing hundreds of names, curses, and dates carved into the soft wood:

Beware! Dominick DiBello is a gun-packing fellow, 1939
Lefty Rosenthal marks cards and loads dice, the schmuck
1952, Good for me, bad for you!—Jimmy "the Bomber" Cattura
And finally, nearly obscured but still visible:
NR, C-a-L, era qui

"Nunzio Rispoli, Counselor-at-Large, was here," I murmured, tracing the inscription with a finger. Doug was just inside the tunnel leading to the Riviera Theatre, moving a flashlight around. I started after him and hesitated—the pharaoh key chain was in one pocket, a pocketknife in the other. I took it out, returned to the bar, and began to scrape into the wood.

"Sara Jane," Doug said, "let's go!"

"On my way!" I said, staring at my handiwork, carved directly below Nunzio's:

SJR, C-a-L, was here.

The mouth in the brick wall beckoned and I went to it. I glanced around the room once more, unsure if I'd ever pass this way again, and then the tunnel swallowed me up.

9

HEADED TOWARD THE RIVIERA THEATRE, TIME
no longer slipped away. Instead, we tracked it by the minute,
having calculated that the walk from the tunnel intersection
to the Troika of Outfit Influence would take an hour. That,
combined with our true north direction—GPS was useless
underground but Doug had thought to bring a compass—
meant that we were close to our destination.

We traveled on, knowing we were close and saying little.

A long descent had begun after we left the tunnel intersection and now the rotten perfume of human waste reemerged.
The mossy brick walls, no longer concrete, told us that the
branch of the sewer system we'd entered was very old; Doug
reminded me that some of Chicago's sewers had been in place
for more than a hundred years. Just ahead came the sound of
moving liquid—not the comforting rush of a clear stream but
the spattering echo of something thick and noxious. Moving
the beam through darkness, Doug said, "Whoa," and raised an

arm to stop me. He pointed the flashlight, and there it was—a waterfall of slimy waste spilling from a trio of pipes at the top of a high concrete wall. The brick floor of the tunnel ended a few feet in front of us; a twelve-foot abyss floated between it and the waterfall. We squinted into the stinking drop-off, unable to see the bottom. "Perfect," Doug said, "dead end."

"You're right. Too perfect," I said quietly. "It reminds me of an Outfit guy, Bones something . . . Bones Caputo."

"Quite a moniker," Doug said.

"He goes around with this monstrous pit bull on a chain, Goliath. The dog's like a walking, snarling shark," I said. "Months ago, I presided over a sit-down between Bones and his partner. They're bank robbers, hitting small neighborhood branches for a couple grand at a time. The partner suspected Bones was holding out, not giving him his fair cut. After a dose of cold fury, Bones confessed that he'd hidden the money. Guess where."

"Kind of obvious, isn't it? In Goliath's doghouse."

"You'd think so. But no . . . Bones is dumb, not stupid," I said. "He'd been wrapping the cash in garbage bags and burying it in this disgusting hole in his backyard where he'd trained the dog to, you know . . . do his business."

"Ugh . . . where no one in his right mind would look."

"It's Outfit mentality," I said, staring at the waterfall. "Hide something valuable where there appears to be nothing but a repulsive wall of shit."

"You think ultimate power's behind that wall?"

I nodded, staring at the pipes spewing out gunk. "Nothing

up there but concrete. There's got to be a tunnel or a door at the bottom," I said, looking into the pit. "No ladder. No footholds. Okay, grappling hook it is."

"We're going down there? Into *that*?"

"Not we. Me," I said. "Attach it to something sturdy and lower me down."

"For once, I won't argue . . . Be my guest," he said, uncoiling the rope and hooking it to a nearby pipe.

"If I'm wrong and there's no entrance—"

"Then I'll hose you down and shoot you full of penicillin," he said, "and we'll find another way inside."

I looped the rope around my waist. "Hold on tight."

"Hold your nose."

Doug lowered me by inches until I could see what waited beneath. The waterfall emptied into a circular pool equipped with some type of gurgling pump, like a giant bowl of gross butterscotch pudding. I touched down on a walkway that wound around the pool, leading to a door. "I found it!" I said, pulling it open, hearing a low rumble, and then—

Ka-thump!

—I went down on my hands and knees as Poor Kevin, in his filthy ski mask and greasy plaid suit, leaped from a shadow and punched me in the head so hard, and—

Ka-thump! Ka-thump!

—I was kicked once, twice in the skull and rolled on my back to see Teardrop, its glowing red eyes cutting through the murkiness, as—

Ka-thump!

—Goatee dropped his boot squarely on my face, grinning with the same evil smirk as the devil tattooed on his chin, until—

"Sara Jane!"

I blinked up at my parents and Lou hovering over me, staring silently, not underground but in our living room, which was as violently trashed as the night they'd disappeared. A family portrait made creepy-clownish by our grinning naïveté clung to the mantel, slashed to ribbons. Cabinets were kicked in like mouths full of broken teeth, shelves splintered, the bust of Frank Sinatra shattered to pieces. The couch I lay on was gutted, with its cottony intestines spilled across the floor. I tried to sit up but a hand eased me back to the lacerated cushions, which were cold and sticky beneath my head. I turned from my dad to my mom to Lou, their eyes riveted on me in a troublesome, anxious way.

"See?" I said, "I kept going, kept looking. I'm almost there."

Quietly, nearly inaudibly, my mother said, "We are alive . . ."

"Thank . . . god," I croaked.

"In Sara Jane," she hissed.

"Each day we wait . . . ," Lou said, taking a slow, threatening step.

"For Sara Jane," my dad continued with a blade of contempt in his words. He yanked me toward him, his voice rising as my mom and brother joined in, chanting, "Our daughter, our sister," pausing to spit, "*our savior* . . . Sara Jane." And then my dad did something he'd never done in my life: he raised an open hand and slapped me so sharp and fast across the cheek that I froze, squeezing my eyes shut—

"Sara Jane!"

—and fluttering them open to Doug, his face tight with anxiety. I was on my back just outside the doorway and he was leaning over me, hands pressed together. "Sorry I hit you," he said, "but I was scared you were dead."

"I'm . . . alive?"

"Luck of the Sicilians, I guess," he said, nodding inside the door, where a pile of brick and stone lay. "Part of the ceiling in there collapsed when you opened the door."

"I heard it," I said, struggling to sit up as the universe did a jackknife and a mule kicked me in the head. Pain reverberated through my skull like a controlled explosion. I leaned over, heaved bile, wiped my mouth with a shaky hand, and touched at the cuts and abrasions on my bare head. "Where's my helmet?" I wheezed.

"In pieces. If you hadn't been wearing it, I could've slapped you around all day and you'd still be lying there, forever," he said. "Something hit you hard enough to knock you back outside the door. It sounded like the rest of the bricks and stuff came barreling down seconds later. If it had all fallen at once, you'd be a pancake . . . no, a crepe . . . a crepe run over by a steamroller hit by a—"

"Got it," I said, hawking blood and recalling a blip from my fever dream. "I saw them," I murmured.

"Who? Your family?"

"Yeah. They're angry at me, losing patience," I said, feeling the trail of a tear. "If I don't save them soon, they could . . . all of them will—"

"Sara Jane," he said, touching my shoulder, "you just got hit on the head with something very heavy. This one time, maybe give yourself a break, okay?"

I looked into the tunnel behind the door, and back at him. "We can climb over that stuff, but it might happen again. If you want to stay behind—"

"I just rappelled into a crap-filled pit," he said. "If I was going to bail, it would've happened by now." He pointed a flashlight and we climbed over the debris, careful not to touch a wall or brush the ceiling. The floor was powdery, the air stale and unmoving. The tunnel curved and ended at a ladder descending into gloom. We exchanged a glance and then began to climb down, first one rung, then another, Doug saying, "Relax. It'll hold. The law of averages says—"

And then the ladder collapsed beneath us.

The thing about free-falling is that it's too late to scream.

Your nervy stomach lurches at not being attached to the world any longer and your brain goes into turtle shell–protective mode. It's only when you land on something that's not soft, but that also doesn't kill you, that you're able to emit an oh-my-god-I'm-not-dead! sound. Mine was guttural—a raccoon backed over by an SUV—while Doug's was shrill and surprised, like an elderly nun hit with a water balloon.

I was able to speak first, saying, "Goddamn . . . ladders."

"What are we lying in?" Doug groaned. "Please don't say sewage."

I stood on the pile of stinking, caked dirt that had broken our fall. Pure circumstance had dropped us near an ancient industrial light switch mounted on the wall. Stumbling toward it, seeing its rusty tubing snake toward the surface, I flipped the handle to ON. First came an anemic *buzz* and then three of a dozen large, suspended lights hummed to life. I looked up at the mouth of the tunnel, high upon the wall from which we'd fallen; remnants of the ladder clung to it and the rest lay in pieces around us.

I turned slowly, staring at a vast, triangular room.

"It's, like, the size of an airplane hangar," Doug said in awe, "but V shaped."

I stared at the three soaring walls and said, "Those must be the foundations of the troika—the buildings that hold the Riviera Theatre, Green Mill, and the bank."

"Which one is which?" he said.

I shrugged, brushing a stray lock of hair from my eyes. "I can't tell. But we're in a big, hidden pocket beneath them." The only entrance and exit seemed to have been via the collapsed ladder, and its tunnel and doorway had been craftily concealed behind the disgusting waterfall—this place was not meant to be stumbled upon by random Outfit members traversing the tunnels. It gave me pause, as I wondered exactly how we were going to get out of here, and I stared around the room. Joe Little had fashioned it from a landscape of brick and concrete, leaving a floor of hard-packed soil. Piles of dirt like the one we'd landed on had been pushed into corners to accommodate—

I spotted it, and gasped a little, elbowing Doug.

—a rounded structure built from white bricks, like an over-sized igloo, crouching in the middle of the room.

"Is it possible?" Doug said. "Could it be . . . ?"

"The last chapter of the notebook," I said slowly. "*Volta*. I think it's a vault."

"If so, it's a big one," he said, following me toward it. A pathway hugged the structure's exterior, and as we looked for the entrance, we passed by a hulking, rusty metal box the size of a refrigerator bolted to the wall. It had a sign with a flaking image of zigzagging electricity and a warning:

CAUTION! HIGH VOLTAGE! DO NOT TOUCH!

"You think that old thing's still functional after all these years?" Doug said.

"Let's don't find out," I said, continuing around the vault to a green brass door held fast with thick hinges, studded with bolts. It took only seconds to rub away decades of tarnish, revealing numerals and letters etched into brass: *U.N.B. 001*, and the year *1932*. "Vault number one," I said, "or at least the number one most important vault. All it takes is a key." The chain came easily from my neck and I leaned toward the doorknob. I looked again, felt around it, and turned to Doug. "There's no keyhole."

"There has to be," he said, edging past. Bending, squinting, touching, he stood back finally, confused. "There's no keyhole."

"Then what's the key for? Why does it have U.N.B. 001 on it?"

He shrugged, staring at the door. "You think maybe it's . . . unlocked?"

I stared at him, saying nothing, unable to believe that anything so simple could be possible. Like cracking a safe, moving my fingers with precision, I gently turned the knob. A loud *click!* made us both jump.

The door opened a few inches, creaking on dry hinges.

Now all we had to do was step through.

10

A FEEBLE GLOW EMANATED FROM THE VAULT—
the switch had activated its lights, too—and I pushed into a
room that was completely empty.

Except for a dramatically thin guy sitting with his legs
crossed, waiting.

I scream-jumped and then caught myself, focusing on the
first mummy I'd ever seen in person.

Doug and I edged inside, and he propped the door wide
open, whispering, "If that thing moves, I'm outta here, fast."
For a minute or two, or maybe ten, we stood staring at the
dead human being, while absorbing the barrenness of the
vault. Doug spoke first, saying, "There's nothing here except
him. Where's ultimate power?"

"Maybe he knows," I said.

We crossed slowly to where the desiccated body sat next
to a table holding a dusty glass, a whiskey bottle, and an
ancient cigar. It wore a plain blue suit and dull brown tie,
moldy with age. What grabbed my attention, though, was

its snap-brim fedora and a diamond-encrusted ring hanging lazily from its shriveled pinkie. Even with every trace of life long evacuated, its posture exuded a haughty, intimidating presence. I stared at the leathery flesh clinging stubbornly to its face, marked by jagged scars on the left side. The thing leered with its lips stretched back, and I felt a chilly whisper of recognition. "Holy shit," I said. "Nunzio found ultimate power all right."

"What?" he said, looking around the empty space. "Where?"

"Remember? The one with lasting influence on the Outfit?"

"Wait, you don't mean—" he said, staring at the gristly skin that had been disfigured by a sharp knife long ago. "Oh. Oh . . . god . . ."

"Close, in terms of veneration by mobsters," I said, nodding at the mummy. "Al Capone. Scarface Al himself. Mister Ultimate Power, in the flesh, or what's left of it."

"The cold air down here preserved it, kept him from becoming a complete skeleton," Doug said, gaping at the body. "Can I . . . should I make sure it's him?"

"He won't complain."

Riffling through his pockets with careful fingertips, Doug extracted a snub-nosed .38 revolver, followed by a fat billfold. He flipped it open and said, "Driver's license name . . . Al Brown."

"His go-to alias. Used it for years, according to the notebook."

"This thing was issued in 1951. Every history book on the control center says he died in 1947, in Florida. It was a closed casket, no one saw the body," he said with a smirk. "That's because there was no body. I guess the rumor was true."

"Faked his death and escaped the Feds and the Outfit alike with a hundred million dollars in cash," I said. "There's a scrap of a newspaper article taped in the notebook, some old cop swearing he saw Capone in Chicago, alive, with Joe Little—"

"In 1951," Doug said.

We faced each other then, my friend and I who had been through so much together, not only on (and beneath) the streets of Chicago, but hacking like jungle explorers through the notebook, untangling its secrets, memorizing its facts. Combining truth with what-ifs, I began enunciating a theory. "Joe Little built the vault for Capone so he could hide a hundred million dollars before he went to prison . . ."

"And then four years after faking his death, when he thought the coast was clear, he snuck back to Chicago to make sure it was safe," Doug said.

"Or to make a withdrawal?"

"But it was dangerous," he said. "If the Outfit hierarchy discovered that Capone had hidden a fortune from them, they would've been pissed. After all, he wasn't boss anymore in 1951."

"He needed someone with real influence to negotiate a settlement so they wouldn't snuff him for the cash. The counselor-at-large," I said. "He needed Nunzio." I glanced at the diamond pinkie ring and flashy fedora. "Capone was a showboat. A braggart. It fits that he would've brought Nunzio down here to show off his stash."

"Which is how Nunzio learned about the vault," Doug said.

"Right . . ."

"None of which explains how Capone died," Doug said, inspecting the corpse.

I stared at the body, thinking, *He's an empty shell. The secret of his death died with him—*

"No bullet holes or dried blood," he said, and snapped open the .38.

—and so did ultimate power, which means—

"It's loaded. He didn't defend himself. Also, the door was unlocked. Why didn't he walk out?"

—there's nothing in this vault that can help me. Nothing at all.

"And where's the money?" Doug said.

"I don't know," I replied absently.

"Do you think Nunzio killed him somehow?"

"Maybe." I shrugged. "Or maybe someone else did. It doesn't matter." What had happened in the past—to Capone's fortune, or how he died—was irrelevant to the present. The real question spread through me like winter frost. "Why did Nunzio say ultimate power was freedom," I asked, "if it's just a bag of human bones?"

Doug faced me and said nothing.

"I thought '*Volta*' existed to protect the Rispolis . . . I was so sure the notebook would save my mom and dad and Lou. Poor Lou," I said. "I was a fool . . ."

"No . . ."

"*Yes!*" I cried, my voice bouncing from the white brick dome. "*Goddamn* that notebook! I hate it! I hate myself for relying on it! All the time I wasted believing in it, hoping so hard, while . . ." I said, the truth so painfully evident. "I killed my family, Doug . . . just like everyone else I've killed . . ."

"Sara Jane . . ."

Leaning over the corpse, staring into its vacant eye sockets, I blinked once, feeling the cold blue flame flicker and burn. "You son of a bitch," I said through clenched teeth. "It's your fault, too. You and your Outfit tore my family to shreds."

It sat silently with a smug grin on its shrunken head.

"Right. Okay," I said, extending a hand to Doug without looking at him. "The revolver. Give it to me."

"What for?" he said, handing over Capone's .38.

"He's dead. He can't get any deader," I said, blowing dust from the chamber, aiming it, and squinting down the barrel. "But at least I can have the pleasure of shooting him with his own gun." And I squeezed the trigger, blasting that smile and the rest of his brittle skull to bony bits.

"Good aim," Doug said quietly, looking at the empty neck, and he then stared past it, paused, and walked to the wall. Running a hand over the bullet marks, he turned and muttered something unintelligible.

"What did you say?" I asked, moving toward him.

"A-u seventy-nine," he repeated. "Like the flecks in your eyes. Gold . . ."

"What is? That brick?"

He nodded and I scraped at the white paint, seeing a heavy yellow gleam, like solidified honey. I used the pocketknife to chip away mortar and pry it from the wall.

The brick was the size of a small loaf of bread, heavier than it should've been.

It didn't take much to flake away the rest of the paint. When I'd finished, Doug and I stared at a thick bar of gold stamped with:

SERIAL NO. 260911

1932

BANK OF CALIFORNIA

999.9

FINE GOLD

400 OZ.

"You have any idea what this is worth?" Doug asked solemnly.

"Absolutely none," I said, unable to peel my eyes from it. "Do you?"

"Gold is, like, two thousand bucks per Troy ounce. It's measured according to—"

"Wait. How do you know that?" I asked. He arched an eyebrow in a how-do-you-think? look, and I said, "Sorry . . . movies, movies, movies."

"Anyway, two grand multiplied by four hundred ounces is . . ." he said, squeezing his eyes and doing math.

"Eight hundred thousand dollars."

"Eight hundred large." He whistled. "Motherfu— And we found the one gold bar hidden in an entire wall of bricks? What are the chances?"

The question stopped me since I knew nothing happened by chance in the Outfit, that even the smallest scam, plot, or racket was thought out to every infinitesimal detail. I looked at the thousands of conjoined rectangles from which the domed vault was constructed, licked at dry lips, and said, "It's the other way around. What are the chances we'll find even one brick among the gold bars?" I lifted Capone's .38 and fired at another wall, and another, and at the ceiling; each shot answered with little beams of golden light.

Doug stared at the ceiling, the walls, me. "All of it?" he said in a tone as soft as rustling leaves.

I handed him the pocketknife.

He carried it to a far wall, picking spots at random and scraping gently. "This one, too . . . and this. And this. Capone converted a hundred million dollars into enough gold bars to construct a small building." Poking a finger in the air, counting, and breathing excitedly, he said, "There have to be five thousand of them here."

"Times eight hundred grand," I said.

"Equals . . ."

We held each other's gaze with little calculators clicking away in our brains. I said it first, beginning with a slow, "Ho . . . ly . . . *shit,*" and ending with, "Four bill—wait, can that be right? Four *billion* dollars?!"

"Ho . . . ly . . . *shit* . . ." Doug gasped. "That's an *enormous* fortune!"

"It's more than that," I answered slowly. "It's ultimate power . . ."

My surprise that it wasn't a massive bomb or something

equally destructive proved that while I was *in* the Outfit, I still wasn't completely *of* the Outfit—at least not yet. If so, I would've remembered that bloodshed is merely a tool used to advance a goal. The organization's real weapon was its collective belief that all people were driven by greed. And that the intense, selfish desire for *something*—status, narcotics, sex, whatever—placed every human being into one of two categories: either a customer, or someone who could be bought. In the Outfit, the boss has absolute control of how profits are made and spent, which guarantees his control of the organization. Beyond the murders he can order on demand, it is his authority over every dollar that imbues him with power.

With the gold at her fingertips, Elzy would have that power times four billion.

She could do anything with it. The Outfit could easily be subdued by purchasing members' loyalty while paying to neutralize those who didn't cede to her control. Every shady business could be expanded exponentially, from drugs and gambling to prostitution and shadow construction and far beyond, into territories yet unexplored. Unions could be bought wholesale, along with legions of cops and aldermen, mayors, congressmen, all the way to the White House. If Elzy were crafty enough, her criminal organization could grow from local to global.

Looking around at the painted bricks, I repeated myself. "It's ultimate power," I said, and then in a burst of comprehension, I understood Nunzio's meaning. "But . . . it's also freedom. At least for my family," I said, the words echoing off the walls. "A hundred million in 1951, four billion today. It's enough, much more than enough, to escape the Outfit forever. It could carry my family so far away, insulate us in such deep secrecy, that no one would ever find us."

"Nunzio was right," Doug said. "But also wrong."

I looked at him, waiting.

"He assumed the Rispolis would be intact, that if something terrible happened, they could use ultimate power to escape together," he said. "Your family isn't."

The vault was so quiet that it felt full of ghosts. "Elzy wants the notebook for ultimate power, but she doesn't know what it is," I said slowly. "She wants me for cold fury because she knows what I can do. And she wants both in order to take over the Outfit. But what is the Outfit? What has its sole purpose been since day one?"

Doug answered without hesitation. "To make money. Needs more to make more."

"I'll use ultimate power to buy my family's freedom. As much as she hates us, not even Elzy would turn down a score like this. It's worth a hell of a lot more than the Outfit and the Russian mob combined," I said, "and she can have every damn ounce of it."

"So you're going to tell her what ultimate power is?"

"But not where it is," I said. "When the deal is done and we're safely away, then I'll tell her."

"How can you trust her? Not just to make the deal, but to honor it?"

"What choice do I have?" I said. "Look, all I know is that yesterday I didn't have a single bargaining chip. Today, I have four billion of them."

Doug hefted the gold bar. "Then we'd better take this. She'll want to see one of those chips." When it was zipped inside the backpack we went to the door, stepped out, and closed it behind us. I tried it once to make sure; it opened easily. Doug stared up at the remnants of the ladder hanging from the wall. "So how do we get out of here?"

"I don't know," I said, looking around again. "There aren't any tunnels or—"

"Shh," Doug said, cocking an ear. "You hear something?"

"What? I don't hear any—"

"Quiet," he said, his head swiveling slowly. "This way, it's music." I followed him around the vault in the direction we'd come from, past the electrical box, and he paused. "I think it's coming from there."

"Where?" I said. "From this thing?"

"Inside it," he said, moving his ear near the box, staring at me. "It's a trumpet."

I leaned in, careful not to touch the box, and heard it—a trumpet, drums, maybe a trombone—and thought of the music Grandpa Enzo used to listen to in the kitchen of Rispoli & Sons while he, Uncle Buddy, and my dad baked and decorated cakes, cookies, and all other types of fancy pastries. "It's jazz," I said. "Big band."

"The Green Mill has live jazz five nights a week," Doug said. "Joe Little hid one door behind a waterfall of crap. Maybe he put another one back there."

"Where no one would be stupid enough to touch it," I said.

"Are we stupid enough?" he said. "Let me rephrase . . . Are you stupid enough?"

I stared at the warning on the refrigerator-sized box. The c in CAUTION! seemed slightly raised, but I wasn't sure. With a silent prayer, I pushed it quickly, and the face of the box popped open, revealing a dark passageway. "Stupid is as stupid does," I said, relieved.

"Good old Forrest Gump." He peered inside. "What if the tunnel collapsed?"

"Like everything else, we'll get through it," I said. After a last look at ultimate power squatting in middle earth, I followed Doug into the passageway, feeling the ground ascend. A few steps through the cool tunnel led to a flight of rickety wooden stairs.

He shone his flashlight upward, saying, "It's really steep, as high as the ladder we fell from, maybe higher. You think it's safe?"

"Down here, safe is subjective. It's standing, isn't it, and it leads out?"

"Good enough for me," he said, leading the way. We creaked toward the surface, turning and twisting a dozen times, and freezing when a low groan of old wood and nails sounded beneath us. The stairway swayed back and forth. "Oh shit!" Doug said, "this thing's going down!"

And then it didn't.

"Just keep moving," I said, "carefully."

We kept on, almost tiptoeing, the music growing nearer, until Doug shone a light overhead and said, "Look." A trapdoor—so close we could touch it, held tight by a padlock gone orange with rust. As we inched closer, voices chattered and glasses clinked above us. Heavy footsteps fell again and again, back and forth, and Doug said, "We must be under the bar." We were, and we stood on a narrow landing, praying it would hold, until the last horn bleated, the last cocktail was slurped, the last receipt tallied, and the Green Mill locked up for the night. When we were sure it was empty, I used the .45 surgically, firing one shot to blow off the padlock. The trapdoor swung on antique hinges, sounding like a crow being strangled. I pushed away a floor mat and we climbed back on top of the world, crouching to make sure no one was around. I closed the trapdoor, pushed the mat into place, and Doug followed me around the winding bar. The booths were empty, the bandstand vacated, the glass wall sconces devoid of light.

A clock on the wall pointed at four a.m.

"Late for a school night—or day." Doug yawned.

As we moved to the exit, I noticed a framed black-and-white face leering from behind the bar. Its left cheek was creased with scars and the head was topped by a fedora. In the photo, Al Capone was at the height of his power, truly the original gangster. I knew from the notebook that "Machine Gun" Jack McGurn had once owned the Green Mill, but that Capone was the real proprietor, using it as a base of operations. It made sense that an entrance to his vault—the most important Capone Door of all—would be located here. I felt the brass pharaoh in my pocket, yet another mysterious key, and was flooded with exhaustion and tired of secrets. We moved to the door, unlocked it, and slipped onto the deserted sidewalk. An entire day of sun had been extinguished while we were underground. It felt as if natural light would never return.

"Let's take the El," I said.

We crossed the empty street toward the station as a yellow light changed to red, the *click* audible in the silent air. I paused in the intersection where Broadway, Lawrence, and Racine met. Bridgeview Bank, formerly Uptown National Bank, was ahead, the Riviera Theatre to my right, the Green Mill just behind.

B U R G L R

It was the oddest feeling I'd had since my family disappeared, something like confidence, knowing that ultimate power was in my hands and deep below my feet. In the world I occupied, where murder was for sale and lives could be bought, I was now armed with a four-billion-dollar weapon.

11

MONDAY MORNING, CROSSING THE THRESHOLD
into the old brick fortress commonly known as Fep Prep, I
was at the beginning of the end.

The fall semester was quickly winding down. When holiday break began, I'd lose the seven hours of relative safety
I clung to each weekday. With its checkpoints, omnipresent
guards, and watchful cameras, my pursuers would be foolish
to try to breach Fep Prep.

It was all courtesy of Mr. Novak.

Thaddeus "Thumbs-Up" Novak, Fep Prep's long-serving
principal.

Short and roly-poly, bald except for tufts of gray hair
around his ears, he favored short-sleeved dress shirts with a
rotation of unusually patterned neckties—Tweety Bird one
day, little flying toasters the next, and so on. Mr. Novak was
as committed to the safety of his students as he was to the
concept—which caused most kids (including me) to roll their
eyes and hide under their desks—of school spirit, bringing

the same bouncy energy to both. Whether herding students to class with cattle noises (*Mooo-ve it!*) or gleefully taking a pie in the face at a pep rally, it was as if a little happiness motor whirred inside his round belly at all times. My introduction to Mr. Novak came on the first day of freshman year via the PA as he recited the rules of Fep Prep in his best Dr. Seussian effort—

> *"Doors lock each day at eight fifteen,*
> *dear student, don't make me repeat it.*
> *Get your butt directly to homeroom,*
> *And then, promptly, seat it."*

It was impossible not to like him, or at least admire his relentlessly positive attitude about, well, everything—which is where his nickname came from. As Mr. Novak bustled through the halls, he'd call out to students and give them a smiling thumb's-up, his way, I guess, of saying it's a great day, you're a great kid, and all is well at Fep Prep.

He came chugging past me now, cheeks rosy, tie flapping, thumb in the air, calling out, "Hey there! The sun's out! Smile, Sally Jane!"

After almost three years, he still hadn't gotten my name right.

I'd continued with school to uphold my mom's educational standards, especially important to me in her absence, and for the safety behind Fep Prep's walls. At the same time, I tried to attract as little attention as possible. Besides attending class and Classic Movie Club (two hours, concealed in darkness),

I existed below the radar. If Mr. Novak thought I was Sally Jane while leaving me alone, it meant I was doing something right.

I walked on, my mind racing with thoughts of subterranean gold.

And then it leaped to Max's heartbreaking absence.

Passing his empty locker filled me with nauseating butterflies. Sorrow and loss were the twin feelings that followed me down the hallway. With supreme effort, I willed them away. They weakened me, and besides, it was over between us.

Still, not thinking about him was impossible.

It was ten minutes until homeroom, and three hours earlier in Los Angeles. If I called now, he'd still be asleep and I could at least listen to his voice-mail greeting. It wasn't much, but it would be enough. I dialed quickly, hearing one ring, two rings, and then, "Hello." I was waiting for "This is Max, leave a message." Instead, the newly awoken Max said, "Hello?" again. My finger hovered over the End button but before I could push it, he said, "Whatever. It's too early for a wrong number," and hung up.

Too early. Too late. It was the story of our relationship.

I nearly jumped out of my skin when a text message buzzed seconds later, scared that he'd figured out the blocked number was mine. But no, it was camouflaged in Outfit code. I didn't need the notebook to translate. I'd been summoned to enough secret sit-downs to understand it:

Aunt Betty's making a delicious lasagna for you and Candi, and bought a new pink dress for the occasion. Dinner will be late . . . hot out of the oven tonight at ten p.m.!

"Aunt Betty" was code for Knuckles Battuta, "lasagna" meant a meeting, and "Candi" stood for Tyler (StroBisCo produced the world-famous Wonderfluff candy bar). "Pink dress" was the location—the Edgewater Beach Hotel, painted in shades of Pepto-Bismol—"late" meant early, and "hot out of the oven" signified urgency. "Tonight" (or "today") always meant tomorrow, and vice versa, and "p.m." meant "a.m.," and vice versa. Also, it was crucial to subtract three hours from the stated time. A sit-down called by the VP of Muscle with his counterpart in Money didn't happen every day. My guess was that it concerned the street war—whatever, I'd find out tomorrow morning. At least I'd get to see Tyler.

Mandi Fishbaum and a posse of her tarted-up lookalikes passed by, hugging textbooks, giving me a did-you-buy-those-clothes-at-a-yard-sale look. I was flipping them off in my mind when Doug appeared and said, "I need to be institutionalized."

"Pardon me?"

"That new security guard, the one who looks like a steroidal ape?" he said. "I was walking down the hall and the guy asked to see my school ID—"

"Like you said, he's new. He doesn't know every single kid here."

"Of course, big deal, right? But the size of him, or that he appeared out nowhere . . . it scared the living crap out of me," he said quietly. "I just . . . clammed up."

"What do you mean?"

"I mean, I couldn't say a word. My jaw was swinging and my tongue was flapping, but nothing came out, not a sound.

I was terrified out of my mind even though I knew there was nothing to be terrified of."

"It's PAWS. A slight panic attack. You know that."

He shook his head. "It didn't feel slight. By the time I could actually speak, the guy thought I was crazy. *I* thought I was crazy." He sighed. "Before I screwed myself up with Sec-C, I could sort of, you know, smart-ass my way through almost any situation. Now, I doubt myself all the time . . . who I am . . . and even with the weight loss, how I look . . ."

To be honest, I'd never gauged my friend in terms of physical appearance.

Beyond the fact that he was getting in better shape, Doug's nose was straight and dotted with freckles in a good way, his skin was unblemished, and his eyes were lit with intelligence. The truth was that he was in an early stage of handsomeness.

"You look fine," I said quietly, patting his back. "As far as the PAWS thing is concerned, you have to tough it through until it fades. No matter what happens, just keep moving forward. That's the secret—"

"I *know* the secret!" a voice over the PA announced cheerfully. "Ralph Waldo Emerson, that greatest of teachers, said, and I quote: 'The secret of education lies in *respecting* the student.'"

Doug and I paused, staring at each other.

The empty air crackled, and then the voice said, "Good morning, one and all! It's your principal speaking . . ."

"Thumbs-Up," I said, making the gesture.

". . . but more important, your respecter in chief. I respect, support, and protect each of you, and you, in turn, must do the same for dear old Fep Prep," he said. "For we are but a single organism, a student *body,* in which the sum of all parts make a whole . . ."

"A whole lot of freaks and geeks," Doug said.

". . . and if one of those parts fails, well then . . . you *all* fail." Silence followed, as every kid in the building wondered if those words were meant in an academic or rhetorical context. Mr. Novak chuckled and said, "Kidding! I'm a kidder! But hear ye, hear ye, we have just enough time left in the semester to take action, and action we shall take. So beginning today, I'll visit each and every homeroom to implement my new program. Drumroll, please . . . Fep Prep is *us!*"

"Yippee," Doug said flatly.

"My first stop is Ms. Stein's class. *R*s through *S*s . . ."

"That's us." I sighed.

". . . where, in fact, I am broadcasting remotely at this moment," he said as we entered homeroom, and there he was, round, pink, and beaming, microphone in hand. As we filed past, he straightened his tie (decorated with dozens of tiny Pac-Man images) and continued to address the school. "Here they are now, your amigos and mine. Their faces, shoulders, and droopy gaits say, 'Hey dude, chill out. You aren't gonna get *us* to participate.' Well, we'll see." He clicked off the microphone and smiled around the room with small square teeth. "We . . . shall . . . see."

Ms. Stein rose from behind her desk. "Let's take attendance and then—"

"It's party time!" Mr. Novak said with a fist pump.

When she finished calling our names, making sure we were

all present, he rubbed his hands together, saying, "Fep Prep is us . . . What does that mean? Who can tell me?"

The room was as quiet and unmoving as a warehouse full of mannequins.

Mr. Novak covered his eyes, circled a finger in the air, and pointed. "You!"

"Um—um, well," Doug stammered, "I think it means . . . we're Fep Prep?"

Mr. Novak shot him a thumbs-up. "Very good, Mister . . ."

"Stuffins," Ms. Stein said.

"Aha! Douglas. I remember your file," Mr. Novak said. "Chess Club, freshman year. Classic Movie Club, now. And you've participated in nothing else. Correct?"

"Basically," Doug said in a small voice.

"Well, we're going to change that," he said. "Fep Prep can only be *us* if we interact with one another. To that end, each homeroom will hold an event with a homeroom in another grade, seniors with sophomores, and so on. Ms. Stein's class will host freshmen. This way, instead of remaining in cliques and clusters, you will now be forced, gently, to mingle. The organizing homeroom requires a representative, an ambassador, so to speak, who, well, organizes the event." Mr. Novak lifted a Fep Prep football helmet. "Go-o-o Cavaliers!" he roared, giving it a shake. "I've placed slips of paper in here with each of your names on them. One lucky person will be selected by yours truly." He dug a hand inside the helmet, set it aside, and then unfolded and stared at a slip of paper. "Sar . . . Sar . . . ," he read, squinting, drawing out the syllables.

Wait . . . it's me . . . really?! I thought. *It's like a bad sitcom!*

"Gosh darn these glasses," Mr. Novak said, lifting them from his face, placing them on his forehead.

Oh god . . . just get it over with, I fretted, hating life.

He held the paper inches from his face and then smiled at the room. "Where is she? Sara Jane Rispoli?"

I raised an arm as limp as a dead trout. "That's . . . me."

"Congratulations! Report to my office end of the day tomorrow for instructions!" he said gleefully. "This is going to be fun!"

"Congratulations," Doug whispered.

"By the way, Sally Jane?" Mr. Novak said. "In the spirit of interaction, choose a partner, if you please."

"It's . . . Sara Jane," I said quietly.

"Fep Prep is us!" Mr. Novak said, shooting the room a double thumbs-up and hustling out the door.

I turned to Doug and smiled. "Howdy, pardner."

"Shit," he muttered.

"Speaking of," I said, "we're going to be in it, deeply, if we don't find another member for the Classic Movie Club. Ms. Ishikawa warned me last week."

I'd founded the club as a sophomore in an admittedly flimsy attempt to appear well-rounded when I someday applied to colleges. The problem now was that every school organization required at least three members and when Max moved to L.A., leaving the club with only two members, we'd become ineligible. Mr. Novak now tracking everyone's participation was the last thing Doug and I needed. Ms. Ishikawa, our English lit teacher and activities coordinator, had already threatened to shut us down if we didn't hustle up a new recruit soon.

As it turned out, a new recruit came to me.

After the bell rang, Doug went his way and I went mine. Trudging toward Trigonometry, I became aware of a trailing cloud of perfume.

"You look like you slept in that T-shirt. Could it be *more* wrinkled?" Gina Pettagola said cheerily, appearing beside me. We were best friends in kindergarten, semi-friends in middle school, and now two people who were friendly to each other with little contact. We'd drifted apart over the years, she toward the popular kids who socialized often, I into the Rispoli family habit of introversion. The thing about Gina was that she clung to loyalty, as did I, so we had never quite severed the bond between us. A petite dynamo with the features of a porcelain doll (she'd been proactive in taking care of her own nose "issue") and who wore designer everything, Gina was the reigning queen of gossip at Fep Prep.

"I have no useful information about anything," I said.

"Doubtless," she said, "but I'm about to make your day."

"Oh?"

"I joined your little movie club thingy!"

I stopped and looked at her. "Really? I mean, that's great, but why?"

"Need more stuff on my résumé," she said. "I'm already in six clubs and organizations but I decided to go for lucky number seven. I'm trying to get an internship at DishTheDirt.com. It's the Tiffany's of online gossip." She looked at me closely, inspecting the damage from the tunnel collapse. "What happened to your face?"

"Oh, uh . . . boxing," I said. "Fighting."

"Ick. You still do that?"

"Every day."

"Hey, FYI, I have some dirt to dish, just for you. If you want it, that is."

"No thanks," I said, walking on.

"Are you sure? It's straight from Mandi Fishbaum."

"I saw Mandi this morning," I said. "How does she do it—spend all that money on clothes, hair, and makeup and still manage to look like a stripper?"

"I know what you mean," she said, "but she gave me a juicy tidbit. You know she's Max's cousin—"

That stopped me again. "So?"

"So," she said, "it seems your ex-BF has a new GF . . . and she's an actress! That redheaded chick, what's-her-name, on that vampire TV show!"

I stared at her, feeling as if my heart was being clogged with wet cement. "I didn't need that today, Gina," I said. "In fact, I don't need it any day."

Her face shifted, the smile fading. "I just thought . . . you'd want to know."

"Gotta go to class," I mumbled, turning away.

"See you in Classic Movie Club," she called after me.

I shoved my hands in my pockets, fingers grazing my phone, and thought of the last call I'd made. *One month and he's already seeing someone?* I thought. *I'm that easy to forget?* I knew my evasiveness and refusal to answer his questions had hurt him, but this hurt, too, and—I couldn't help it—made me really angry. I blinked once, feeling the cold blue flame leap and burn brightly. A line of voltage crackled over my shoulders, and there was a buzz at my fingertips, and then another.

It was my phone.

I blinked again, slowed my pace, and stared at a text message from Tyler:

> Tonight, 10 p.m., lasagna with Aunt Betty, can't wait to see u . . . Candi.

Me 2, I wrote back, and meant it.

12

THERE IS NOTHING PRINCIPLED, NOBLE, OR JUST IN an organized-crime street war. It's a dispute over money, and every bill has blood on it.

I put down the pen and looked up from my journal.

The clock read 6:15. It was Tuesday morning.

My meeting with Knuckles and Tyler would happen in forty-five minutes.

The Bird Cage Club was silent. Doug and Harry were asleep on the couch in the other room, the little dog wrapped around Doug's feet. My eyes had popped open at 4:00 a.m., my subconscious churning with questions about how to offer Elzy four billion dollars for my family without getting captured, and how that would fit in with the street war.

At least one of those concerns was on Knuckles's mind, too.

Tyler had sent a text to him (and copied me) late the previous evening. It was a precautionary message, asking what ingredients were being used in the lasagna—the meeting.

"Spinach" was code for a financial issue, and "meat" signi-fied a hit, that someone was targeted for murder. Instead, Knuckles replied with another ingredient:

Red sauce.

The Outfit's code word for the Russians was "Red," as in "Red hit on my girlfriend" (Russians are moving in on my prostitution trade) or "Red stole a cup of sugar" (Russians are taking over my cocaine biz). Knuckles wanted to discuss the street war, urgently.

There's a saying in real estate . . . "Location, location, loca-tion." That's what the war's all about, I wrote. *The Outfit controls neighborhoods on the South and West Sides where it sells drugs and hookers . . . where there are money-laundering front busi-nesses, chop shops, and meth labs . . . neighborhoods that are prime hunting grounds for "zombies" (gambling addicts, drug addicts, sex addicts, whatever addicts), and Elzy wants those neighborhoods . . . no, scratch that: she's using her Russian soldiers to take over those neighborhoods.*

I bit a thumbnail, trying to think like her.

Once she controls all of that area, she'll control the Outfit's cash flow, which means she has the Outfit. But members won't merge seamlessly with her mob. There will be deep distrust and resentment, I wrote. *That's why she wants me. Whatever Juan Kone did to my dad, he must be unfit to serve as counselor. It's so clear: my job will be to force Outfit members into compliance. Along with the notebook—ultimate power—she thinks she'll have it all.*

I thought of what I'd seen and heard over the past month, and what I knew.

In a series of sit-downs, the tenor of the discussion about

the war had begun to shift from "we need to fight harder" to "the longer we fight, the more money we lose." The conflict was bad for business—it required cash for weapons and cash to bribe law officials to look the other way, and worse, it took members away from their daily rackets, so they were unable to earn. While a small group of Outfit old-timers advocated fighting until the bitter end, the younger contingent, now the majority of members, were muttering about making a deal with the rival mob—to cede certain territories to the Russians and allow everyone to get back to the business of money, money, money.

What I knew was that Lucky, the Boss of Bosses, would never stop fighting.

He was Elzy's last barrier and he was formidable.

Chicago had belonged to the Outfit alone for a century, and Lucky was determined that it wouldn't change on his watch. At the outset of the war, he ordered me to be prepared to use cold fury to interrogate hostages, and said that if they had no useful information, it would be up to me to decide if they were tortured or killed. His directive came after Johnny Eyeball, the poor kid who was on his way to becoming an ice cream creature, escaped Juan Kone but was captured by the Outfit and mistaken for a Russian mobster. I took a huge risk, setting Johnny free, hoping that he'd find his way home. And then I lied to Lucky, telling him I'd killed the kid myself. But the Russians—the real Russians—were quick and crafty, and not one had been caught. With the rank and file's growing hesitancy to fight, along with mutterings about the hostilities being bad for business, morale within the Outfit was slipping. As VP of Muscle, it was Knuckles's job to keep the Outfit doing battle, swinging lead pipes and firebombing the Russians.

Is that what the meeting's about? I wrote. *Maybe Knuckles wants me to use cold fury to force members to fight? Or needs Tyler to authorize money for . . . more weapons?*

The alarm clock buzzed twice—6:30 a.m.

I closed the journal, rubber-banded my hair into a pony-tail, thought about Tyler again, and removed the rubber band. After jumping into fresh jeans, I found a T-shirt that wasn't too wrinkled (thanks, Gina), and did battle with my hair until it looked like it belonged on a human head. At the last second, I touched my mouth with lip gloss.

As I moved across the Bird Cage Club, Doug rose on an elbow and said, "Good luck with Aunt Betty."

"Thanks."

"Tell Candi I said hi," he said, followed by smooching noises.

"Shut up. Don't forget to walk Harry."

"He won't let me, will you puppy-boy?" he said, scratching the little dog's head. "Take your aspirin?"

"Of course," I said, averting his gaze. "Take a break from smoking."

"No can do. That's the thing about a habit. You have to be consistent."

"See you at school," I said, stepping onto the elevator.

"Don't forget our meeting with Novak, after last period."

"Damn school spirit." I sighed. "Why does the guy have to be so gung ho?"

"Because Fep Prep is we," he said lying back down, "or is it 'are us'?"

I nosed the Lincoln from the parking garage, scouting for garbage trucks, street cleaners, taxis. Wells Street was deserted. Wacker Drive wound around to Lake Shore Drive, and then I was speeding north to Bryn Mawr Avenue. The pink colossus that was the Edgewater Beach Hotel sat a few blocks away. I parked on a side street and hurried to the rear of the building where a sign was posted above a brass pipe: FIRE HOSE CONNECTION. Making sure no one was around, I pressed the slightly raised *C*. A Capone Door sprang open and I stepped into an elevator that rose quickly to the roof.

I was the first to arrive and crossed the pebbled surface, watching sunlight push through clouds over Lake Michigan.

Knuckles's reason for choosing the location was obvious: it was empty, and miles beyond earshot of anyone. The Outfit built the hotel in 1928, with all the old villains—from Capone to Accardo— having spent time here. When I turned, Tyler was walking toward me, smiling. His green eyes and smooth dark skin sent a tingle across my shoulders, and then I had a heartbreaking flashback—not long ago, Max took me to the roof of an old church to watch the sunrise. Marble angels stood guard along its parapet, gazing mournfully at the beautiful, broken city. As the sun appeared, bathing us in a golden glow, Max called it "the light of Italy," and I knew then that I loved him. But he was gone and Tyler was here, opening his arms for a friendly hug. I smelled his sweet citrus scent, felt his arms around me, and pushed away thoughts of Max.

Tyler inspected my cuts and bruises. "What happened to you?"

"Oh . . . I got into the ring. Did a little sparring," I said.

"Must've been with a heavyweight," he said.

"Yeah, you could say that," I said, thinking of the debris that had fallen on me.

"Anyway, you look beautiful."

"I look like it's seven a.m.," I said, feeling a blush spread over my face.

"Yeah," he said with a smile that was an ad for proper dental care, "beautiful."

"Okay, well . . . you too, as usual," I said.

"Hey, by the way, that loan shark over on Peterson Avenue? Mario something?" he said, dropping his voice even though we were alone.

"Caminetti," I said. "I fined him twelve grand a couple of weeks ago. He's pissed off at me, huh?"

"Just wanted you to know. Safety first," Tyler said.

"Thanks," I said, giving his arm a squeeze, as a metal door slammed, followed by the crunch of wheels.

"Whatever you're doing, knock it off. I just ate," Knuckles growled, rolling toward us. He was an enormous old man, slabs of geriatric muscle confined to a Scamp—a scooter-wheelchair—his face bisected by a scar inflicted long ago by someone who'd fought back; whoever that someone was, I was certain his last breath came soon afterward. Each time I saw Knuckles, I reminded myself that this giant, grandfatherly type had personally murdered dozens of people and orchestrated the beatings and deaths of hundreds more. He pulled a dandruff-flecked fisherman's cap back on his broad forehead and scratched a wooden match. The turd-cigar in his mouth flamed white and orange. Coughing out smoke, he said, "If I could personally rip the hearts out of every damn one of those Russians, I'd do it yesterday."

"You didn't bring me all the way up here to tell me that," I said.

"You didn't need to tell me at all. I could've guessed," Tyler said.

Knuckles glanced around, seeing only indifferent seagulls, and said in a low, resentful tone, "I do need you, damn it. Both of you."

"Oh?" Tyler said, interest firmly caught.

"From what I hear, Lucky ain't exactly in the healthiest frame of mind and body to be making decisions," Knuckles said carefully. "Especially about this street war."

"What are you saying? Is he sick?" I said, feeling slightly sick myself. After the incident with Johnny Eyeball, Lucky and I had come to a sort of understanding. He didn't ask about my dad's protracted illness and I followed his orders like the most obedient of counselors-at-large. I had no idea how I'd be affected if someone else were in charge.

"I'm saying what I'm saying and nothing more," Knuckles muttered.

"Get to the point," Tyler said. "Why are we here?"

"VP of Muscle," Knuckles said, throwing a thumb at himself, and then pointing at Tyler and me. "VP of Money. Counselor-at-large. Only Lucky has more power in the Outfit than the three of us . . . at least individually. But if we join forces," he whispered, "then we'll have enough combined power to take control of this *maledetto* street war."

"Let me guess"—Tyler smirked—"you want to escalate it. Show those sissy Russians what it really means to fight? Enough of the firebombs, bring out the nukes!"

"No, smart-ass," Knuckles hissed. "I want to end the violence."

"Wait, wait—you, the VP of Muscle, whose life has been devoted to maiming and killing," Tyler said, "want to passively resist?"

"You ain't understanding me," Knuckles said. "I want to make a deal with the Russian mob."

Tyler and I exchanged a look and I said it first. "You? A deal?"

Knuckles nodded his massive skull. "The Outfit has flourished for so long because we always put business first. That means we don't practice Sicilian vendetta. Someone offends you, pisses you off, and you start shooting, or worse, rat to the Feds? All it does is interrupt business. Instead, you take your beef in front of the counselor-at-large because that's the rules, and rules make money. And if a guy can earn, who cares if he's Sicilian or Jewish or—or whatever the hell you are," he said, nodding at Tyler. "We even held our nose and let you in, sister," he added, "with all due respect to broads."

"Speaking for women everywhere, gee, thanks."

"Look." Knuckles sighed. "I've been around long enough to know that everyone—us, them, whoever—would rather make money than war. We stop fighting over the turf the Russians already took, maybe concede to them a little more, and it'll end, trust me. The Outfit will earn less, but we'll be earning. Besides, we've always been innovative when it comes to new sources of revenue. Hey, we're moving into online gambling, big-time, ain't we? The stinking Russians can't invade that space."

"You think Lucky's judgment is . . . impaired," Tyler said. "That his insistence on fighting is based on something other than business."

"No one loves his job as much as I do." Knuckles sighed. "Splitting heads is the poetry of my goddamn soul. But fighting a war works only when it *improves* business."

"You mean, when we're winning," I said.

Knuckles pursed his lips and gave a small nod. "In this case it's killing it."

"I meet with our accountants every day," Tyler said. "With members fighting instead of earning income and the Russians stealing our customers, profits are down. Way down. If Lucky's too old, sick, or whatever to make competent decisions—"

"You didn't hear that from me," Knuckles murmured.

"So . . . what's your plan?" Tyler said.

"Send an emissary under a white flag, one of my guys . . . tell the Russian boss we're ready to deal," Knuckles said. "If we don't put the guns down and start talking soon, we won't have any turf left."

Surrender was the smartest thing for business but the worst thing for me.

If the three of us somehow managed to wrest control from Lucky, not only would I lose the old man's protection but also, making the deal would further embolden Elzy. The turf she'd taken and, as Knuckles said, a little more, wasn't nearly enough for her. She wanted everything, especially the notebook and me. I shook my head. "No. I have to stay loyal to Lucky. He's the boss. What he says goes."

"What's gonna go," Knuckles said through gritted teeth, "is more cold, hard cash, right down the crapper!"

"Lucky's orders are clear. We have to keep fighting," I said pointedly, "instead of surrendering like cowards." The old killer stared daggers at me and then turned away, muttering under his breath.

"Sara Jane," Tyler said. He looked at me closely, narrowing his eyes like a mind reader. Something in his gaze made my heart take an extra beat as he turned to Knuckles and said, "She's right. We have to stand by Lucky. You said it yourself—the Outfit is nothing without rules."

Knuckles swallowed the obscenity that must have been tickling his throat. He'd taken a risk proposing we sidestep Outfit protocol; now that he'd been outvoted, he needed to secure his position. "I want to make it clear," he growled, "that I had no intention of . . . displacing, so to speak . . . Lucky, as boss. I'm just as loyal to him as the both of you! My suggestion was in the best interest of business, and if I hear otherwise, if rumors are whispered about this meeting, I'll dispute it using every weapon in my arsenal." He sat back and chewed the cigar. "Besides, if we're going to keep fighting this damn war, every one of us needs my boys on the front line, with me leading 'em."

"It's confidential," Tyler said, grinning slightly. "You have my word."

"That and a plugged nickel will buy me Wrigley Field."
Knuckles snorted.

"You have my word, too," I said. "If I say it, you know that
I mean it."

Knuckles paused and nodded curtly. After a few formali-
ties, he rolled across the roof and was gone. Tyler turned his
face to the lake breeze and exhaled, relieved, I supposed, that
the old killer had left us. Without his knowing it, Tyler's support for my position had helped me tremendously, preserving
my relationship with Lucky and withholding more power
from Elzy.

It made me want to thank him, but to my surprise, he
thanked me first.

13

WITHOUT TAKING HIS EYES FROM THE LAKE, he said, "I mean it. I'm totally grateful."

"Okay, well . . . you're welcome," I said, "but for what?"

He turned to me. "For reminding me to take Lucky's side. It's dangerous for *anyone* in the Oufit not to support him, but especially us. A black guy in charge of Money and a woman serving as counselor? Everyone, *including* Lucky, already regards us as second-class citizens. Besides, Knuckles is a devious old bastard. After what he did to my parents . . ." He shook his head, saying, "Who knows if his plan was even real? What if we'd agreed to it and then he double-crossed us, said it was our idea, that we were planning a coup?"

"Even if it's real, we can't afford to oppose Lucky," I said. "He's old and he may be sick but he's still . . . Lucky."

"In name only," Tyler said. "My dad tried to explain to me once what it meant to be the boss of the Outfit and it didn't sound like the luckiest job in the world. Never sure who you can trust, constantly looking over your shoulder for a knife in the back."

"Comes with a lot of power, though, and a ton of cash," I said, "if you're willing to sell your soul."

"I asked him once, my dad, if he was ever chosen boss, would he do it."

"What did he say?"

Tyler half smiled, a little sadly, green eyes crinkling at the edges. "Yeah, but only if he could neutralize all his enemies inside the Outfit, which is impossible, since even friends are enemies. Money makes it that way. Everyone wants what everyone else has."

"Not me," I said.

"Me neither," Tyler said, placing a hand on my shoulder, strong and warm. "Look, we have to support each other in this thing. Speaking of backs, you watch mine and I'll watch yours. Okay?"

"Absolutely," I said with relief.

"Hey, remember the movie we watched on the plane?"

"Yeah?"

"If you ever need my help, or if something's really important, that will be our personal code word."

"Shawshank?"

"Shawshank," he said with a nod and a smile, and then his gaze hardened. "You know what I wish? That the Outfit never existed. I mean, I understand why my dad didn't defect. It's a spiderweb, and once you're in, they won't let you out. I take my duties seriously because I have no choice . . ."

"Me too. Exactly."

". . . and don't get me wrong, it comes with perks, so it's not like I'm suffering. As the next Strozzini in line, even being black, it was inevitable that I'd get the job. But having it happen the way it did, being so young. It was a surprise, you know?"

"Yeah. I know."

"And so damn confusing. All of a sudden, I had this responsibility and power," he said quietly. "Not really sure what to feel other than—"

"Trapped?" I said.

"Hatred," Tyler replied coldly. "My dad told me once that the Outfit runs on hatred, and that the only way to survive is to hate it back."

"No problem here."

"In a perfect world, I'd walk away from it," he said, "far away."

"If that perfect world ever happens, I'll go with you."

"Then I guess we're not going anywhere together," he said, "unless you want to give Rome another shot." He was smiling differently now, charming and a little sad.

"Maybe someday," I said. "I'm just . . . so busy . . ."

"I know, I know," he answered, extending an arm. "I'll settle for walking you to the elevator."

"Done," I said, hooking his elbow.

We rode down quickly and stepped onto the sidewalk. "Be careful out there. I need your eyes on my back," he said with a wink, kissing me on the cheek.

"Me too," I said, watching him walk to the curb, where a sleek black car had pulled up. He waved once, got inside, and disappeared.

I glanced at my phone—7:42 a.m.

Just enough time to get to Fep Prep before homeroom.

I hurried down the sidewalk and climbed into the Lincoln with the hope that traffic wasn't too heavy. Being on time for school was strictly enforced at Fep Prep (as Mr. Novak would say, *Don't hesitate and don't be late, or detention, my friend, will be your fate*) and I headed toward Lake Shore Drive.

The southbound morning commute had begun and it was already thick with people going to work in the Loop. I had moved past a station wagon and around a minivan, and was traveling at a fair clip when a school bus came up alongside of me.

The little kids threw me off.

I glanced at the two in each seat, and turned away until my paranoid gut screamed, *Anything is possible!* The bus edged nearer and when I looked again, those kids were actually large, crouching men in crimson-tinted goggles.

It was an *oh-shit!* moment followed by rapid acceleration.

The bus swerved in behind me, flying like a huge yellow torpedo. I wove through traffic, trying to shake it off and get distance between us. The big vehicle moved with disturbing speed, sticking to my bumper, coming even closer, and then it hit the Lincoln with a jarring blow. I flew forward in my seat, squeezing the steering wheel, and it hit me again—trying to cause an accident? It could work, taking my car out of com- mission with more than enough guys to subdue me, maybe even another vehicle nearby. I had to get off the drive, try to escape through narrow side streets where the bus would be forced to slow down. I gunned it toward the nearest exit ramp. Angry horns and screeching tires warned me that the Russians were following my lead. I veered onto North Avenue, blowing through a red light and barely avoiding a collision as two cars coming from opposite directions squealed to a halt in the intersection behind me.

The bus didn't pause, smashing through them, sending the cars spinning out of its way as it continued after me.

I leaned on the gas, squealed onto Clark Street, and slalomed in and out of too much traffic. Eyes flicking from the windshield to the rearview mirror, I watched the bus gaining speed, coming inches from plowing down a motorcyclist, swerving wildly around the poor guy, and then it was behind me again. I had a choice—continue up Clark Street into even heavier traffic or slide to the right, down Lincoln Park West—and I went right, careening past a pair of bicycle cops who could only watch openmouthed as I sped by with the bus on my tail. I knew now that city streets had been a stupid idea, there were too many obstacles; I had to get back on Lake Shore Drive and head north, away from the commuters, where traffic would be light and the road open. Ahead, at Fullerton Avenue, a car idled patiently at another red light, suddenly green, and it slowly turned onto Fullerton. With no time to wait, I made a wide, stuttering right turn around it, and flew down Fullerton back to the drive.

In back of me, far too close, came the thunderous blast of the bus's horn, as it, too, went around the car.

The speed limit on Fullerton was twenty-five miles per hour, which I tripled, howling past the Lincoln Park reservoir and hanging a murderous left onto the Lake Shore Drive on-ramp with the bus only a few feet behind.

Gears grinding and brakes shrieking, it went onto two wheels, and then no wheels.

I watched in the rearview as it flipped into a toppling roll, smashing into the underpass wall. It creaked once and settled onto all four blown tires, motionless and smoking.

I drove away, free and breathing.

Doug was at his desk when I entered homeroom. "How was the lasagna?" he said.

"There was a bus full of Russians," I said, still shaking a little. "I barely made it."

He bit his lip, eyes worried, as Ms. Stein took attendance and made announcements. Then the bell rang. In the hallway, he gave my shoulder a quick squeeze. "You okay?"

"It was close. Too damn close," I said with a nervy shudder. "Anyway, it's the lasagna that matters."

"Tell me about it during Classic Movie Club. We're watching *Amarcord*. There are parts in it we can talk through without missing a damn thing."

Mrs. Ishikawa had set third period as our club time at the beginning of the year; it was only a couple of hours away but that wasn't the problem. I shook my head. "Gina, remember? We can't discuss it in front of her."

"And I have a mandatory study session during lunch," he said.

"After school, then."

"You mean after Novak," he said.

I nodded and turned down the hallway. The rest of the day crept past. After the final bell, walking toward the meeting, I was hit with the familiar sense of guilt that accompanies a trip to the principal's office whether you've done anything wrong or not. There's just something about turning the doorknob that feels like doom is waiting on the other side.

Instead it was Doug, waiting in a chair, twiddling his thumbs.

Mr. Novak's secretary looked up, said nothing, and nodded me into a chair, too.

"How was Aunt Betty?" he whispered.

"Hideous, as usual," I answered just as quietly.

"Candi?"

"It was just business. Mostly," I whispered, looking at the framed portraits lining the wall—the president, the mayor of Chicago, a painting of old Casimir Fepinsky himself on horseback wearing a Polish military uniform and thick sideburns—and seeing not one woman among them. I sighed and glanced at Mr. Novak's secretary, catching her eye as she looked away, and knew she'd been inspecting me over her computer.

"Very good!" Mr. Novak said, standing in his office doorway. "Right on time for our powwow! Come in, Douglas . . . Sally Jane."

I considered correcting him, shrugged it off, and followed him inside with Doug behind me.

Mr. Novak edged around his desk, sat with his stubby legs crossed, and cradled his fingers behind his head. "Welcome to my humble abode," he said. "My casa is your casa." I looked around the office crowded with memorabilia—little figurines with their thumbs up, photos of Mr. Novak posing with students making the sign, even a framed Cubs jersey stitched with *Thumbs-Up Novak*. "What you see here is a lifetime in education," he said proudly, as his phone buzzed. He leaned forward, lifted it from the cradle, and said, "Novak here!" He listened for a moment and a smile creased his chubby cheeks. He spun around, his back to us, and spoke in a low tone, saying, "Of course I'm happy you called. Oh, don't be like that . . . Yes . . . Yes, Bootsie . . ."

Doug turned to me and mouthed, *Bootsie?*

". . . Me too. Until then," Mr. Novak murmured, then he turned and replaced the phone. He straightened his tie, a loud, tropical number adorned with palm trees and coconuts, and said, "Now then. Why are we meeting today?"

"Because you told us to be here?" I said.

Mr. Novak shook his head. "It's because . . . ," he said, lifting his eyebrows, making them dance, "Fep Prep is . . . ?"

Doug shrugged slowly and said, "Us?"

"Pre-cisely!" Mr. Novak said, slapping the desk. "Fep Prep is *us*. And making sure it's the best school in Chicago is the responsibility of every educator and student here." He opened a folder, studied its contents, and moved his gaze to me. "*Every* student . . . even a serial nonparticipant like yourself. Your attendance record has been a little spotty, and to date, you have not one team, charity, or academic competition."

"I founded the Classic Movie Club," I said feebly.

He shot me a thumbs-up. "Kudos for that. It's a great start. But otherwise, you've been largely invisible during your time at Fep Prep."

"I'm busy . . . outside of school," I said, uttering the mother of all understatements.

"We all have lives beyond these hallowed halls, my dear, but that's no excuse," he said. "If it will help, I'd be happy to call your parents and talk about your schedule."

"No, thank you," I answered, as calmly as possible, thinking of a phone ringing in our empty house on Balmoral Avenue. With all my might, I wished he would shift his focus to Doug, who'd become small and unnoticeable in the classic please-don't-let-him-call-on-me posture. "I'll do more," I said, "*participate* more."

This time it was a double thumbs-up. "*Wunderbar!* Now, for the good of Fep Prep, you and your partner will lead a group of freshmen on a field trip to the Skydeck atop the Willis—or as it was called in my day, Sears—Tower. You'll present a short talk to them about the history of the building, and then you'll mingle with your classmates. That's how mentoring is born! How does that sound?"

"Awesome," I said, forcing a smile of my own.

"Super awesome!" he replied. "The view from a hundred and three stories is a wowzer. I'll accompany you and the group one week from today. And I expect you to be *fully* prepared, yes?"

"Yes," I answered.

"I'll make a participant out of you yet, Sally Jane! Today

the Willis Tower, tomorrow, glee club! Becau-u-u-se . . ," he said playfully, drawing out the syllables.

I stared at him, trying to read his mind.

"Fep Prep is us," Doug said robotically.

Mr. Novak slapped his desk. "You guys rock! Now get the heck out of here!"

We did, without hesitation, hurrying from the office, down the hallway, and outside. The meeting had lasted long enough for most kids to have vacated the school yard, with only a few stragglers loitering on the sidewalk. I heard the lighter snap and smelled smoke as Doug stood next to me, lighting a cigarette. "I'll tell you something about that guy"—he coughed— "he's got enough school spirit to choke a pig."

"I don't need it, Doug. More scrutiny at school, blowing valuable time on field trips," I said. "You know what I really need?"

"What?"

"A whole new life." I sighed.

"I can't give you that. No one can," he said, holding up the pharaoh key chain. "But a little diversion wouldn't hurt."

14

I DROVE CAUTIOUSLY TOWARD CLARK STREET, wary of a garbage truck that seemed to be tracking us— turning when I did, grinding gears ominously, staying a little too close behind—but then it turned off into an alley and disappeared.

Nonetheless, I charted a circuitous course to our destination.

To be honest, I'd nearly forgotten about Great-Grandpa Nunzio's stash house.

I resisted going; it fell into the category of why-am-I-doing-this-when-my-family's-missing? Not to mention this was the day of the week when I made sure my house on Balmoral Avenue was secure. But I gave in when Doug wisely reminded me that investigating my family's past often yielded clues to the present.

A half an hour later, I stopped outside Reebie Storage.

We climbed from the Lincoln and I made sure to pay the

meter. The Chicago parking authority was as relentless as the Outfit when it came to collection.

Approaching the entrance, seeing the ornate twin Ramseses guarding the door, I marveled again at the web of duplicity constructed by my family. I'd passed the building a million times in my life, never remotely suspecting that it harbored Rispoli secrets. Without a word, Doug and I pushed through the door. The clerk was an elderly guy, frail and doddering, in a Reebie T-shirt. He lifted his glasses and scratched at the back of his head while turning the skeleton key in shaky fingers. "Huh. Wouldja look at that? Old one, ain't it?"

"I suppose so," Doug said impatiently. "Look, how long is this—"

"Oopsy," the clerk said as the key slipped from his hand, clattering to the floor. He bent beneath the counter, saying, "Gosh darn it all . . . clumsy me . . ."

Doug leaned toward me, muttering, "This is *exactly* why I say senior citizens shouldn't have driver's licenses," and turned back to an Uzi submachine gun aimed at his—*our*—faces.

The old guy squinting down the barrel suddenly didn't seem so frail. He held the gun as steady as a rock and his voice lost its quiver. "Where'd you little bastards get that key?" he said. "You got three seconds to spill before I blow your brains out the back of your heads. *One . . .*"

"He means it," another guy said, appearing out of nowhere and leaning casually on the counter next to the gun-toting grandpa. He was twenty, maybe younger, with little visible skin that wasn't covered in tattoos. In contrast to the Russians' crude ink on flesh, his were precise, artistic images, burned

136

with care. I habitually search strangers' faces for a twitch or flicker that could reveal hidden knowledge or imminent violence, and what I saw in Tat-boy's face was dead seriousness. He pointed behind us. "You have no idea how many times I've had to scrub that wall. It's not the blood so much as the skull bits."

"*Two . . . ,*" the old guy said between clenched teeth.

"Skull . . . bits," Doug gasped, sucking air, consumed by a full-body tremble.

I glanced at Tat-boy's forearm, where a familiar scarred visage leered up at me—Al Capone seared in deep lines of black and gray. Other faces covered other parts of his body and I nodded at them, saying, "Frank Nitti. Momo, Giancana." Blinking once, feeling the blue flame flicker and leap, I grabbed his gaze. "Where's Tony Accardo?"

"On . . . my back," Tat-boy said quietly. His eyes widened as we both stared at the shared image of his rising internal terror—his own skull shattered and stuck to the stained wall. His hand groped for the Uzi, clumsily pushing the barrel down. "You're—you're her," he stammered, chewing back tears.

"*Who?!*" the old man barked.

"Counselor-at-large," I said, blinking, and freeing Tat-boy, who leaned on the counter, sucking air. "Sara Jane Rispoli."

"Oh. Uh-oh," the old man said, dropping the gun on the counter. "Crap," he added by way of apology, removing a hunting knife from the small of his back and throwing it down, too. "Please excuse me, Miss Rispoli . . . *counselor!*" He coughed. "Ray here will be happy to take you to unit—?"

"You have the key," I said.

"Oh . . . right!" he said, hastily dropping Ramses into my hand. "Ray! Take 'em!"

"Follow me," Tat-boy wheezed, knocking a fist against his chest, leading us down a hallway. He opened a door marked *Employees Only* and we stepped inside to a dripping slop sink, the air ripe with the smell of bleach and floor wax. Mops stood in a bucket, jugs of cleaning solution shared space on a shelf with paper towels and garbage bags, and a stained janitor's uniform hung from a hook. He locked the door and his eyes moved to Doug. "May I speak freely?" he asked. I nodded and he said, "Ray Capezio Jr. Fourth-generation Outfit . . . fourth-generation Reebie man. We've been guarding the big boys' stashes since forever. Sorry about granddad. The old man loves his job."

"Clearly," Doug said, pulling a hand over his sweat-soaked forehead.

"Why didn't you use the Capone Door in the alley?"

Clueless, I faked it as usual, saying, "I . . . wanted to make sure you guys were on your toes, considering the Russians. Look, we're in a hurry—"

"Oh. Sure," he replied, giving the mop handle a pull. The room shuddered and fell. The sink kept dripping and the janitor's uniform swayed on its hook as the disguised elevator carried us down. Ray cleared his throat and said, "Speaking of the war, we've heard rumors about Lucky's . . . *fitness,* I guess is the word. I was just wondering . . ."

I stared at him until he shut up. "Rumors are a no-no, Ray."

"Right. Rumors, gossip, all that crap is for broads." He

heard his own words and blanched. "Just not a broad like you . . . I mean, a *chick* like you! A *lady* like you!"

"Try *person,*" I said as the closet came to a stop. "The more you think of women as people, the easier it gets."

"I'll try that," he said weakly, opening the door to a long hallway covered in glazed brick. Its walls were lined with brass doors similar to Al Capone's vault, and I knew I was seeing Joe Little's handiwork. "Your key is what . . . R-nineteen-twenty-nine?"

"Ninety-two-ninety-one-R," I corrected him.

"You're reading it forward," he mumbled, looking at doors. "It's the reverse, of course. *R* for Rispoli and then the year your family rented the space. Everybody does that if they haven't been here in a while. Even your pop did it."

"Pop . . . my dad?"

"Had to be a year ago. He was here looking for the unit when I came down to oil the door hinges. I remember, it was right after the Hawks won the Stanley Cup." Politely, he added, "How's he doing by the way? Pretty sick, huh?"

"Yeah. Pretty sick," I said quietly. What my dad had been doing here was a question that couldn't be asked without seeming even more clueless, but another had been solved—Nunzio had been stashing stuff since 1929. As our footsteps echoed around the hallway, I glanced at each unit and said, "What's inside all of these?"

"No idea. Never been in any of them, and never will. One thing about the Outfit—make the mistake of sticking your nose where it doesn't belong and say good-bye to that poor old nose. Here we are. R-nineteen-twenty-nine," he said, stopping outside the last door. After a polite smile, he turned and left.

I looked at the skeleton key in my hand. A quick breath filled my lungs as I turned the lock and stepped inside to the perfume of mildew and gasoline.

"Light switch," Doug said, flipping it.

First a buzz and then yellow illumination erased the darkness. It was more a garage than a storage room, with high ceilings, a loading dock at the far end, and something large with four wheels beneath a tarp. The rest of the space was empty. We moved toward the hulking form, silently inspecting it, and then unrolled the cloth, flap over flap. A slab of tarnished chrome revealed itself, nearly the same height as my shoulders, topped by a hood ornament of a tiny, shiny lady with wings, about to take flight. Large glass headlights gaped like the eyes of a great steel insect, bisected by a metal plate bearing the engine size—V-8. The hood's long nose was the same gunmetal gray as a great white shark, lined with air vents like vertical gills. Its wide fenders were rolling steel waves above whitewall tires with mesh covers; extra wheels were secured to the car's body by heavy straps. We walked around it slowly, meeting and passing at the rear where a leather trunk sat above the back bumper, and then paused to stare at each other through opposing front-seat windows. "Why the hell am I always finding cars?" I said.

Carefully, Doug opened the driver's-side door, stepped onto the running board, and lifted himself into a springy leather seat. "Manual gearshift, on the floor, just like my mom's old Mercedes, except this bad boy is a *lot* older."

I climbed into the passenger side, opened the glove box, removed a perfectly preserved booklet, and read, "'Cadillac LaSalle Shop Manual, 1929.' Same year Great-Grandpa Nunzio stashed it down here."

Staring at the instrument panel, Doug said, "Fuel gauge. Speedometer. Battery gauge. Hey, look at that, a radio. Who knew cars had radios back then?"

"I wonder *why* he stashed it?"

"There's a key in the ignition," Doug said. "Is it possible . . . ?"

I shrugged, looking around at the small rear glass window and the long plush bench seat with three boxes on it—a large cardboard one marked *Ace Uniform Supply,* a medium sized wooden crate, and a smaller box so familiar that it drew me into the backseat. All three were ancient. The cardboard had gone soft and the crate's wood was spongy. I knelt before the small one, a cake box, whispering the words on its faded cover: "Rispoli & Sons Fancy Pastries." I opened it to rows of cash. The currency was larger and greener than it is now, some of it smudged with muddy brown fingerprints, like—old blood? Fifty bound sheaves of hundred-dollar bills, each marked with the total value of a thousand dollars, were topped by a handwritten note:

NR,

    Happy Valentine's Day. Hope this satisfies your sweet tooth.

                                                C

I felt little hairs rise on my neck as I set it aside and opened the Ace Uniform Supply box. Inside, half eaten by mold, were two carefully folded blue wool Chicago police officer uniforms, complete with badges tarnished by age. "Valentine's Day," I murmured, thinking of blazing tommy guns and bodies sliced by bullets. Seconds later an explosive roar filled the room. Diving for cover, I threw myself to the floor of the car, feeling it rumble beneath me, smelling oily exhaust.

Doug grinned sheepishly from the front seat. "So . . . it starts." He got out, looked beneath the car, and climbed back behind the wheel. "It's connected to one of those electrical chargers that keeps the battery alive for, like, years," he said. "Your dad must have kept it running. We could probably drive it right out of here."

"If so," I said quietly, "it would be for the first time since 1929."

Doug reached for the key and cut the engine. "How do you know?"

I lifted one of the uniforms, showing him the badge. "Right down the street, like, two blocks from here, at a place called SMC Cartage Company, Capone's guys killed seven rival gang members, execution style. Lined them up against a wall and cut them to ribbons with tommy guns on February 14, 1929. The Saint Valentine's Day Massacre."

"Same year Nunzio stashed the Cadillac. Same *year* as the Cadillac," Doug said.

"Witnesses heard gunfire, called the cops, and then were surprised to see two cops running *away* from the scene and fleeing in a Cadillac instead of a police car."

"That means—"

"They were the killers."

"A pair of Outfit guys *disguised* as police," Doug said. "Pretended to be the law and assassinated the other gang. Sick and brilliant."

"The real cops couldn't figure out how the fake cops and the Cadillac disappeared without a trace," I said, shoving the pastry box full of cash at Doug. "Here's the answer. My great-grandpa gave the killers a place to hide a few blocks away. The car has been here ever since. Al Capone was grateful . . . he filled one of my family's pastry boxes with a fifty-thousand-dollar thank-you to Nunzio. It's blood money, literally."

"So many secrets in your family," Doug said, staring around the old car, his gaze stopping on the crate. He pulled on a slat, snapping it off like a brittle bone. "Oops," he said, "the wood's rotten," and he went silent, reached inside, and came up with a brown bottle. It was marked with the image of a maple leaf and MADE FROM 100 PERCENT CANADIAN MOLASSES. "A dozen bottles." He grunted, pulling a cork and taking a sniff as his nose climbed up his face. "Damn! You know what this is?"

"Something tells me it's not for pancakes."

"Bootleg whiskey," he said, "probably made from Nunzio's own molasses. It's hundred-proof alcohol . . . this stuff could peel paint." He licked his lips and took a drink.

"Whoa, whoa," I said. "What are you doing?"

He gasped for air and croaked, "Smooth . . ."

"Doug, seriously!"

"I am serious," he said, shuddering with wet eyes. "We

should at least, you know, taste what drew your family into the Outfit to begin with."

He was right—the Rispolis' criminal history could be distilled to the moment when Nunzio began selling molasses to Al Capone in order to make illegal whiskey. My great-grandfather's use of ghiaccio furioso to control bootlegging thugs led to his role as counselor-at-large, and to my family's fate, all the way down to my own misdeeds.

The bottle was cool in my hand as I took it from Doug.

I sloshed whiskey against glass and sipped it, feeling it burn my throat and, milliseconds later, my brain. The overall effect was like having gasoline pumped into my head and I squinted, nostrils flaring, jaw squeezed tight, trying not to puke.

"Nice face," he said.

"Ugh, it's disgusting!" I spit. "All the bloodshed . . . for *that* crap?"

"On the other hand, it goes nicely with a smoke." He lit a cigarette and took the bottle from me. "Maybe one more pop."

I stared at him for a moment. "What's going on with you?"

"W-w-what do you mean?" He choked, gagging back the booze.

"I know what you said. Nicotine has a calming effect on PAWS. But come on—whiskey and cigarettes? You're like a washed-up country-music star," I said. "I don't buy it. You're smarter than that."

The smile faded from his face. "Right. I'm smart," he said. "I analyze everything down to its most obsessive, infinitesimal detail . . ."

"That's part of the reason we've come so far. A big part."

"Okay, so maybe this stuff makes me feel less deliberate," he said holding up the cigarette in one hand, the bottle in the other. "More in the moment."

"You can't become something by using props," I said. "Putting on a big hat and jumping on a horse won't make you a cowboy. It's illogical."

"I'm *sick* of logic. It didn't save me from Poor Kevin or those Mister Kreamy Kone groupies or Sec-C. *You* saved me, remember?" he said. "I want to be fearless . . ."

"Doug . . ."

". . . like you."

"Oh god, I'm not fearless. You know that. Far from it."

"But you don't flinch. You make yourself do things, what needs to be done in a bad situation."

We faced each other silently. "You mean kill people?" I said.

"No. Well, yeah, that too . . ."

"You want to talk about fear?" I said. "I'm scared every day that I'm not *making* myself do it. Dead bodies have become things to jump over as I keep running."

"You have to survive—"

I shook my head. "Outfit enforcers, murderers . . . they weren't born that way. It happened to them just like it's happening to me. They killed someone, maybe it bothered them, but they did it again, it bothered them less, and they did it again and then again, until . . ."

"Human life doesn't mean anything to them. They kill for money."

"What's the difference?" I said. "Dead is dead, and I'm the one who did it and may have to do it again."

"Sara Jane—"

"This noble-quest bullshit has taken too much of me," I said. "All I want now is to salvage what's left—the part of me that still believes even a justified murder is wrong. I lose that, I lose myself for good."

He said it again. "You have to survive."

"I know. If I don't, my family won't." I sighed. "But I can't do it without you, Doug. Take this the right way, okay? I can't tell you what to do, but relying on cigarettes or booze or whatever to become fearless? It make me nervous."

"Like you can't count on me?" he asked.

"Like you're not the logical Doug I trust my life with," I said. "Besides, let me ask you a question. Who smokes more than anyone you know?"

He scrunched his brow. "Dope or cigarettes?"

"Both."

"Uh . . . my dad. My real dad. Always has something burning."

"And who has a cocktail within reach at all times?"

"Oh my god," he whispered. "My mom. Shit."

"You really want to follow those examples?"

"Okay, you convinced me. Time to quit," he said abruptly, dropping the cigarette into the whiskey bottle and setting it aside. He reached into his pocket and removed the lighter. "I'm keeping this, though, as a reminder."

"Of what?" I asked.

"Just . . . to be myself, I guess. Something corny like that."

"It's after five," I said, glancing at my phone, and climbing out of the Cadillac with Doug behind me. "I need to check on my house. Let's get going . . . I hate being on the street when it's dark."

As we moved to leave, Doug nodded over his shoulder at the big old car. "What about that thing? What are you going to do with it?"

I stared at the car, perfectly preserved by decades of sitting in one place. "Leave it for the next generation of Rispolis," I said, turning out the lights and locking the door. "If there is one."

15

A HALF HOUR LATER, I DROVE SLOWLY PAST THE front of my house, three stories of brick and slate set among hundred-year-old oak trees.

The street was wet and quiet, the rain having paused while clouds gathered again. I turned into the alley, pausing at the entrance, looking for garbage trucks, utility workers. It was empty. A moving truck blocked the other end, crowding the narrow alley as a sweaty guy in overalls struggled to wheel furniture up a ramp. I stared through the windshield, seeing a familiar figure appear. It was elderly Mr. Belford, who'd lived on the street forever, tall and bent, leaning on a cane, giving instructions. Neither he nor the guy gave us a second look. I continued to the garage, pushed the button, parked inside, and closed the door. Ice cream creatures had taught me a lesson about leaving the Lincoln in front of my house.

Making sure no one was watching, Doug and I hurried across the backyard, up the porch steps, and slipped inside.

Quickly, I moved to the front hallway and punched a code into the alarm, disarming it. I'd been careful to have the mail held, pay the utilities in cash at a currency-exchange place, and leave a lamplight burning. We'd always been a reclusive family, but I couldn't take the chance of drawing unwanted attention from nosy neighbors.

The grandfather clock wasn't ticking.

I wound it and the hands came to life, continuing to mark the minutes of my family's absence.

My weekly routine never varied—check windows and doors, make sure nothing is leaking, the furnace is okay, and circuit breakers haven't popped. Intellectually, I knew it was mostly unnecessary. Emotionally, the ritual assured me, as though I were preparing the house for my family's imminent return.

Afterward, Doug and I went into the kitchen for a glass of water.

I leaned on the counter, looking at my mom's cooking utensils placed just so, untouched for half a year—knives, garlic press, a well-used rolling pin. "I used to stand here and watch my mom make gnocchi, my favorite," I said. "Her hands were really beautiful and delicate, but strong."

Doug said nothing, watching and listening to me.

"She pulled her hair back when she cooked, and wore this faded blue apron," I said. "We'd just talk, about everything. If I had a problem or an issue, something that seemed like the end of the world, she'd say this Italian phrase her mom used to say to her. *Finchè c'è vita c'è speranza.*"

"Which means . . . ?"

"Where there's life, there's hope," I said. "She knew how to make me feel better."

"You're talking about her like she's dead," he said quietly.

"It feels that way sometimes. Like they all are."

"You know they're not, Sara Jane."

"Yeah, but Elzy has them," I said. "And she hates me so damn much."

"You hate her, too."

"I think she hates me in a different way," I said. "My brother is alive. Hers isn't."

Doug nodded, and then I led him upstairs. The boards creaked beneath our feet as we climbed to the second floor, where we opened closets, pulled back the shower curtain, made sure windows were secure. I glanced into my bedroom. The posters of Jake La Motta and Roy Jones Jr., my two favorite middleweight boxers, scowled back. The shades were drawn, furniture dusty. Nothing had changed from the previous week.

I paused outside Lou's bedroom and turned to Doug. "Hey, do you mind giving me a minute alone?"

"Huh? Oh, sure," he said, turning away. "I'll just go down the hall and . . . stare out the window."

I entered my brother's room, seeing the made bed, the poster of Albert Einstein sticking out his tongue, the books carefully arranged on shelves, and I thought of people who'd lost a loved one at war—how they preserved the dead soldier's room as if he were still alive. I sat in the desk chair, using my foot to turn in a lazy circle, staring at book titles—*Venice: Art*

& Architecture; *Man and His Symbols*; *Mineral Deposits of South Africa*; *Training a Recalcitrant Dog.* My little brother was the smartest kid I'd ever known, his interests wide and varying, his brain bursting with knowledge. I looked at a thin volume, its spine reading *Geometrics of Bridge Building.*

Its bookmark, a faded strip of newspaper, caught my attention.

I pulled the book from the shelf and opened it to the page.

Instead of typeset words, it was filled with Lou's handwriting.

He'd been keeping a journal of his own, hidden behind a title he knew no one would reach for. The bookmark was a slim article, headlined: TWO REPUTED MEMBERS OF CHICAGO OUTFIT FOUND SLAIN IN FACTORY. The story was vague. I didn't recognize the names of the dead men. I put the slip of paper aside and paused; reading the journal would be an invasion of Lou's privacy, but the fact that he'd been reading about the Outfit drew me in. I turned to the first page. Lou had scribbled the date in the corner—a little over a year ago. Flipping forward, I saw that he'd made entries every couple of weeks, some covering several pages, others just a paragraph or two. Turning back, I read the very first sentence:

My father is a criminal.

"Oh, Lou . . . ," I said, knowing how much it must've hurt him to write those words.

The pages told a tale of discovery of the worst kind—from secret to secret, leading to a heartbreaking conclusion. It opened with a slow afternoon at the bakery. Lou had been hanging around with Grandpa Enzo (Lou loved working at

151

the bakery) when my grandfather employed the rule of all food-preparation businesses—in the absence of customers, clean the place. While Grandpa polished display cases in the front of the store, Lou mopped the kitchen, washed pots and pans, and then turned his attention to Vulcan, the huge iron oven. We'd each been warned since forever never to go near it, but the oven wasn't being used and Lou was being his usual proactive self.

If he hadn't done such a thorough job, actually climbing inside, he may never have found the little red button.

It was only minutes later that my inquisitive brother realized Vulcan was an elevator.

At the time, he said nothing to anyone; it was his nature to investigate first and ask questions later.

After a few days, he snuck into the bakery when it was closed and rode down to Club Molasses, taking Harry with him for protection. Knowing Chicago history as he did, he recognized a speakeasy when he saw it. Club Molasses was full of artifacts of our family's criminal history, from the old wall map to the Ferrari and more. Still telling no one, he did exhaustive research on the Outfit, piecing together scraps of information about Nunzio and Enzo that finally led him to a confrontation with our dad. As the journal progressed closer to the present, it was clear that my dad had confessed much to him, but not all. There was no mention of the notebook or ultimate power, but Lou was acutely aware of cold fury, the role of counselor-at-large, and another fact that chilled my blood.

In precise script, he'd written:

The Outfit rewards disloyalty with death.

There were other phrases of his that pierced my heart with their familiarity:

If he weren't my dad, I'd hate him for what he's capable of, and what he's done.

And:

Parents, grandparents, Uncle Buddy . . . liars of the worst sort. "I love you," to your face . . . and a knife in your back.

And:

They've betrayed my sister by not telling her what she possesses.

"Why didn't you tell me, Lou?" I said. The answer wasn't in the pages. Maybe my parents had made him promise not to; maybe my dad had confessed to Lou what Uncle Buddy alluded to, that he was planning to make a deal with the Feds to become an informant; maybe Lou was waiting until he formulated a plan to fix a situation that seemed intractable. As I neared the end of the journal, my feelings turned with the pages—from shock at their existence to dismay that he'd withheld the information from me to pure empathy. I knew what it felt like, assembling piece by piece a puzzle that, in the end, created a shameful picture of our family.

"Sara Jane . . . ," Doug said from the hallway.

"Just a second," I answered, turning to Lou's final entry, made two weeks before Juan Kone kidnapped my family:

When the truth comes out, Sara Jane will despise the Outfit as much as I do. She's strong, and unafraid . . . a fighter. She'll never serve it as counselor-at-large, no matter what happens.

I stared at the words, thinking, *I'm sorry, Lou. I had no choice.*

"Sara Jane," Doug called again, his voice urgent.

"You won't believe what I found," I said, carrying the book down the hallway.

"How many Russians does it take to write a parking ticket?" he asked, his face drawn as he looked into the street below. It sounded like a bad joke but his tone was ice cold. I pushed hair from my face, following his gaze through the window. A white SUV was parked at the curb, its door bearing the words CHICAGO PARKING AUTHORITY. Three men in khaki uniforms prowled the sidewalks, two on one side of the street, the third on the other. They almost looked legitimate, but the goggles on their faces and tattoos creeping up their necks told a different story. I couldn't help but think they resembled nesting dolls—small, medium, and large versions of a bodybuilder type with a blond crew cut. Small and Medium peered through car windows while Large looked up and down the street, and then stared at my house.

"Did they follow us?" Doug asked.

"Maybe. Or maybe they cruise the house every day and got lucky."

"Let's call the cops. Scare them off," he said, backing away from the window.

I stepped away, too, shaking my head. "Elzy used to be Detective Smelt, remember? She might still have people planted on the force."

"So what then?" he asked.

"We make a break for it," I said. "Drive like hell." I moved back to the window, peeked outside, and—the SUV was gone. I looked up and down the street, and Doug did the same.

"But what if they're still out there?" he asked in a shallow voice.

"They *are* still out there," I said. "Now it's matter of who's faster, them or us." He took the lighter from a pocket, gave it a nervous click, and I led him downstairs, into the front hallway. Right there, behind drawn window shades, a shadow moved across the front porch. It had to be Large, and he was, way over six feet tall and half as wide.

"Oh my god . . . ," Doug whispered.

I faced him with a finger to my lips, nodded toward the kitchen, and realized I was alone. Turning back, I saw him planted to the floor like a statue, eyes wide and jaw quivering. I motioned at him urgently to follow but he shook his head stiffly, mouthing, *Panic attack.* Sidling up to him, I murmured, "Doug, you *have* to move!"

"Can't. So scared . . . legs don't work . . ." He gasped. "Freeze . . . response."

I threw his arm over my shoulder and tried to drag-walk him, but he lurched into me. Stumbling sideways, we hit a small table and I watched a vase tip back, forth, back, before shattering on the floor, the noise echoing through the house, and—

Boom!

—Large hit the front door like a wrecking ball as I screamed, "Doug! Move!"—

Boom!

—trying to yank him along, but he was deadweight, and—

Boom!

—the door splintered, Large kicked it open, staring at us. There was a pause, a grin, and he charged like a blond bull in a china shop. I shoved Doug out of the way and spun for the kitchen but Large was too fast, hurtling down the hallway and throwing a huge fist at the back of my head. It was like being hit by a two-by-four, pain exploding through my skull, the force throwing me against the counter. I saw a knife, reached for it, and lifted the rolling pin instead, swinging it blindly as I turned. There was a double *crunch!* of goggles and nose, and I swung again, connecting to Large's Adam's apple. He gurgled, grasped at his neck, eyes bulging, and I used the rolling pin like a mini–baseball bat against his jaw, the hard, solid *crack!* dropping him to the floor. I stood over him, sucking air, and when I was sure he was out, I shouted to Doug. He staggered into the kitchen, moving awkwardly, but moving.

"We have to go. Now," I said.

He nodded dizzily.

I stared into the backyard. It was surrounded on all sides by a high wooden fence, constructed by my dad for maximum privacy, and the garage at the back had an alley running behind it. We counted to three and rushed across the lawn, through the garage door. I peeked out of a grimy window at the moving truck, which hadn't budged, and crossed the garage to another smudged pane of glass. The front of the white vehicle was a few feet away, idling in the alley with Small at the wheel. I couldn't tell if Medium was beside him, but the fence had prevented them from seeing us enter the garage.

"One guy is right outside, in the SUV. The other one might be in front of the house," I said, biting my lip, thinking. "Can you drive?"

Doug was taking deep breaths, calming himself, and his eyes were steady. "I'm good, I'm fine," he said.

I handed him the car keys. "When the door goes up, I'll run straight at the moving truck. When the guy chases me, tear out of here, in the other direction," I said. "I'll slip past the truck and make for Glenwood Avenue. Be waiting for me there."

"What if you run into the other guy?" Doug said, climbing into the Lincoln.

"At least he'll be on foot, too. I'm fast when I'm scared."

"Get ready," Doug said, pushing the remote control, and the door began to rise.

I took a deep breath and sprinted from the garage. The SUV's engine roared to life, the vehicle immediately speeding after me, as Doug squealed from the garage going the other way. The report of a gun was followed by a bullet whizzing past, pinging the moving truck I was running toward. I glanced back at the SUV, and at Medium in the passenger seat—they were *both* in the SUV—leaning out the window with a pistol, as another bullet bit into the gravel near my feet. If I stayed out in the open any longer, the next one might find me. I reached the moving truck and scrambled into the cab, praying for keys in the ignition.

Nothing, no luck, while footsteps on the run sounded behind me.

I reached over and pushed down the passenger-door lock,

spun toward my side, pulling my knees to my chest, and when Medium yanked open the door, I hammered him in the face with both feet. Small grappled uselessly with the locked passenger side with one hand, a gun in the other. I swung out my door, lifted myself on top of the truck, ran its length, and jumped onto the SUV. Doug was coming for me, speeding backward, as I leaped to the alley floor, hauling ass. Small was on the run, too, gun raised, when I threw myself into the Lincoln. There was a *ping!* against the trunk, another against the bumper, but we were gone, grinding out of the alley and squealing away.

"I told you to wait for me on Glenwood Avenue!" I said, jittery.

"Too risky," he said. "Too much running through the neighborhood, exposed."

"But I told you—"

He cut me off with a shrug. "Partners don't *tell* each other . . . they discuss. Short of that, if one's wrong, the other one takes appropriate action to correct her. Consider yourself corrected."

Knowing he was right, I mumbled, "Well . . . all I'm saying is, Glenwood Avenue was the plan."

"A good plan, but not great," he said. "There was no way I would leave you alone back there. If something happened, I was going to ram the shit out of them in reverse."

I nodded. "Great plan."

Doug stared through the windshield, driving carefully. "Thanks, partner," he said with a small, satisfied smile.

16

WEDNESDAY MORNING ARRIVED WITH A BOOM of thunder that sounded as if half the planet and my skull—had exploded. I sat up on both elbows, still feeling Large's fist to the back of my head. Standing unsteadily, hearing a distant buzzing noise, I wondered if I'd suffered neurological damage. The buzzing stopped, started, and I kicked the blankets aside, bent, and lifted my phone. The text message read:

Ed Debevic has invited you to a football game on Friday, noon, at Soldier Field. A Redskin running back is in town! Be wise, bring a friend, and prepare to have a swell time!

It was a text message from Lucky—I was being whistled in, digitally. It surely hadn't come directly from the old man himself; few things in the Outfit, especially an order from the Boss of Bosses, traveled in straight, traceable lines. Although

I regularly dumped my phones, I had to at least give my ever-changing number to Knuckles and Tyler for business reasons. One of them had passed it to someone else who had handed it over yet again, to the shadowy underling who'd sent word that Lucky demanded to see me.

"Ed Debevic" was his code name, one he'd been using for decades.

"Football game" meant a private sit-down with the man himself.

"Soldier Field," one of Chicago's most well-known landmarks, referred to one of its least known, Lucky's headquarters at the Algren Hotel. A specific day of the week required a single-day subtraction (so "Friday" meant Thursday, tomorrow) and the time, "noon," meant 9:00 a.m. "Redskin" ("Red" for Russian) was obvious and "running back," a player, meant a mobster. "In town" meant under lock and key—that is, a Russian mobster had finally been captured and I was being called in to interrogate him. A tingle of opportunity went through me. If by chance an officer had been captured then, as Goatee had told me, he'd know where Elzy was holding my family.

I looked at the text again, rereading the last line:

Be wise, bring a friend, and prepare to have a swell time!

Its true meaning was a warning—be stupid enough to bring someone to watch your back, and prepare to die—which signified that the sit-down was so important that anyone other

160

than me even knowing about it was strictly forbidden. It was odd. By now, everyone in the Outfit was probably aware that we had a Russian prisoner, so what was the big secret? And why did it come with the threat of death?

I'd be a fool to question it.

Not that I hadn't considered asserting myself with Lucky.

When he'd told me I would have to decide the fate of Russian hostages—either torture or kill—I hesitated at the prospect of ordering even more violence. The only way I could refuse would be to use cold fury—to hold his gaze and command him to absolve me of the duty. But then I learned that someone was always watching when the counselor-at-large met with the boss. Lucky's girlfriend, Peek-a-Boo Schwartz, told me as much—she monitored every one of the old man's sit-downs via closed-circuit camera and other methods. If she or anyone else saw me administer cold fury to the Boss of Bosses, I wouldn't escape the Algren Hotel with my eyes, much less my life.

The other reason I'd never use it on him was the one that nagged me most—I still wasn't sure how long the effect lasted on someone. I'd ordered Knuckles never again to question me about my dad's supposed illness or my family; months later, he'd continued to comply. And although the past half year felt like a lifetime, ghiaccio furioso was still new to me. There was nothing in the notebook about its lasting effects. I directed it at Outfit members without compunction only because I was protected in my role by Lucky.

Using it on my protector would not only be foolish; it could be a death warrant.

I would present myself at the sit-down as his loyal counselor.

More than anything, I needed time with the Russian prisoner.

I hoped that I'd be allowed to interrogate him alone, but if not—if hidden eyes were watching—I could at least force him to tell me where Elzy's headquarters were. I might not be able to free my family, but I'd contact her and offer her a deal—four billion dollars in gold for them. And then the question Doug posed in the vault came back to me: *How can you trust her? Not just to make the deal, but to honor it?*

I couldn't, but it was all I had left.

A growl of thunder sounded overhead as clouds massed outside the window.

I left the Bird Cage Club, headed for school with Doug, looking over my shoulder every five seconds for Small, Medium, and Large. The attack and narrow escape at my house had driven my internal paranoid-meter through the roof; instead of a safe haven, Fep Prep now felt permeable and open to attack, too. Entering school that morning, even a happy thumbs-up from Mr. Novak failed to calm me. The rest of the day passed in gut-churning anxiety, and when it mercifully ended, Doug and I spent the evening formulating how best to interrogate the Russian without raising suspicion about my true motives. He wondered aloud what the ominous warning meant. I brushed his concerns aside, but by the time I returned to my mattress, one thought dominated my mind.

Be stupid, bring someone to watch your back, and prepare to die.

It wasn't the most comforting lullaby.

I lifted the aspirin bottle, stared at the little white pills, and put it down. There was no way I'd use cold fury on Lucky. But I also wouldn't walk into that sit-down without a measure of electrical security.

Staring at myself in the mirror Thursday morning, trying to subdue my hair like a lion tamer with a whip, I sighed, gave up, and clipped it back. Rain oozed down the glass block window—it seemed biblical, like it would never stop. The way my life was going, plagues and locusts would be next. As I reached for my toothbrush, Doug said, "You already did that."

He was leaning in the doorway, flicking the lighter, an old Cubs cap jammed on his head. At his feet, Harry lifted his soft, gray skull and blinked at me.

"I did?"

"Nervous, huh?" he said.

"Did you make the call?"

He dropped his voice an octave and said, "Good morning, this is Anthony Rispoli. My daughter, Sara Jane, is under the weather today with her monthly . . . well, ha-ha, you get the picture. She'll be back at school tomorrow."

"Did you really need to add that detail?"

"All great actors improvise," he said. "No one will question that excuse."

"Time?" I said, walking past him to my room.

He glanced at his watch, following me. Harry's claws tick-tacked behind him. "It's seven forty-five. Thing with Lucky is at nine?"

"Sharp," I said, taking my standard sit-down outfit from the closet—black skirt, starched white blouse, black heels.

"Okay, well, I'm going to walk Harry before school. Seen his muzzle?"

"In the front closet," I said. "Why?"

"He's been going for the pigeons lately, haven't you, naughty boy?"

"I hate that thing. He can't bark when he's wearing it, can barely even whine."

"That's okay," Doug said. "He could use a little quiet time."

"You have to take his collar off for the muzzle to fit," I said. "Don't lose it. Lou made that collar for Harry."

Doug slipped it off Harry, inspected it, and handed it to me. "It's cool."

I looked at the small rectangle of copper into which Lou had etched *Harry* in curlicue script; it was attached to a band that fit snugly around the dog's little neck. "He's getting aggressive with pigeons, huh?" I said.

"You know what they say—dogs feels the stress of their owners."

"In that case, he should be going for something a lot bigger than a pigeon."

"It's going to be fine. Just be careful," Doug said, turning away. "Break a leg!"

"If that's all that gets broken, I'll be a happy girl," I muttered.

I heard the closet door shut, the elevator clank and whirr, and I was alone. If I were someone who prayed regularly, now would've been the time. I started to dress, thinking of a helping hand, how welcome it would be, and recalled what Tyler had said about watching each other's backs. Lucky had made it clear in his text that our sit-down was a secret, but— screw it. Tyler had been correct; he and I were outliers in the organization. If the results of my interrogation of the Russian were as dire as I thought they might be, it would affect him, too. Short of any information I learned about my family, I resolved to tell him what I learned.

I finished dressing, and as I went for the elevator, noticed the rain had eased back. Looking closer, I saw that the sky was like a boxer between rounds—brooding, restless—*Waiting for the bell,* I thought.

At the last moment, I grabbed an old raincoat of my dad's I'd taken from the house, a huge, truly hideous thing.

I needed all the protection I could get, even if it was only from precipitation.

I threw it in the backseat, roared from the parking garage, and splashed through the Loop. It occurred to me then that the first time Lucky summoned me, he'd requested three dozen Rispoli & Sons famous molasses cookies.

This obviously wasn't a cookie sort of meeting.

Twenty minutes later, I eased to a stop across from the Hotel Algren on a bland side street off Michigan Avenue. Lucky didn't occupy a suite or a wing; all thirteen floors were the Boss of Bosses' personal residence and fortress, a multimillion-dollar address as purposely plain and deceptively unremarkable as the man himself. At 8:58 a.m., I walked briskly across the puddle-filled street. Like the last time I was here, the lobby's single occupant was an anemic potted palm.

The elevator doors parted, I stepped aboard, and was soon creaking upward. The thirteenth floor was tomb-like in its stillness. I walked slowly down the hall, crinkling my nose at a bitter, medicinal scent.

Outside Suite 1306, I made a fist and knocked once.

A slot opened, revealing a pair of stone-cold eyes. "Password," a voice demanded.

"Password?" I said, trying to remember from the last time I was here. "Um . . . oh! 'I refuse to answer on—on the grounds that it may incriminate me'?"

The slot closed, a lock was released, and another, and the door swung open.

The figure filling it was tall and lean in a slate-gray suit. Just as on my previous visit, he stared down his aquiline nose at me, his brow furrowed beneath cropped silver hair. The difference was that then he hadn't been holding an AK-47. Now he nodded me quickly inside the drab room with its scuffed furniture and small, neatly made bed, looking both directions down the hallway before shutting and locking the door. The street war had made everyone in the Outfit jumpy, but the assault rifle set off alarms in my gut—the atmosphere was bristling with urgency, as if something was just about to happen. I crossed toward the pink-tiled bathroom where, on my previous visit, I'd stepped through a Capone Door into Lucky's lair.

"Not there. Over there," the guy said in Chicagoese, sounding like, *Not dere. Over dere.* He pointed the gun at an ancient, scarred wardrobe.

"Oh . . . okay," I said, pulling open its tall wooden door to find a small elevator. I stepped inside, ready to push the Down button, when the guy shook his head. "Up?" I said. "But I thought we were as high up in the building as possible?"

He gave me a shows-how-much-you-know smirk as the elevator doors closed. I rose quickly, trying to figure out how many floors I was passing—three maybe, which meant the thirteenth was actually the tenth?—and smelled the medicinal odor again as the elevator reached its destination.

There was nothing there but a steel door with a red light next to it.

I moved forward as a disembodied voice said, "Look up," and I craned my neck at an eye-in-the-sky camera. "There's an antibacterial dispenser by the door, counselor. Use it." I did as instructed, the light turned green, and the door opened to a room that was half medical center, half guard post. A nurse in scrubs stared at a beeping digital monitor. Rows of pill bottles stood next to plastic bags filled with clear liquid. Several armed thugs milled around, the types regularly used for Outfit security—thickly muscled with hard guts, dead eyes, and rifles strapped over their shoulders. A tall, gaunt man stood inspecting a clipboard, wearing a white coat with the word *Doc* stitched on it; if the guy was a real physician, he was the first I'd ever seen wearing a shoulder holster filled with a .38.

He looked up as I approached, handed me a surgical mask, and said, "Put it on." I did, and he nodded me toward a circular staircase.

I twisted up the steps, ending at another steel door and another watchful camera, followed by a metallic buzz.

I pushed inside a world made of glass.

The room was a dome, thirty feet high, its vast panes spotted with rainwater. I looked up and around at the idling clouds over Lake Michigan to the east, at surrounding buildings everywhere, and finally at a hospital bed in the center of the room. A large TV stood at its foot. Closed-circuit cameras were attached at intervals to the steel skeleton holding the glass panes. The rest of the space was empty except for a bank of flashing, blipping machines with tubes snaking to the bed.

Drawing near, I saw human remains lying beneath a thin blanket.

Lucky was beyond skeletal, as if constructed from brittle twigs. His flesh clung to him, its texture parchment-like and the color of a rotting banana peel.

The balance had clearly tipped, the old man so much more dead than alive.

I cleared my throat, drawing his attention. He turned to me, rheumy eyes behind thick glasses, breathing with effort. "You're . . . pretty sick, huh?" I said.

"There's the no-shit statement of the day," he said, shaking his head. "Take off that silly mask, it's too late for me to get any sicker. It's the Big Casino . . . cancer everywhere, eating me alive." He pushed weakly at a button attached to a tube in his arm. "Morphine on demand. Kills the pain before the pain kills me. They tried chemo, that filthy poison, but no use. It was sadistic . . . which reminds me, Knuckles Battuta ought to use chemo as a torture method for Muscle. Make a note of it, kitten . . ."

"Oh . . . uh, okay . . . ," I said.

"Not you-kitten. Me-kitten," a sultry voice said, and I turned to see Peek-a-Boo Schwartz, Lucky's ex-stripper girl-friend. She was as senior-citizen voluptuous as the last time I'd seen her, blond hair swooping over her face, lips just as glossy. But now weariness dominated her face; she was an old woman caring for an old, dying man. Peek-a-Boo gently pushed Lucky's glasses up his toucan nose, patted his spotted head, and said, "Need anything, killer?"

"Just you, baby doll," he said. "Everyone needs someone who's unconditionally loyal. Who tells you the truth, no matter what." He flicked his shark eyes at me; as broken as he was, they remained as black and penetrating as ever. "You better have at least one person like that, girlie."

"I do," I said, thinking of Doug, wondering about Tyler.

"That broad right there," Lucky said, nodding at Peek-a-Boo, "that *lady* . . . has been my most trusted adviser for a long, long time. She could've been boss—"

"Quit kissing my ass, you old bastard," she said softly.

"—but no broads in the Outfit, right? Until you came along, filling in for your dad, who's gone . . ."

I swallowed thickly and said, "Sick. You mean, he's sick."

"I meant what I said," he murmured, his eyes pinned to mine. "He's gone. The Russians have your family. You've been lying about it the whole damn time."

I trembled on the inside and my paranoid gut screamed

that there was no lie I could tell or excuse I could make that would help me now. I was seized by pure panic, my brain expanding and contracting as I tried to figure a way out of an inescapable situation.

The wall made of glass was all around me.

If I got a running start, I could smash through it and scream for help all the way down before I met the concrete.

In that long moment, it seemed like my last, best option.

17

"HOW . . . DID YOU FIND OUT?" I SAID.

My words sounded as small and defenseless as they were.

"We'll get to it," the old man said coldly. There was no *aha!* or accusation; he was all business, which terrified me, since Outfit business included broken heads and severed limbs, and that was gentle. "So this whole time your family has been gone—"

"I've been trying to find them, to *save* them!" I said, feeling my throat catch, failing to hold back a tear. "I wasn't trying to fool you. I was scared that you would think my dad had turned informant . . ."

Lucky shook his head in a weak, barely perceptible back-and-forth. "We got guys inside the FBI. I would've known long before now if he was a rat."

"I only want my family back," I said, wiping the moisture from my eyes. "It's been one long, endless nightmare."

"Welcome to the club, girlie." He snorted, sick and moist. "You got any idea what was done to my poor sister, how my father died? Or what *I've* done to other people's sisters and fathers and everybody else they loved, in the name of the Outfit?" He pushed himself forward and his voice rose as he pounded the bed with a bony fist. "There are hundreds of Outfit nightmares like yours, and thousands even *worse!*"

"Lucky," Peek-a-Boo said, laying a hand on his shoulder, easing him back.

The old man gasped for air, biting at it until he'd regained his composure. "Hear me now . . . ," he wheezed, "I ain't gonna see Jesus until we *crush* those Russians and regain our rightful place in Chicago. It's my last order of business before I check out. That's why you're here. *You're* going to make it happen."

He flicked a remote. The TV at the end of the bed showed a closed-circuit image.

A guy crouched over a table, face nearly touching it, and when he whipped his head back I saw powdery lines smeared around his nose. He pushed at it with the palm of his hand, sniffing wetly, and then looked directly at us. "Ah . . . I hear camera moving its little eye," he said. Using his fingers to comb at his stringy hair, he moved boldly toward the camera with a body built from coiled springs and small hard stones. A thick gold chain hung around his neck with an Orthodox cross dangling from it. He touched the cross, smiling with pointed teeth. "You see me but I can't see you," he said playfully, cracking his knuckles, showing star tattoos. "But if you're out there . . . hello, baby!"

His Russian accent made it sound like, *Halo, beh-bee.*

The wolfish smile stayed in place, and I knew he was

talking to me. I couldn't help notice his lack of goggles, but his eyes were the same shade of crimson.

Oh my god, I thought, *contact lenses . . . like Juan Kone's.*

"Our hostage, or guest, as the case may be," Lucky said. "Haven't laid a hand on him, making him think we're reasonable. Besides keeping him locked up, we've treated him like the king of coke, giving him all he wants. The junk burns right into his eyes."

They didn't get that way from cocaine, I thought uneasily.

"Tell her what the boys call him," Peek-a-Boo said.

Lucky grinned, more like a grimace. "Vlad the Inhaler. Get it?"

I nodded, watching the guy pace the room.

"I was about to whistle you in for an interrogation when the creep started blabbing about how they have your family," Lucky said. "We didn't catch him as much he let himself be caught. That junkie was sent to make a deal. In fact, he hasn't stopped saying it over and over again—the Russians will call a truce if we trade *you* for your family." He leaned so close I could see spidery veins beneath translucent skin. "We agreed."

We faced each other, the air dead between us, as my mind went into overdrive.

Did Vlad tell Lucky who his boss was? I thought. *Did he tell the old man about Elzy's other object of desire, the notebook?*

But no—that would undermine Elzy's plan to conquer Chicago. If Lucky knew I had a decades-old record of Outfit secrets and crimes, I'd be strapped to Knuckles's torture chair at this very moment. Instead, I was about to be traded to the

Russians, who would do even worse to make me give up the notebook.

With all my might, I kept a blank face and shrugged. "They'll never call a truce. It's a lie."

"Of course it is," Lucky said. "You know what I think? The Russians snatched your family hoping the counselor would be a strong bargaining chip with me. Your father's no shrinking violet, though. He would've used ghiaccio furioso on those bastards, but they somehow figured out a way to disable it. Now they know he has that cold blue power, and they must know you have it, too. Maybe your mother caved and told them, or that brother of yours." His gaze narrowed behind thick glasses. "I believe they intend to use you as a weapon, to flip you to their side and force you to use ghiaccio fusioso *against* us."

I swallowed once, thickly, feeling how close he was to at least part of Elzy's reason for wanting me. "My dad didn't do it. Why would I?"

"Because you're a girl. They assume you're weak . . . unable to stand up to whatever torture they're inflicting on your father," he answered. "Anthony Rispoli is a tough son of a bitch. They obviously don't believe you're as tough."

"They're wrong."

He shrugged bony shoulders. "It doesn't matter either way. Get this straight—I'm not in the business of saving your family or anyone else's. I'm making the trade for one reason only . . . to find out where the hell their mob . . . their goddamn *boss* . . . is holed up." He grunted painfully.

"But why do the Russians *think* you're making it?" I asked, the question slipping out before I could stop it.

Lucky's black eyes were pinned to mine. "Because they believe we're losing the street war. And that we're desperate for their bullshit truce."

"Well, we are, aren't we?" Peek-a-Boo said. "Losing, I mean."

The old man faced her, the stoniness in his expression softening slightly. "That's what I meant about having someone close by to tell the truth. Yeah, we're losing the war," he said, turning to me. "This trade is our best chance, maybe my *last* chance, to end this street war the way I want it to end."

"How's that?" I asked carefully.

Lucky thumbed the morphine button, slowly lying back. His voice was shallow when he said, "Kitten . . . take over . . ."

Peek-a-Boo's gaze lingered on him until his eyelids fluttered, and then turned on me. "It's the oldest play in the book, honey," she said. "You're the rabbit. Everyone follows you."

I'm used to it, I thought, listening to her.

"We're letting Vlad walk out of here, just you and him, on the pretense that you've been exchanged for your family," she said, moving away from Lucky's oxygen tank. She lit a cigarette, staining the filter hot pink. "Doubtless, Vlad will deliver you to his boss. A battalion of our guys, the invisible ones, will follow close behind."

"So they know about the trade? The invisible guys?" I asked, worried as always about the secret of my family's captivity.

She shook her head. "They were handpicked by Lucky. They don't need a reason to obey an order—they follow it, without question, and keep their mouths shut. The only people who know about the trade are you, me, and Lucky. It's no secret that the rank and file, maybe even his own VPs, wouldn't support what he has planned, so to hell with them," she said, handing me a device. "Take this just in case."

I looked at the GPS in my hand, thinking of the school buses, scooters, and other anonymous vehicles that had chased me for the past month. "Don't you think Vlad will have men on the street, too . . . waiting?"

"Maybe. It's a chance we're willing to take," she said. "Besides, our boys will spot them a mile away."

It didn't reassure me. I bit my lip, saying, "He takes me to his boss. Then what?"

"What do you think? It's not going to be subtle. A bloodbath never is. Your family taught me all about that." She was referring to the infamous Catacomb Club massacre, when my great-uncle Giaccomo Rispoli—Uncle Jack—gunned down dozens of innocent people, and nearly killed her, too. The Russian mob was far from innocent, but it was plain that Lucky had planned a mass murder of his enemies on an even larger scale.

It also meant that the rabbit would be directly in the line of fire.

"I'm walking in there unarmed. What happens when bullets start flying?"

She squinted through smoke with a grim half smile. "Duck."

"If by some miracle my family and I make it out of there," I said, "what then?"

Lucky sat up like a corpse coming to life, pointing a waxen finger. "You *will* make it out of there . . . our boys will see to that. And then, if he's able, your father will resume his role as counselor," he croaked, as raindrops pock-pocked the dome. "If not, you'll take over for him, permanently."

"But . . . I'm a woman," I said. "I thought—"

"You thought *nothing*!" he barked. "Broad or not, we *need* a Rispoli! Besides, no one walks away. Those are the rules . . ." The old man crumpled into the bed, squeezing morphine into his veins, waving me away with a fluttering hand.

The room was silent except for the rain. Lucky's breathing rose, shallow but steady. "Speaking of rules," Peek-a-Boo said quietly, "you know it's the counselor-at-large's responsibility to choose the boss's successor?"

"No . . . I mean, I do now. Why?"

"Why do you think? Only the counselor can enforce the decision among Outfit members through ghiaccio furioso," she said.

"But how?" I asked. "The rank and file is scattered all around Chicago. Is enforcement done, like, person by person?"

"The opposite. The entire organization is whistled in to one place at one time," she said. "They're called and they come. They're ordered to face the counselor, eyes wide open, and they do. Following the rules is their religion."

"It's hard to believe that no one looks away from the counselor."

Peek-a-Boo smoothed her hair. "Maybe some do, but the

majority do precisely as they're told. They want to be led, like any another zealots," she said. "By the way, there are only two candidates to replace the boss, based on rank. Either the VP of Muscle or the VP of Money."

"I guess that will be up to my dad when he's counselor again."

"If he makes it out of there."

"Lucky said he would. That my whole family would make it out," I answered, feeling the sickening truth in her words. In the end, there would be no real guarantee of their safety.

"Lucky's an optimist," Peek-a-Boo said, glancing at her watch. "It's time. Get Vlad into your car. Our guys are already in position. All you have to do is drive, not too fast, not too slow, wherever he tells you to go."

I looked back at the old man. "So how long does he have?"

"Days, maybe. He's about to prove himself wrong. There's a way to escape the Outfit, all right, and that's to die," she said, staring at me. I saw something in her eyes—not sympathy, but more like commiseration from one woman to another, both bound to an organization that resented their existence. "Ironic, hm? The thing that's killing him is doing it the only way the Outfit could ever be destroyed, too."

"I don't understand."

Peek-a-Boo looked around at the cameras watching us, and back at me. "Like cancer," she said, almost in a whisper. "From the inside out."

The moment passed, her smoking, me thinking about what she'd said. "After he's, you know . . . gone, what happens to you?" I asked.

"I'll be protected until a boss is in place. Then the new regime will squeeze me for the information and secrets I've learned from Lucky over the years. After that . . . ," she said with a shrug. "All I know for sure is that there's no place in the Outfit for a woman who knows more about their business than they do. I'll be of no use to them."

"That's not true, not if they're smart."

"But I am a woman, just like you. They're no different from the Russians, just like Lucky said . . . they think we're not as tough as they are," she said, opening the door. "Well, are we?"

I stepped outside without a word and the door locked behind me.

Vlad the Inhaler was down there somewhere, waiting to take me to the Russians.

"Let's find out," I said aloud, descending the spiral staircase.

18

THE OUTFIT GUY POURED FROM CONCRETE was still holding the AK-47 when he told me to wait downstairs. I was to drive Vlad wherever he told me to go, without question.

There was nothing more to say.

I was the rabbit.

The lobby was airless and damp with the rain falling steadily outside, ricocheting off the sidewalk. I crossed the tile floor, counting my steps—sixteen, wall-to-wall—until the elevator binged. Vlad the Inhaler stepped off, jangly and cocky, looked left and right, and then aimed a smile at me as if we were long-lost pals. His crimson eyes gleamed as he pinched at his nose, wriggled it like a hyperactive bunny, and said, "There she is! Miss Counselor-at-Large herself! Cute *and* tough!"

I said nothing, feeling my left hand curl into a fist, and resisting it.

He moved closer, trailing an acrid smell of sweat. "You're a fighter, eh?" he said slyly, fingering the gold chain. "Well, give up the notebook, or be ready to fight for your life." He grinned, smoothed back his hair, and drove a hard-knuckled fist deep into my stomach, doubling me over.

I didn't make a sound, sucking in the agony and the instinct to fight back.

Vlad wiped a hand under his nose, saying, "Let's go have some *fun,* yes?!" He led us into the downpour, across the street, me trying to find my breath, him humming a frenetic tune. "You drive," he said. "I want your hands where I can see them. I hear you like to throw punches." With a yank of the door handle, he shoved me behind the wheel, walked around, and slid in on the other side, shaking his head like a soaked wolfhound. Whether it was nerves or a subconscious desire not to go anywhere with the guy, I dropped the keys. I bent for them, and as I sat up, he grabbed a handful of my hair and jerked my head back. "Drop them again, girl. I dare you," he said, running his hand through my hair, caressing it gently, and then slamming my face into the steering wheel. The horn made a sharp bleating noise, like a lamb at slaughter. "Now drive," he said, "south, down Michigan Avenue. South. We can see the sights, like young lovers."

I sat back tasting blood and when the starlight explosion cleared from my brain, pulled slowly from the curb. Snaking rivulets streamed down the windshield. The thumping wipers barely kept the road visible. I turned onto Michigan Avenue and drove past the limestone water tower into a line of creeping traffic.

"You know Wicker Park?" he said, drumming fingers on his thigh.

"Yeah," I said, glancing in the rearview mirror as a black town car moved toward us. In the other lane, a brown Buick edged into position, rolling slowly.

"Hoyne Avenue, near Division Street. There's a place, Czar Bar," he said. "Your family is waiting. Maybe not well, but alive."

A real location, and that word, *alive,* uttered so casually. My heart beat rapidly as traffic inched through the storm.

I eased to a stop at a red light.

The gray, Gothic Tribune Tower loomed on my left, its spire lost in mist, while the Wrigley Building squatted to my right like a huge, rain-soaked wedding cake.

A flick of my eyes in the rearview mirror showed the town car and Buick several car lengths behind. In my mind, I paced off what would happen next—I'd park on Hoyne Avenue and enter Czar Bar while the Outfit guys arrived outside. There would be a short interval before the onslaught began as they loaded guns, took positions. Those few minutes would be the only chance to save my family.

A brutish wind picked up, rocking the Lincoln.

The red light seemed to be eternal.

Just ahead I could see waves below the Michigan Avenue Bridge throwing themselves against its concrete foundations, leaping like wet, caged animals. Vlad stared out the window and read my mind, murmuring, "These are the long minutes, eh? Like before walking into a prison cell. Who's waiting for you in there? What will they do to you? Your stomach fills with moths and ears ring like church bells. You wait, you wonder."

He turned and grinned, tracing my jaw with a clammy finger. "But for now, it's just you and me, baby."

"And me, asshole."

We spun around to Doug sitting in the backseat, shoving away the old raincoat he'd been hiding under. Harry crouched next to him, teeth bared behind the muzzle; in a quick motion, Doug removed the muzzle from his face. The little dog growled from deep in his belly while Doug held the .45 toward Vlad's empty face. Astonished and alarmed, through gritted teeth, I said, "Doug, what the *hell* are you doing here?!"

"That weird warning in the text message—I was worried about you. I thought you might need me . . . us," he said, as Harry growled again.

As unnerving as their presence was, even worse was the steel briefcase on Doug's lap. We'd agreed never to leave the notebook alone at the Bird Cage Club, and now the Russian mob's object of desire was right here in the car with us. I wanted to scream at Doug to flee but my tongue went numb.

Vlad was staring into the backseat and spoke first.

"Briefcase." It sounded like *brif-kes,* and his tone was so languid it was as if guns were aimed at his head several times a day. "Could it be the one your father told us about? Under duress, of course. I waterboarded him myself. Funny what comes out when you're drowning on dry land." He pretended to gag and spit, bugging his eyes, and then melted into a sly smile. "In that briefcase, there is a notebook. *The* notebook, yes?"

Doug said, "But I have a gun, so—" and that split second

was all Vlad needed to launch himself into the backseat. The grappling was quick and ugly as he drove a fist into Doug's startled face while Harry howled and lunged.

"Harry! Heel. *Heel!*" I screamed, sure Vlad would do just as bad to the little dog, or worse. Harry froze on his haunches, teeth bared, hair bristling, eyes locked on the Russian. He trusted my voice and obeyed it, despite his instinct to attack.

"Doggy is smartest one in car," Vlad said, jammed between Harry and Doug with the .45 pointed at me. He lifted the briefcase onto his lap and said, "Look behind us. Typical, eh? Raining like hell, streets a mess, and a garbage truck just happens to break down now. No one can get past, not town cars, not Buicks . . ."

I glanced back at the hulking vehicle. It was stopped sideways, hazard lights flashing, blocking every car behind it. Large, flower-filled concrete planters ran down the middle of Michigan Avenue making it impossible to get around the garbage truck. I looked from dazed Doug to whimpering Harry, and said, "Now what?"

"Your friend just made everything easier," Vlad said, tapping out a cokey beat on the briefcase. "We proceed to Czar Bar, where you say good-bye to your family."

"Because you're letting them go," I said. "That's the deal. Them for me."

"Oh, sure, you hug and kiss, say, *See you soon, Mommy!* and we wave bye-bye," he said, picking at his teeth. "No. We kill them. Only reason it hasn't happened by now, we want you to watch."

Something painful spread through me, a cancer of defeat, and I turned, placed both hands on the steering wheel, and stared through the windshield. "Your boss hates me that much," I said.

"Drive carefully, baby, it's wet outside. We don't want the gun to go off and have something happen to this fool," he said, blithely driving an elbow into Doug's gut. As he groaned painfully, Vlad said, "At least your brother put up a fight. It took a hell of a lot more than punch to stomach to—you know—get his mind right."

I blinked once, coming awake, and met Vlad's eyes in the rearview mirror. "Lou," I said, as the cold blue flame began to flicker and burn.

"Very strong kid, physically, mentally, at first," he said. "I learn techniques in Russian prison, some with fists, others with ropes, that break any man, make *any* man loyal to his torturer. Your brother, no—he kept fighting." Vlad leaned forward, his breath warm on my neck. "Until I bring out the knives."

A zing of electricity crossed my shoulders, a reminder of aspirins untaken and of how easy it would be to kill someone I hated. "You brainwashed him."

"Washed his brain, inked his skin, and now he's one of us," Vlad said. "At least that's what he thinks. It amused my boss to see how his transformation hurt your parents, how he screamed at them, spit in their faces."

"Lou wouldn't do that—"

"He did it, and more. But if necessary, my boss would kill him like stepping on a bug. Hey, green light," he said, nudging me with the .45. "Anyway . . . just another dead kid on a Chicago street. Who would give a crap?"

"I would," I hissed, jamming my foot on the gas, demanding all the power contained in the Lincoln's V-8 engine. The back end fishtailed as the tires chewed wet pavement, and we flew ahead like a missile. I had no real plan, only to shake the gun loose from Vlad's grip and allow the deadly voltage surging through my brain and body to take its course. We barreled onto the bridge, rain pounding the car, as I whipped the steering wheel back and forth, swerving wildly side to side.

"Slow down, *bitch*!" Vlad screamed, digging a hand into my neck and screaming again at the painful electrical current coursing through me, biting and burning his fingers. I craned my neck at him, seeing the blue glow of my eyes reflect from his suddenly pale face, and grinned like a Sicilian demon from hell. Somehow the Russian had managed to hold on to the .45. But a guardrail ran along the side of the bridge and I yanked the steering wheel, hitting the railing hard, metal on metal shrieking, throwing Vlad, Doug, and Harry against one another, and then I did it again.

There was no traction beneath the tires, not even a skid, only a frenzied slide.

The street was too wet, the car too heavy, the speed too intense.

The Lincoln did not bounce from the guardrail but seemed to stick to it, and then the earth began to turn as we went up and over the side of the bridge.

There was a short period of silence, a tiny sliver of floating peace like when astronauts bounce around a space capsule, and then—a deafening impact as two tons of Detroit steel collided with cold river water. We'd flipped in the air and come down with the wheels beneath us, water rising over the hood, and then the doors, rushing into the car and sinking us so quickly it was like being on a roller coaster going over the highest hill.

The convertible top ballooned outward and was torn off in a brown liquid rush. I removed my seat belt and pushed away from the car as a cloud of bubbling suction pulled the Lincoln to the river floor. I dug at the water, seeing quivering light above the river's surface, and broke through, spitting mud and sucking air. Curtains of rain swept over me. I splashed and quivered in the current, hair plastered to my face, and then began paddling anxiously in a circle—

Where's Doug?! Where's Harry?!

—and spotted Vlad swimming toward me with one arm. He was so close I could see his wild brown eyes—he'd lost the crimson contacts—as he pushed against the water, grunted while he lifted the briefcase in an overhand motion, and hit me in the head.

It was a sledgehammer blow, snuffing out the world.

I sank beneath the waves inhaling water, comforted by the dark weightlessness, and then panicked, clawing my way back to the surface. With fiery pain rippling from my skull, and weary from fighting the river, it was all I could do to hold on to consciousness and watch Vlad prepare to hit me again, realizing that I wouldn't survive another blow, when something tore from the water—black homicidal eyes, flaring nostrils, sharp, snapping teeth—and Harry flung himself into

Vlad's face. Canine snarls mixed with human screams, and I bobbed helplessly, peering through the downpour at the little dog's head wildly twisting from side to side. Vlad went under, pulling Harry with him, a cascade of silent bubbles rose up, and then both of them popped to the surface with Vlad screeching in Russian, and then in English, "Devil *dog*! You took my *nose*!"

"Harry!" I screamed. "Get away from him! Please, Harry!"

"Goddamn *demon*!" Vlad bellowed. They were thrashing and biting, and I pushed myself toward them as their heads bobbed and then sunk rapidly beneath the waves.

Beneath the waves!

Where's Doug?!

I turned, and turned again, filled with panicky adrenaline, searching the face of the river, spotted a slime of rising motor oil, and dove for it. I opened my eyes as I descended, unable to see farther than my hand, but there—the hulking shadow of the Lincoln was impossible to miss, looking as if it were parked on the river floor! I pulled toward it, feeling my way through to the backseat, touching Doug's hair that was like a waving mass of seaweed. Drawing closer, lungs burning, I saw his leg wedged beneath the front seat. I held his ankle in both hands and yanked with all my strength, doing math in my feverish brain—*How long had he been under, two minutes, four, was he already dead?*—until the leg came free and his body slowly rose toward me. I hooked the back of his shirt and tried to pull but he was too heavy, we were too deep.

The old raincoat was wedged in the backseat.

I grabbed it, looped it tightly around Doug's wrist, and

burrowed madly through brown water toward the surface, counting each jerk of the raincoat, and at ten broke into the rain, literally eating the air. With one arm beneath Doug, the other pulling toward the weedy shore, I tried not to feel his motionless chest. We came aground on a muddy spit just feet from part of the bridge's foundation. His face was ashen, eyes open and staring at nothing, lines of greenish liquid snaking from his nostrils.

My head jerked up at a commotion on the other side of the river.

There were shrill calls for help as Vlad was hauled onto the dock of Wendella boat tours. He bent at the knees, face streaming blood and water, and then rose and scanned the river until he saw me kneeling next to Doug's limp form. Even from that distance, it was evident something was wrong with his face, as if a small, nasty explosion had occurred beneath his eyes. Two men tried to help but Vlad shoved them away, lifted the briefcase with one hand and a middle finger at me with the other, and pushed through the crowd. I watched him jerkily climb a flight of steps toward Michigan Avenue; if I scrambled up the embankment to the walkway above, it would be possible to catch him. I could use cold fury not only to get the notebook but also to try to save my family.

The choice was stark—Doug, or the notebook and Vlad.

I leaned over my friend and used what I'd learned in first-aid class at Fep Prep, clearing his mouth of as much gunk as possible. Hands trembling, I tilted his head, held his nose shut, and began mouth-to-mouth resuscitation. There was no response, just me pushing air down his throat, and I paused, saying, "Come on, Doug! Not like this!" and resumed, breathing for him until he kicked and bucked, and I rolled him on his side as he vomited river water, gasped, puked once more, and drew in a huge gulp of air. I sat him up and held him in place like a big, awkward baby until he was breathing on his own. Kneeling next to him, pushing the rain from my face, I said, "Doug . . . thank god . . . you were . . . I mean, you almost . . ."

He quaked with a full-body shiver, blinked at me, and turned his head slowly. "Where's Harry?" he mumbled.

"Harry?" I said, looking out over the water. It was an expanse of gray ripples, swallowing up and smoothing over all signs of a crime scene. "He saved me," I said, feeling my throat tighten. "Harry saved my life, again."

"But . . . where is he?" Doug tried to stand but failed, his hands sinking into mud, eyes desperately sweeping the river.

"Vlad tried to kill me. Harry attacked him . . . they went under . . . Vlad came up . . ."

Doug looked at me with his face twisted in disbelief. "You—you let him go? You didn't go back for him?"

"I went back for you."

He looked through me, and then back at the river. "Oh," he said, biting at his bottom lip. "That's . . . too bad, because . . ."

"Doug," I said, touching his shoulder, but he shrugged me off weakly.

". . . because, you know, I love him," he whispered, eyes shimmering with tears. "Harry's my friend. He doesn't care what I look like, or who I am, and . . . I think he loves me, too. I think so." He spread a muddy hand over his face. "Yeah, he did. Harry loved me," and he spoke other soft words that melted from his lips, mixing with tears.

Gratitude and guilt spiked my heart. Lou had rescued the little dog from a pound, using slow, kind patience to tame a wild nature spawned through mistreatment. The Italian greyhound took on aspects of my brother's personality—intelligence, fierce loyalty—and losing him was like losing Lou again. There was nothing I could say to make Doug or myself feel better, so I didn't. I kneeled, looking into the water until sirens cut the air, and then helped Doug up the embankment to the walkway. I hurried him onto Lower Wacker Drive where we wouldn't be seen; he moved as if sleepwalking, stealing glances at the river as we walked deeper into the Loop toward the Bird Cage Club.

I didn't look back, not once.

Harry was gone and we had to keep moving.

We could sit around forever hoping someone we loved would come back from the dead. But the only thing we'd probably get from that was dead ourselves.

19

THE RAIN STOPPED FOR GOOD ON FRIDAY
while lingering clouds bumped and swirled in the early-
morning sky.

It was a day filled with reflection of the worst kind.

Doug sat on the couch wrapped in a blanket, bruised and
sighing. He'd slipped Harry's dog collar around his wrist,
vowing to never remove it. The ghost of our little friend per-
meated the place. Just as Eskimos can identify different types
of snow, there are multiple variations of silence. The Bird
Cage Club rang with the absence of soft whining demands to
be petted, the tap-shoe sound of claws crossing the floor, and
barks of joy at being fed snacks. Harry was gone, but he was
all around us.

I lay on my mattress staring at the ceiling, suffering the
loss of the notebook as well. My hope was that it had become
waterlogged and unintelligible; if not, Elzy was surely
scouring it for the secret to ultimate power. It was there, in the
final chapter, *"Volta,"* handwritten decades earlier in Buon-

diavolese, an obscure form of Sicilian, by my uncle Jack. He had translated it for me, but in a fit of rage and ignorance, his daughter, Annabelle, destroyed his work. If Uncle Jack hadn't recorded the Troika of Outfit Influence in his screenplay *The Weeping Mafioso,* I would never have discovered the vault made of gold bricks. The problem now was that my dad was one of the few people in the world who read and spoke Buondiavolese; Uncle Buddy once confronted him about it in my presence, referring to it as a secret language shared by my dad and Grandpa Enzo. I assumed that my dad had denied knowing the secret to ultimate power, but now Elzy had proof of its existence, and would use every torturous method available to force my poor dad to translate "*Volta.*"

Gingerly, I touched the painful spots on my neck where Vlad's fingerprints were burned into my skin; in electrifying him, even that short burst, I'd inflicted the same damage on myself. It hurt all the way to the bone. I sat up slowly, grimacing with the effort, and shook an aspirin from a bottle. I turned the pill in my hand and considered swallowing it dry; after the previous day, I wasn't sure I'd ever go near water again. The sensation of drowning had invaded my dreams, and a text I'd received from Tyler minutes earlier brought back that stifling feeling:

> Are u okay? Heard Red attacked out of the blue.
> Let me know u r safe.

—which meant news of the incident had leaked back to the Outfit. Tyler's 'out of the blue' comment assured me, at least a little, that Lucky had told the truth—only the old man, Peek-a-Boo and me had known about the trade. But the text meant my failure to lead Lucky's handpicked men to the Russians had reached him, as well. I had no idea what the repercussions would be other than swift and unpleasant. I was about to text Tyler back when my phone rang. I put the aspirin aside and looked at the familiar number flashing on the screen—Knuckles. I lifted the phone, expecting him to try to coax information out of me, and said, "Don't ask about the bridge."

"Came at you when you weren't looking, huh?" he said gravely. "Well, forget that for now. We got other fish to fry."

I paused, bit my lip. "What do you mean?"

"Ed Debevic . . . has left the building."

The room was perfectly still, but somewhere Outfit tectonics shifted. Lucky was dead less than a day after our sit-down, and all his power and secret plots were gone with him. It meant my fiasco on the bridge was gone, too, or at least on a back burner until the succession of a new boss.

At the other end, Knuckles sucked on a cigar and hacked like an old dragon. "Are you aware of your responsibility? What happens next?" he asked carefully.

"Yeah. Looks like I have an important choice to make."

Knuckles cleared his throat. "According to the rules, you have to name Ed Debevic's replacement in precisely one week, at an Outfit-wide sit-down," he said. "All members will be present, from the lowest pickpocket and pimp all the way to the top."

"Next Friday," I said quietly.

"Take the Gray Line subway train from Lawrence Avenue. Be in the station at 5:03 p.m. on the nose. Not 5:02, not 5:04. It'll take you to the meeting place."

"Wait, you said 'subway,' but the Lawrence Avenue stop is for an elevated train," I said. "Besides, Chicago doesn't even have a Gray Line subway."

"Chicago doesn't. But the Outfit does," Knuckles replied.

I could almost hear him biting his tobacco-covered tongue, wanting to ask why I didn't know that, and hadn't my poor, sick dad told me about it? Apparently cold fury still held him in check. Instead, when he spoke, his tone was ingratiating, or more accurately, ass-kissing. "You know I've always respected you," he growled sweetly. "Hey, *come due piselli in un baccello,* eh? Don't we work together like two peas in a pod?"

"Oh, sure," I said. "I wake each day wondering what new joy my trusted colleague—by that, I mean you—will add to my life."

"Ha-ha!" He fake-laughed. "You're a kidder. By the way, speaking of kids, the last thing you want to do is select one for a man's job. Your other choice, that smooth-talking pretty boy, is a treacherous little turd. I've said it before and will say it again, he'll flash his pearly whites while cutting your throat."

All I heard in his screed was the term, "man's job."

Knuckles thought of me, and all females, as inept and of a lower intelligence, and choked on the fact that I served as counselor-at-large. The belief in gender superiority was endemic in the purely male Outfit—except for Tyler. If I had to choose a boss, of course it would be him. But I was unsure that he would agree to it, unwilling to go any deeper into the Outfit he despised. I'd never use cold fury to force him to serve, which left me with a true conundrum—who would I name as Lucky's replacement?

And just like that, I had the perfect answer, and a plan to save my family.

On the danger meter, it pushed the needle past red.

I put the aspirin back in the bottle. If the plan went awry, which was very possible, I'd need the voltage to zap my way free. "Anything else?" I said impatiently.

"Just remember, counselor, I'm at your service at any time of the day or—" Knuckles said, as I hung up on him and hurried into the other room.

Doug was slumped on the couch like a depressed burrito, brown eyes gone red from crying. I sat on the other end with Harry's curling-up spot miserably vacant between us. "I know that I should apologize for everything . . . messing up your chance to reach Czar Bar, losing the Lincoln, and oh my god . . . especially the notebook," he said. "I'm so sorry, really, but none of it compares to the fact that I brought Harry along, and he—"

"It's not your fault."

"Yes it is," he said, wiping his nose. "I was trying to be your hard-ass partner, ready for action with a gun and a tough little dog, and . . . I got him killed."

"Doug," I said, "Vlad's men in the garbage truck were onto me from the beginning. They cut off the Outfit guys. I would've been walking into Czar Bar unable to use cold fury, without backup—who knows what would've happened to me? If you hadn't hidden in the Lincoln and brought Harry, I might have been dead."

He sniffled, looking at me. "I'm still responsible. But they are, too."

"Which they?"

"All of them," he said bitterly. "Elzy, those Russian assholes . . . and the animals that make up the Outfit, it's their fault, too. Everyone striving for ultimate power, and all it led to is the death of my friend. It makes me want to . . . to . . . ."

"Give up?"

Doug's eyes were suddenly dry and hard. "Kill every one of them."

An image of that homicidal fantasy rose up before me, the still, cold bodies of my enemies, all the threat and danger vanquished in one fell swoop. If I had the chance, would I do it—*could* I do it? It chilled me thinking about that scope of murder, hundreds of lives, maybe more. "There's a difference between wanting to do it, and doing it," I said.

"I know." He sighed. "That's why I'm just sitting here. There's not a damn thing I can do."

"Yeah, there is," I said. "You can drive a stick shift."

I told him about Lucky and then explained my plan, starting at "*Volta.*" With every Rispoli bone in my body, I was sure Uncle Jack's scrawled Buondiavolese revealed that ultimate power was actually billions of dollars' worth of gold. But there were factors on my side—it would take time for Elzy to dig through the notebook, and even longer for her to force my dad to translate the last chapter. She didn't know that

I'd located ultimate power, so before she made any progress or hurt my dad further, I'd beat her to the punch.

I'd tell her what it was.

Doug listened to the details, and said, "You mean you're going to lie."

"Am I going to tell her about the gold? Hell no—at this point, why should I? Look, according to the rules, I'm supposed to name either the VP of Muscle or the VP of Money as the boss, but screw the rules. Elzy thinks the notebook will lead her to total control over the Outfit, so I'll give it to her," I said. "In exchange for my family, I'll name her as the new Outfit boss, and I'll present it—that level of total control—as ultimate power."

"That's some risky business," he said, sitting forward, throwing off the blanket. "Lying to her about what it is when she has the notebook. Using your role as counselor-at-large to sell out the entire Outfit. It'll cause a genuine shit storm."

"There's no way to avoid it."

"So," he said, "what does driving a stick shift have to do with all of this?"

"If Elzy agrees to the deal, I won't waste a second waiting for her mind or mood to change. I'll go directly to Czar Bar and get my family," I said. "That means a hasty retreat. The Lincoln's gone, all we have is the Ferrari. You're the wheelman, Doug—the getaway driver."

"Getaway driver? I've been waiting to do something like that since forever!" he said with a fist pump.

"You won't panic and freeze up?"

"No way. I'll be thinking about Harry the whole time," he

said, the ruddiness coming back to his pale face. "Make the deal and I'll drive like hell." I held his gaze until his determined grin died, frowning at him. "What?" he asked.

"What you just said about the deal. How do I contact Elzy?"

He went to his laptop on the control center, tapped some keys, and pointed at the screen. "There it is. Czar Bar's phone number."

"Wait, you think I should just *call* her?"

"Why not?" he said. "Just ask for the boss."

"What if they don't believe it's me?" Doug raised an eyebrow in a *seriously?* look. "Right. Of course," I said. "How many me's are there?" I lifted the phone, took a deep breath, and dialed. It rang once, twice, and then the phone on the other end was lifted from its hook. It was quiet, not even an intake of breath. "It's . . . Sara Jane Rispoli," I said.

There was no reply, but something lived in the silence, evoking an odd memory.

I was seven or eight, with my mom at a crowded street festival, and we stopped to have our palms read. The fortune-teller peered at my hand, and then into my eyes, and while I couldn't recall what she'd said, the experience then and now was the same—the creepy feeling of being known.

"Elzy?" I said.

The pause was filled with dead air and breathing, replaced by the sound of a palm held over the receiver. Behind it, I heard a muffled conversation, and then a familiar voice said, "Hello, baby!"

"Vlad . . ."

"You should've checked brakes on that clunker! Shame, shame! No safe-driver award for you!" He snuffled. "Hey, by the way, thanks for notebook and, *oh so sorry* about your friend!"

"My friend?" I said, looking at Doug watching me.

"It's no fun, dying that way, drinking Chicago River water, but hey, he had a big goddamn mouth so maybe it happened quickly, yes?"

"Yes," I said quietly, "I hope so."

"At least you got his body, so maybe you have nice little going away party. The doggy, on the other hand, the fish are chewing on his furry ass by now, I bet. He was a fighter, though. You should see my nose, or what's left of it! He bit, he clawed, and then, how do they say? All dogs go to heaven?"

The cold blue flame danced in my gut and a line of electricity crept up my spine as I said, "I want to talk to your boss."

"You go through me or I hang up."

With supreme effort I choked back the rage coursing through my body. "You'll find out soon enough, but I'm telling you first. The boss of the outfit, Lucky, is dead."

Vlad repeated it with his hand over the phone, and said, "So?"

"So, tell *your* boss I want to make a deal. An exchange. Give me my family, and I'll give up . . . ultimate power."

The line was quiet for a moment. "Go on," he said.

I explained the counselor-at-large's responsibility to choose Lucky's heir—if they didn't believe me, they could ask my dad. "That's the deal. The entire Outfit will be gathered when

I name her boss. At the moment of the announcement, all eyes will be on me, and I'll enforce the decision with ghiaccio furioso," I said. "But that's all I'll do for her. I won't serve her as counselor. From then on, she can use her soldiers to keep the rank and file in line." Vlad covered the receiver and the muted conversation grew more urgent. One voice, high and commanding, rose above the garble.

Vlad returned to the phone and asked, "Who else in Outfit knows you're offering deal?"

"No one," I answered.

"You have officers, yes? VPs you call them. Muscle and Money, your comrades? You didn't warn them?"

"No." I swallowed, thinking of Tyler.

"Good. Easier to get rid of them when time comes." He chuckled. "So how soon until you use that witch power to make Outfit obey your decision?"

"The sit-down is a week from today, with every member present."

He relayed my message, and then said, "Do it, and you can have family. By the way, don't be disappointed. They look much like my nose."

"No—I get my family first, *now.*"

Vlad chuckled again. "You have sense of humor. In another time and place, we could've had fun. I would've shown you tricks I learned in prison," he said, and cleared his throat. "Okay. We're all businessmen here—business*people,* I mean. You take mommy and brother. We keep papa until deal is done."

"How do I know you'll let him go?"

"Because we don't need him no more," he said. "Your papa's days as counselor are over."

"What does that mean?" I asked carefully.

"It means he's retired," he said. "Mommy and brother only."

Elzy would have the same crimson eyewear as her Russians, which meant I couldn't force her to free my dad. My mind raced, with one thought in the lead—saving my mom and Lou was better than saving no one. "Okay, I said, "I'm coming to get them now."

"No, no, no," he said. "Don't be silly. We need a time to spiff them up and, how you say, wash their brains? Make mommy and brother forget things they've seen and heard? We're like Outfit, we have little secrets that can't just walk out door."

There was no way to protest. All I could say was, "When?"

"You call back, after weekend, Monday—no, Tuesday," he said. "An extra day to make you suffer, yes?"

"Tuesday," I said.

"Hey, look on bright side. We got no more reason to chase your ass. Or maybe we do it just for laughs," he said, covering the phone again. "One more thing. My boss comes with you to meeting. Outfit sees new leader face-to-face so clear they are under control of *Mafyia*." It was another deadly wrinkle, a dangerous complication that could ruin my plan, but I had no choice except to agree. "By the way," he said, "notebook is fascinating! So many secrets! You want to hear my favorite?"

"No."

"Those Capone Doors! I *love* them!" he barked. "Your daddy denied they were real, just made-up stories in case cops ever find notebook, until we use jumper cables to make him tell truth! Now I'm looking for those crazy doors everywhere! So anyway, we talk soon, yes?" And he hung up.

I stared at the phone and looked at Doug.

"Well?" he asked.

"We have a deal." I sat on the couch numbly and gave him the details. When I finished, I looked at him and said, "They think you're dead."

"I'm a lot of things, but not that."

"They're going to get rid of the VPs of Muscle and Money. Knuckles . . . he made his own bed," I said solemnly, "but Tyler—"

"You have to warn him. Soon."

"With Lucky dead and the Outfit in transition, it's a chance for him to escape, the opportunity he's been waiting for," I said. "Same for you, Doug. Take the gold bar and get the hell out of here while you can."

"Where?"

"I don't know. New Mexico or Fiji . . . someplace where the Outfit doesn't exist and there's no Russian mob."

"And no you. I just lost Harry. You're all I have left. Besides, I love Chicago. Those bastards can't run me out of my town." He pushed his bushy hair from his eyes, filled with resolution. "I'm in it to the end, friend."

I knew what "friend" meant; the perfect definition was sitting across from me.

It was the other phrase, "the end," that gave me pause.

It meant that something stopped forever, but greed, violence, and deception—the things that breathed life into the Outfit and the Russian mob—would continue long after the sit-down a week from today. They would continue forever.

I didn't care. I could live with that as long as my family was free.

20

SATURDAY NIGHT. MEETING TYLER IN AN HOUR.
Need to warn him, I wrote in my journal. I glanced at the clock,
which read 7:01 p.m.

I'd texted him yesterday and he'd responded immediately,
relieved that I was okay. When I asked if he could meet this
evening, he answered with a smiley emoticon, wondering if it
was a date. I replied that it was business, and told him to be at
the Davis Theater at eight, surprising myself.

The Davis had been Max's and my special place.

The night my family disappeared had been the Fep Prep
spring dance. Before we parted that evening, Max asked me
to a movie the next day. Of course I never made it, but later,
during relatively (understatement alert) calm periods, we saw
an overblown action flick there, and then another. We ate salty
junk, watched some great films, some crap ones, and yeah,
made out like crazy, since the place is really dark, usually empty,
and one of those special old theaters that seem to encourage

playing around. The fact that I wanted to take Tyler to the Davis meant—what? That Max having a girlfriend meant that I was over him? That I wanted to make out with Tyler?

It's business, I wrote, underlining it. *Serious business . . .*

Voices murmured from the other room followed by a muted shriek.

It was just something Doug was watching on his computer. He was alone on the couch, and he'd placed a pillow where Harry usually lay, absently petting it from time to time. I read the journal page I'd just filled, trying to recall details from the previous day that I might've skipped, but it was all there, from Lucky's death to the upcoming sit-down to the deal with Elzy. I bit the end of the pen and then wrote:

After I name Elzy as boss, both of our worlds, Tyler's and mine, will change. If possible, he's in greater danger than me . . .

I flipped forward, seeing that the journal was almost full, and backward, amazed at how much I'd written in just six months. I'd made the first entry the night my family disappeared and then, page by page, connected old secrets to new ones. The longer my family remained missing, the more detailed the information I'd recorded, linking the Outfit's past with the present. Suddenly a lightbulb went on in my mind, and I carried the journal into the room, showing it to Doug. "We didn't lose it, after all," I said. "The notebook . . . it's right here."

He looked up from the screen. "What are you talking about?"

"I recorded everything," I said. "Every fact and secret,

every Capone Door, rule, and rumor. The entire notebook is in these pages."

"You should turn it in," he said. "Give Thumbs-Up the surprise of his life."

"Not unless I want to graduate in handcuffs." I glanced at the computer, seeing velvety flesh, oozing blood, and gratuitous cleavage. "What are you watching?"

"*Sucker for Love*," he said. "The vampire TV show. With Max's girlfriend."

My stomach dropped hearing his name. Face burning, I said, "What the hell for?"

Doug looked at me, saw my expression. "Oh . . . sorry. I just wanted to see what she looked like, and—"

"Forget it." I sighed, sitting next to him. "So. What does she look like?"

"She hasn't been on yet. I'll tell you one thing, there's a lot of sucking going on, but it's mainly the acting," he said, "and—wait! That's her!"

"Which one?"

"The tall redhead in the thigh-high boots, with the crossbow made from a wooden cross. Get it?" he said, shaking his head. "Seriously, is there *anything* left in the vampire canon to exploit?"

"She's . . . curvy," I said, staring at the screen, folding my arms over my chest.

"More like buxom. Busty even."

"I've seen enough," I said, rising from the couch. "Gotta get ready to go."

"I'd be jealous if I wasn't so depressed," he said, petting the pillow.

I dressed in something other than a Cubs T-shirt (something with an actual collar) and the jeans I chose didn't look as if they'd been stitched together from cast-off denim. I'd already subdued my hair with about a gallon of conditioner and now brushed the wild curls into black shiny waves. A smear of lip gloss, a mist of perfume, and I stared in the mirror at the final product. I still wasn't wild about my nose—that Italian cliché in the middle of my face—but it was part of who I was. I was okay with it.

Doug was slumped sideways on the couch when I crossed to the elevator.

Going closer, I saw that he'd nodded off hugging the pillow.

Onscreen, the busty vampire was literally sucking face with a guy who was either her victim or her boyfriend or both. I stared at her—sexy, tough, undead—and turned off the computer, her image disappearing in a flash.

It wasn't a stake through the heart, but it was the best I could do.

With no Lincoln and no time to uncover the Ferrari (it, too, was stored in the garage beneath the Currency Exchange Building) I was stuck with public transportation. It was a twenty-minute train ride to the Davis Theater; I hoped Vlad had been serious about not chasing me anymore. I took the elevator down from the Bird Cage and stepped through the Capone Door urinal in the Phun-Ho to Go men's room, then into the fast food restaurant itself. The place was empty; it was always deserted, for both lunch and dinner. The fuzzy TV on the counter was blaring something screechy and joyous from an Asian channel while the guy who ran the joint leaned on the counter as usual, focusing on the screen. I'd realized months ago that it was some sort of Outfit front business, and that he probably knew who I was, since I used his men's room as my own private entrance and exit. He was always there, in the same spot, early in the morning when I cut through with Harry (poor Harry) for a pre-school walk, and at all other hours; I wondered sometimes if he lived in the place and what type of criminal activity he fronted for.

I passed by him now and he didn't look up from the TV.

The train ride to Lincoln Square, where the Davis is located, was quick and blessedly uneventful.

Tyler was waiting in the lobby with popcorn, 3-D glasses, and a look of genuine relief. "Hey," he said, kissing my cheek, smelling lemony fresh, "you *are* okay. The Russians just appeared out of nowhere, huh?"

"Something like that. I'm okay . . ."

"Better than okay. You look great, like you could star in one of these movies."

"It would have to be a drama," I said.

"Ed Debevic," he said with a nod.

"I've got a big decision to make. Next Friday."

"Yeah. I thought that's what you wanted to discuss," he said, holding up the glasses. "That's why I picked the crappiest film."

He wasn't kidding.

It was one of those films where you knew from the first

second how it ends—the interplanetary cop with a chip on his shoulder redeems himself by trying to prevent Earth from blowing up, *yawn*—and the theater was empty. We put on our glasses, stared for a second, and turned to each other. "So." Tyler sighed. "You have to choose a new Boss." His face was taut, less curious than concerned.

"That's the rule. Either Knuckles or you."

He nodded, saying, "Listen to this. I was meeting with Knuckles—more cash to fight the Russians—when news came in about you on the bridge. Guess what he said."

"I'm sure it was tender and heartfelt."

"The old bastard snorted and said, 'That's what you get when it's a girl versus men. She took a dive, literally. Fighting is a man's job.'"

"'Man's job,'" I repeated. "I've heard that one before."

"Could you ever imagine that dinosaur as the boss, as the guy *we'd* have to answer to?" He chuckled, shaking his head.

"No, of course not. It'll never happen, not in a million years," I said. "But . . . it's not going to happen for you, either."

His eyebrows rose with the corners of his mouth, the grin amused and a little surprised. "What makes you think I'd accept being boss?" he asked.

"Nothing, but you knew I wouldn't name Knuckles," I said, tucking a strand of hair behind my ear. "So that leaves you. You had to be thinking about it."

"Sure, it was on my mind," he said. "This sounds crazy, but I even wondered, if I became boss, could I change the Outfit? Legitimize it somehow. Turn it into a real corporation instead of a criminal one. The organizational structure is in place—"

"It's impossible," I said. "The members obey rules, mostly, but you know what really drives them."

"Money," said the VP of Money, as the film flickered around us. "It's all about the cash."

"Wads of it, dirty and tax-free," I said. "Greed trumps everything—loyalty, friendship . . . I've seen it in sit-down after sit-down. The rank and file are a bunch of violent psychopaths for a reason. It allows them to do *anything* for money."

"They'd never settle for normal jobs and salaries. You're right. The Outfit will never change. It's our life," he said, pursing his lips, "the only one we've got."

"Maybe not."

"What do you mean?"

I hesitated, unsure how to say what needed to be said without revealing too much information. "I've still got to name someone boss," I said, lifting the 3-D glasses.

Tyler lifted his glasses, too, his green eyes cutting the gloom. "But not Knuckles or me. You're going outside the rules?"

I nodded once, slowly.

"Who?" he said.

I wondered then—what would happen if I told him about my family and Elzy? I'd asked myself if I could trust him, and I thought now that I could. As my Whispering Smith, he'd passed on information for no reason other than my safety, asking for nothing in return. I'd helped him with the smash-and-grab guy, but that was by choice. Tyler had gone further than me when it came to watching out for each other, alerting me to the threats dangerous men might act upon if my cold fury lost its hold on them. But something held me back—maybe a calcified instinct to keep my family's secrets, or perhaps I'd become too Outfit, too wary of showing all my cards—and I said, "I can't tell you. Not yet. You have money set aside, right? A stash of your own?"

"Yeah, of course, but whoever it is, you can trust me with it. You should know that by now."

"I do, I trust you, Tyler. But I have reasons, personal ones, why I can't tell you," I said. "Look, if there was ever a time for you to escape this life, it's right now, before I name the new boss. I don't want to do it. I hate this person as much as I've ever hated anyone. But I don't have a choice. Afterward, things in the Outfit are going to change. Muscle and Money are too important. The VPs . . . Knuckles and you . . . won't be allowed to keep your jobs."

He looked at me solemnly. "How about our lives?"

A tingle of terror went through me, knowing Elzy's cold-blooded philosophy. "It's questionable," I said, and paused. "No, it's not, it's certain." I leaned close and put my hand on his. "I'm telling you this because I care about you. You have to trust me in return."

He pursed his lips, looking into the distance. "I wish my dad was here. He'd tell me what to do."

"He'd tell you to run," I said. "You don't have a choice either."

Tyler turned back and said, "What happens to you?"

"I have to see it through, name the boss, and then . . ." I shrugged, thinking of my family, and of escape. I'd told Tyler all I could. The rest belonged to me.

"One week until a new boss," he said. "So are we saying good-bye for good?"

It struck me then that I was pushing him away for his own safety, losing him almost like I'd lost Max. A friend, someone I could trust, gone. "I think so," I said, swallowing the words.

"I have so many questions—"

"I know you do," I said. "But even if I answered them, it wouldn't help you now."

He slid an arm around me, pulled me close, and we kissed briefly. "Thank you, Sara Jane," he said. "I just wish it wasn't this way. We could've been—"

"I know. Me too. I wish . . ."

We sat back then, staring at the screen, waiting for the world to blow up.

We hugged outside the theater, holding on to each other until a sleek black car pulled up. Tyler got inside, lowered the window, and waved as it sped away. I watched until it was gone, then hurried down the sidewalk and onto a train. It took off with a lurch and then the tracks were clattering beneath me as I traveled toward the Bird Cage Club.

I stared out the window thinking of Tyler's words, *We could've been—*

This day had proven it. There were no happy endings.

Why are you so surprised? I thought. *This is real life, not a movie.*

The trip was as uneventful as the one to the Davis. I walked down the stairs and hit the sidewalk looking for utility vehicles and delivery scooters. Taxis passed by without pausing and a cop car sped around a corner barely slowing its pace. It was almost eleven p.m. when I passed through the grease-clouded door of Phun-Ho to Go.

The guy was behind the counter as always, the TV blaring into his face.

Something was different—I saw it immediately.

His eyes were pinned on me instead of the screen, tracking me to the men's room. He cleared his throat and I stopped. "Your carryout is ready," he said.

"My . . . carryout?" I said suspiciously, surprised the guy could actually talk.

"Deliver itself, scratching on door," he said, looking into the kitchen, whistling.

I heard the *tick-tacking* first, and then a low whine.

Harry limped out from behind the counter.

I'd been wrong in my meeting with Lucky—my tears hadn't dried up, not completely, not for the joy of seeing the little dog. "Oh my god," I whispered, dropping to my knees, scooping him up, and burying my face in his fur. "Harry . . . you're here . . . you're *alive!*" If dogs can hug, Harry did, and when I nuzzled him, he nuzzled me back. It was like holding a dream.

"Dog smell like river," the guy said, wrinkling his nose. He was right, Harry stunk, with crusty mud coating his body. I inspected his head and snout, seeing the deep cuts and scratches inflicted by Vlad, all of it matted with dried blood. "Also, hungry as bear. I wrap up sliced chicken to go."

"Thank you . . . thank you so much," I said, standing with Harry in my arms.

"It's just chicken."

"Not for that. For him, for taking him in," I said.

"No thank me, counselor." He shrugged. "You do your job, I do mine."

I hurried through the men's room and into the elevator, the ride seeming to take forever. When I looked at Harry, he was looking back. "You saved my life again," I said. He breathed through his nose and seemed to smile as the elevator reached the penthouse.

The Bird Cage Club was dark.

I saw Doug bundled on the couch, heard him snoring. Gently, I placed Harry on the ground and whispered, "Go to him." He did, his claws announcing his approach, making my friend sit upright. Doug rubbed sleep from his eyes, blinked at the little dog, and rubbed them again. First disbelief, and then slow joy spread over his face.

In the quietest of voices, he said, "Are you real?"

21

SUNDAY WAS A DAY OF CELEBRATION, OF unrestrained joy, and the scrubbing of a small, gray, Italian hero with four legs who, like Lazarus, had risen from the dead. The idea of it made Doug consider going to church, briefly, but instead we gave thanks to Harry for being such a little badass. He'd fought for us, almost died for us, and best of all, found his way back to us.

Monday, by contrast, was a day of suffering.

Vlad had predicted it, and it was true—waiting another twenty-four hours to call Czar Bar to find out when I could pick up my mom and Lou was torture, as was the idea of leaving my dad behind. Each minute seemed like an hour, on and on it went, from the Bird Cage Club to Fep Prep and back again. The sun went down, I stared at the ceiling, and when the sun rose Tuesday morning, I dialed Czar Bar. It rang for six thousand years until a heavily accented voice said, "Czar Bar . . ."

"This is Sara Jane Rispoli, may I talk to—"

". . . leave message."

I hung up, paced, dressed, and tried again, allowing several jangling millennia and "leave message" to pass through my ear again before breaking the connection. I'd just hit Redial when Doug called out that we were going to be late for school.

As I entered the room, he said, "Hooray. Field-trip day."

"Crap," I said. "I forgot about it."

"It's covered. I worked out the details with Thumbs-Up yesterday, even wrote our little speech," he said. "The bus leaves Fep Prep at noon with him, us, and seventy-five pimply freshmen. Including Classic Movie Club during third period, it's a complete blow-off day."

"What are we watching?"

"*A Fistful of Dollars.* It's about a violent loner out for justice. You can probably skip it," he answered, "since you live it."

I looked at my phone. "With everything that's happening, the past few days just seem so . . . absurd. Field trips, movies . . . all I care about is the safe return of my family."

"One family member made it," he said, leaning down and kissing Harry.

"How many times have you kissed him this morning?"

"Too many to count," he said. "Can't get enough of that puppy love."

I tried Czar Bar before homeroom and after, before Trigonometry and after, and was standing outside the Theater room, phone in hand, when Gina approached.

"Texting," she said, arching an eyebrow, "or sexting?"

"Trying to call a friend," I said, putting my phone away.

"You only have one, and I just saw him go into the Theater room."

I stared at her for a moment. "Why are you so mean to me?"

"Excuse me?" she said, taken aback. "You were mean first. *You* stopped hanging out with *me.*"

"Yeah. In seventh grade. When your social life started and mine stopped."

"Not my fault. Your parents were so protective, they barely let you out of the house," she said. "Are they still like that?"

"Yes and no. I mean, I'm not home much."

"God, remember Mandi Fishbaum's birthday party in sixth grade? When Walter J. Thurber kissed you?"

"Mandi's still pissed off at me."

"Can you believe what a pothead Walter's become?" she said. "I was sworn to secrecy, but his sister's hairstylist told me—"

I held up a hand. "Please. I don't care. It's none of my business."

She nodded, smiling a little. "I'm sorry about the thing the other day, the Max thing. It was asshole-ish of me."

"It's okay."

"If I hear anything else about him from Mandi, should I tell you?"

I thought about it, feeling how useless it was. "No."

"What if it's juicy?"

"Especially if it's juicy."

"Suit yourself," she said. "So what are we watching?"

"It's old, you've probably never heard of it. *A Fistful of Dollars.*"

"Nineteen sixty-four, directed by Sergio Leone, starring Clint Eastwood," she said. "I'm more than just gossip, Sara Jane. I love movies."

Apparently.

She and Doug sat next to each other during the movie, whispering about cinematography, spaghetti Westerns, and other things that I stopped listening to. It was impossible for me to concentrate on the screen, and I left the room several times, dialing Czar Bar to no avail. After the movie was over—after Doug and Gina continued arguing in the hallway about the meaning of the ending and after she departed, insisting we watch *Vertigo* next time—Doug said, "Who would've guessed?"

"What? That Gina was a such movie nerd?"

"Yeah, but something else. That she'd inspire me," he said with wonder. "I was talking about Clint Eastwood's moral justification, and she says—this is a quote—'Stuffins, you're a complete idiot if you don't become a film director someday.'"

"Wow," I said, seeing the perfect logic of it, "she's right."

"I know," he said. "It's so weird. All the years I've spent watching movies. I mean, I considered it, of course, but never thought I could actually make them."

"You know what I like most about it? You're thinking about the future. What you're going to do after, you know, this all ends."

"This?" he asked with a little smile. "School today? The field trip?"

"You know what I mean," I said. "Anyway, yeah, you'd be an awesome director, Doug. That's my opinion."

"Yours means the most," he said. "Now come on, let's go

to the Willis Tower and look at the view from almost fifteen hundred feet in the sky."

"School spirit. It's killing me."

"True fact. *Rah-rah* is the last sound many nerds and geeks hear before dying," he said, leading me out the main entrance and down the steps to where a bus idled.

I stared at the long yellow vehicle and said, "That thing makes me nervous."

"Relax," he said, "it's a goggle-free zone."

A torrent of students rushed past and began piling on, jockeying for places to sit, which reminded me of something. "Seats," I murmured.

"There's room for everyone," Doug said, pulling a clipboard from his backpack.

"In the Ferrari, I mean. There are only two. We're going to have to take out the passenger seat so we can fit in my mom and Lou."

"So now we have an after-school project," he said, as we climbed onto the bus. He moved away, checking off kids' names as the driver revved the engine and Mr. Novak bounded aboard. Grinning like a chubby jack-o'-lantern, tufts of hair encircling his ears like fuzzy gray earmuffs, he clapped his hands vigorously, shushing students, and cried:

"It's on to Willis Tower
aboard this fine bus!
Let's make our school proud,
because . . . !"

He paused. No one said a word.

"Becau-u-u-se . . . !" he repeated, louder and more forcefully.

"Fep Prep is us!" the kids shouted.

"Exact-a-mundo!" he said with a thumbs-up as we chugged away. He sat on the seat across from me, gave my knee a friendly tap, and said, "Excited?"

"Absolutely," I answered, pressing a smile onto my face.

"You should be." He winked, straightening his tie, which was decorated with rubber duckies. "It's not every day you get to have an adventure in the city!"

I nodded, staring out the window, thinking, *If you only knew.*

22

THERE'S A POINT, WHETHER YOU'RE ON A FERRIS wheel or an airplane, or in my case, a superfast elevator climbing toward the sun, when you realize you're way, way higher in the air than a human being is ever supposed to be.

It's called the Willis Tower now, although it's still referred to as the Sears Tower, but whatever; it stretches 108 stories into the sky while most birds fly at one-third that altitude. My ears popped and my guts flipped during the ride, and when we climbed out on the 103rd-story Skydeck, with its floor to ceiling windows, the unnaturalness of riding so high in a metal box sunk in.

As students filed from the elevator, I stepped aside and broke one of my rules.

For the past six months, I'd rigorously avoided giving out any information that could be used to track or trap me, but now I dialed Czar Bar, waited for the tone, and left my number for a callback. I'd reached the point where there was nothing left to lose.

I hung up, walked into the Skydeck, and had a mini-freak-out, watching kids lean their foreheads against the windows and stare straight down.

That was nothing compared to the Ledge.

Years of head smudges had inspired Skydeck management to install four large, enclosed glass rectangles extending several feet out into nothingness; all that exists below a person standing inside a Ledge box—each strong enough to hold an elephant—is pure stratosphere, and farther down, people like ants, cabs like toys, and rock-hard concrete. Doug and I made our factoid presentation to the bored students gaping out of windows or taking pictures with their phones. Afterward, Mr. Novak told us we were fortunate to live in a city of such architectural splendor, and that no one, under any condition, was to leave the Skydeck. I moved among the throng of kids, asking questions, chatting with them—mingling, as Mr. Novak said—until Doug waved me over before ambling inside a glass box. The way he glanced casually between his shoes, clipboard at his side, made my knees sweat. He rocked on his heels, saying, "You ever see *The Towering Inferno*? Nineteen seventy-four, with Paul Newman and Steve McQueen."

"Don't add a fire to this, please."

"Come on, wuss. It's weirdly cool and . . . ," he said, looking up. "Holy shit!"

"What?" I asked, still hesitant to step into the box.

"Window washers! *Above us!* We're on the hundred and third floor, so they're—"

"Out of their minds," I said with a shiver.

"The platform they're standing on is basically a plank

223

attached to ropes, swaying in the wind. It looks like it could snap at any moment."

"Doug," I said, feeling green. Since Uncle Buddy plummeted to his death from the Ferris wheel at Navy Pier, too-high locations made me depressingly nauseous.

"I'm not kidding, if that rope broke, he'd—oh, my bad," he said, sealing his lips when he saw my distressed face.

"Please, will you—" I said, as my phone buzzed, the display showing *Czar Bar*. I answered, hearing Vlad's voice cut by static, and then empty air. I redialed and heard garble until it died away. "I need reception," I said, looking around desperately, "and privacy. This isn't just any phone call."

"You won't get past Thumbs-Up. He's everywhere."

"There's an emergency exit on the other side of the room," I said.

"But it's armed. There's an alarm."

"Do you have a small piece of metal?" I said. Doug patted his pockets, shifted the clipboard, and handed me a pen. I snapped off its pocket clip and bent it into an L shape. "Chapter six of the notebook, '*Metodi*—Methods.' It has a section called 'Picking Locks and Disabling Alarms.'" I held up the metal L. "This should deactivate it . . . hopefully."

"Thumbs-Up has his back turned," Doug said. "Now's your chance."

I was gone without a word, sneaking from one group of students to another as I made my way across the room. Mr. Novak turned abruptly and I crouched behind a kid the size of an upright buffalo. When he shuffled his feet, I moved with him like a shadow, and when Mr. Novak turned away, I spun for the exit. The keyhole thing that disabled the alarm was right where it was supposed to be; a quick turn of the clip and I slipped soundlessly through the door. The stairwell was vast and silent. I felt a cool breeze and peered up at a crack of natural light—something nearby was open to the outside.

I ran up three flights to a metal door marked *106*.

It was slightly ajar and as I pushed through, I gasped at being in open air with Chicago spread before me like an urban map in 3-D. The Willis Tower had multi-level roofs; the one I stood on was a flat, gravel-covered section with several huge, humming air vents and a few buckets scattered around. The space was obviously used for maintenance only. The window washers' platform now sat on the roof, but several ropes trailed over the knee-high ledge, bolted to heavy rungs set into steel girders. A pair of hard hats, gloves, and long poles with squeegees at the end lay nearby—maybe the window washers had gone on break and left the door open? A stinging wind lashed hair into my face as I peered up at the 108th floor. The tower's immense, dual antennae stretched into the sky, each tip blinking *red-red-red* behind a wall of dusty clouds.

It was now or never, and I quickly dialed Czar Bar.

I cursed each ring of the phone, myself for blowing the call, and Novak for making me be here. I waited for the *beep,* but then Vlad said, "Hello, baby."

"When can I come for them?"

"Relax. Aren't you happy to hear my voice?"

"When?" I asked through clenched teeth.

"Where are you, anyway? It sounds like wind tunnel," he said. When I didn't answer, he continued, "Okay. Big sit-down is Friday? You come Thursday, eleven thirty p.m."

"No, no way. That's too long."

"For you. Not us. Washing brains is all done, spick-and-span," he said, "but we think it's good idea to give you little time as possible between getting mommy and brother, naming new Outfit boss. Too much time and maybe you think, forget papa, two out of three is okay, I take them and run for it."

"I wouldn't do that. I'd never desert my dad."

"See, that's what I told my boss! I say, girl is committed, she drive off bridge without blink of an eye," he said. "Speaking of, ouch, you shocked shit out of me."

"I wish I could've done more than that."

"Doggy did enough. No nose puts real crimp in coke habit," he said. "So Thursday, eleven thirty p.m. Don't make mistake of bringing weapon, and come alone or *no one* goes home. And remember, my boss goes with you to sit-down on Friday."

"I know, I understand, but tell Elzy—"

"Who?"

"Your boss," I said, "Elzy."

Behind me, metal scraped gravel.

Vlad said, "I don't know no Elzy," as I turned, watching the door open slowly.

I ducked behind an air vent. "You're lying! That little red-headed witch—"

"Baby, my boss is lot of things," Vlad said, "but not little, and hair is farthest thing from red—"

Footsteps crunched toward me and I said, "I have to go!"

"Don't tell me there's other man."

"I'm not kidding!"

"You break my heart," he said, and hung up.

And then the other man spoke.

"Sally Jane!" Mr. Novak said. I stood slowly, seeing the dismay on his face as he hurried toward me. "Do you know how many rules you've broken by coming up here? Good heavens, my dear, this is *not* in the spirit of a Fep Prep student!"

I listened to his words, but my mind was far away.

Vlad's lying. Of course Elzy is his boss.

"Your safety is my utmost concern," he said, cheeks flushed, his loud tie flapping in the breeze.

But the deal is done.

"And I'd never forgive myself if something happened to you!" He stopped in front of me with his hands on his hips.

So why would he lie? I'm going to see her soon, face-to-face.

Mr. Novak's eyes softened as he said, "I'm sorry to say, but we're going to have to meet with your parents to discuss this."

"If you can find them," another voice said behind him.

It was a gargle-growl inflected with the nasal undertones of West Side Chicago—one that had sung Frank Sinatra tunes as lullabies to Lou and me long ago. Mr. Novak turned, I looked past him, and he spoke first.

"Bootsie?" he said, confused.

"Elzy," I whispered.

"What in the world are you doing here, my sweet?" Mr. Novak asked.

She moved toward us from the open door, smiling, as

petite as ever, red hair ablaze. The shock of seeing her was intense but muddled, she was out of context—why *was* she here if the pickup was on Thursday, at Czar Bar? All I could do was stare, forgetting even to blink, and I remembered too late as she hurried up to us, quickly lifted an aerosol can, and sprayed me in the eyes with a thin stream of liquid. One flashing realization—*my eyes are on fire, oh my god, someone put out the fire!*—as I screamed in agony and bent at the knees, palms pressed into my eyes, feeling a thousand angry bees invade my head. Tears popped and fell, and I wiped at them desperately, trying to clear away the awful searing pain and terrifying semi-blindness.

"What have you *done*?" Mr. Novak yelped.

"Pepper spray, a cop's best friend," Elzy said, yanking my arms behind my back, twisting on plastic cuffs, and throwing me to the ground. "I hoped it would be a defense against ghiaccio furioso. I also assume it's temporary."

I couldn't see anything other than shadows, nullifying cold fury. With urgency in his voice, trying to help me up, Mr. Novak said, "Sally Jane—"

"It's Sara Jane," Elzy said. There was a sharp thump and the sound of a body falling. "The butt of a pistol. Cop's second best friend."

Mr. Novak groaned nearby, twisting in the gravel. "I don't . . . understand."

"I used you to get to her," Elzy said vacantly. "That school is like Fort Knox. You were my inside man. So trusting. All I had to do was suggest Willis Tower for a field trip."

"Oh, god," he whispered, "after all these months together."

"You didn't even check the slips of paper I wrote out for you with the names of Ms. Stein's students on them. Every one of them read 'Sara Jane Rispoli.'"

Mr. Novak shifted around. I heard him trying to rise, and then silence. "What are you doing?" he asked.

I waited for Elzy's reply but she said nothing.

"Bootsie! *Please!*"

The pistol's silencer made a soft flitting noise, quiet and deadly. Squinting, I watched the blurry image of Mr. Novak dab his chest, look at blood-smeared fingers, open his mouth to say something, and collapse on his side.

"No . . . no," I whispered. "Why?"

Elzy's footsteps sounded on gravel, moving closer. "You and I have unfinished business." Her tone was no longer vacant; it was smoldering rage kept in check only by the weight of misery. "My brother, Poor K-K-Kevin," she said, choking on his name, "was the only person who *ever* loved me."

"He attacked us. Lou and me, and—"

"I . . . want . . . him . . . *back!*" she shrieked, the outburst cutting the air like hundreds of screeching bats taking flight. My skin went cold, the chill crawling over my body. Elzy was breathing hard, maybe fighting tears, maybe preparing to scream once more, but no—it was all contained rage again, teeth grinding, when she said, "But I can't have him. Can I? He's gone. Forever," and she kicked me deep in the stomach.

Pain rocketed up into my chest and throat and I rolled onto my side, groaning.

"I was lost after Buddy Rispoli killed him," she said, circling me, kicking me again, her boot finding my face.

The sour taste of blood was on my tongue, leaking from my nose.

"Nothing matters anymore, not the Outfit or that damn notebook, if my brother isn't here to share it with me." The wind rose up around us and faded, and she halted in her tracks. "It's your fault he's not," she said slowly, "as much as your uncle's."

"No—"

"And now you're going to die in the same way Poor Kevin did," she said, grabbing a handful of my hair and yanking my face to hers. "Only higher, and much, much worse."

23

THEN I WAS PULLED TO MY FEET AND PUSHED across the roof. Even half blind, I knew the edge and empty sky loomed ahead. "Sometimes things come together," Elzy said, shoving me forward, talking more to herself than to me. "That last detail . . . how would I get you up here? I was going to use the gun. Even better, you had to use your phone."

"We had a deal!" I cried.

"What are you talking about? Move," she said, as I dug my heels into the gravel, fighting every inch.

"The Russian mob! My family in exchange for ultimate power!"

"So that's who has them. I wondered," she grunted, fighting me back.

"Elzy, don't do this! If I die, they'll kill my parents!" I cried, my feet stuttering across the roof. "They'll kill Lou!"

It slowed her, but only a little. "When I was your nanny, I liked him so much better than you. A smart, sensitive boy," she said, resuming her efforts. "But now, my brother dead—

move, damn you!—and your brother dead! Justice, with you as a bonus."

"You can have it! Ultimate power! It's real, it's what you wanted! *Please!*" I said, flooded with the type of despair that comes from begging an enemy.

"Killing you is the only ultimate power I need," she answered, as a punishing wind whipped around us.

The cold blue flame flickered and burned, but the pepper spray kept it contained within me. I thought of chapter 6 of the notebook again, "Methods." It contained a list entitled "Disabling Your Enemies"; I knew the only way to recover from the spray was to cry it out, and that it took at least fifteen minutes. My hands were bound. I was out of options, thinking, *Use your head, Sara Jane!* And I did, driving it backward, making hard contact with Elzy's face. She shrieked, faltered, and I was free, scrambling away, trying to find the door to the 106th floor, but seeing only gauzy circles and foggy squares. I ran toward what appeared to be the exit and was hit linebacker style, low and behind the knees, going down face-first. Gravel bit into my chin and cheek as I was dragged back toward the edge and jerked to a standing position. I felt cold metal pressed to my neck. Elzy spit blood and I spoke first, gasping, "It's so . . . much money. Ultimate . . . power . . ."

"Don't insult me," she hissed. "I wouldn't let you go for *any* amount. I have one ambition left, to avenge Poor Kevin."

"Sara Jane!"

Elzy and I both turned to see Doug standing near the open door, but before I could warn him she lifted the pistol and put a bullet in his chest, the quiet *f-f-f-t!* followed by a metallic *ping*.

Doug let out a whimper of surprise and crumpled backward. I heard his body hit the roof and then nothing else. Elzy gathered up my hair and jerked me around, walking, now running.

She leaned in and whispered hoarsely, "Tell Buddy *hello.*"

In one shoving motion I was thrown into space.

Oh my god! No, no, no, this can't be real!

I tried to scream but the oxygen was sucked from my lungs, my tongue fixed in my throat as I bicycled through the air, kicking at nothing. Reality and horror blended seamlessly— *I am dying, I am dead*—as I somersaulted toward earth and landed hard on my back. I squinted up at the blinking antennae and a blue sky pushing through clouds. Pain raged beneath me, my wrists cut and bleeding but freed from the plastic cuffs on impact.

I pushed into a sitting position, squinting painfully around and under me, and saw that I was floating 103 stories in the sky.

I'd landed on top of an ultrathick glass Ledge.

No one was inside it. My vision was clearing; wiping away a face full of tears, I looked straight through to the ground far below and that one tiny peek yanked me back to the outsized danger of the moment. Terrified that the slightest shift, slide, or errant breeze would send me toppling to earth, I gripped the glass around me, hearing my hands squeak with terror-sweat. And then my head tingled, my skin crawled, and ever so slowly I looked up at the 106th floor where Elzy's enraged face, as red as butchered beef, stared back. She opened her mouth and the words cut through the wind as she shrieked, "You goddamn *Rispolis.* You're like Sicilian *cockroaches!* I should've done it this way to begin with!" The gun led her hand over the edge, pointed squarely at me, and all I could do was wait for the bullet, but then her arm was in the air and she disappeared from view. She screamed, loudly and plaintively, as the gun flew over the side of the building.

And then she did, too.

Elzy fell, clawing at the air, and grabbed the window washers' dangling rope. With her feet pressed against the building like a mountain climber, she gripped the rope with one hand while using the other to frantically coil the remaining length beneath her arms, and then looked up to the roof.

Doug stared back, holding something high in a trembling hand. The sun reflected from it, blindingly silver.

"She shot me in the lighter!" he cried.

"Pull me up!" Elzy yelled, as she gaped beneath her and then back up at Doug.

"You threw my friend off the roof."

"You threw *me* off the roof!"

"I hit you," he said. "You fell."

I looked into the Ledge below, at students pointing up at me, and heard screaming sirens. "Doug!" I croaked, bathed in cold sweat. "We've got to get out of here!"

"What about *me*?!" Elzy shouted.

"The cops can have you. Maybe you'll know some of them. Maybe they'll let you go, but I doubt it," I said. "A dead principal is hard to explain." I stood slowly, cautiously, with every nerve in my body twitching, arms held out at my sides like an acrobat. Doug tossed me a rope. I secured it at my waist, exhaled as much fear as possible, and rappelled up the building. He hauled me onto the roof and we hugged quickly, urgently. "You're alive!" he cried into my shoulder.

"You too," I gasped.

"Don't leave me here, Sara Jane!" Elzy wailed. "I was your *nanny*!"

I stared down at her. "You're the devil."

"You little *bitch*!" she screamed. "I hope those Russians cut your family's *throats*! I hope Lou suffers until he's *dead*!"

My hand was on the ledge, inches from the rope that held her. *It would be so easy*, I thought. *Use the lighter, burn the rope, another enemy dead, and . . . what would that make me?* I swallowed the temptation and said, "You're on your own, Elzy."

"I'll survive this! I'll come for you again! You'll *never* escape me!" she cried, trying to climb, kicking at the building, raging against it as the coil beneath her arms unwound with a wild whipping noise. Her scream pierced the air and she slipped, grasped the rope with one hand, swung like a human pendulum, and fell.

In contrast to movies, where a person yells "No-o-o!" as she hurtles to her death, Elzy let loose a string of obscenities that faded but didn't end until it was blotted out by the faraway screech of brakes and blowing horns. I stared over the edge at the toy cars and ant people already converging, and then we hurried across the roof, pausing only when we came to Mr. Novak.

Doug bent down, closed the chubby little man's eyes, even straightened his tie.

Staring at him, I could only think, *A good man, dead.* Elzy had killed him neither for self-preservation nor even as a twisted form of justice, but because he'd served his purpose and become useless. She'd paid, of course, but her evil goal—revenge—had come with a price. Poor Mr. Novak had owed nothing and paid far more.

"Sara Jane," Doug said quietly, "we have to go."

And then we sprinted down 106 floors without stopping. The door at the bottom of the stairwell was equipped with an alarm, but I had the metal clip. I disabled the alarm and we peeked into the north lobby, watching hell break loose on the street outside; it was choked with cop cars, fire trucks, ambulances, and gawkers. I was a mess, eyes red and swollen from the pepper spray, dried blood from Elzy's kick to the face spattered on my nose and shirt. Doubtless, Fep Prep students were reporting to security that they'd seen me on the Ledge. Doug and I needed a way to escape without drawing too much attention, but catching a cab would be impossible. I eased the door shut as Doug said, "Now what?"

I thought for a moment, biting my lip. "Everything's happening on the north side of the building, where Elzy landed. But there's a south lobby, too."

"So?"

"So. Shawshank," I muttered, taking out my phone.

"Starring Tim Robbins and Morgan Freeman . . . what are you talking about?"

"A long shot," I said, texting furiously: *Are you still here? In Chicago?*

Tyler answered: *Making final plans. Leaving tonight. U okay?*

I used the code word, telling him that I needed one of his sleek black cars sent to the south lobby of the Willis Tower as quickly as possible—that I was doing confidential counselor business and needed a ride, right now, no questions asked.

He texted back: *No ?'s necessary. Car there in five mins.*

You thanked me at the Davis, I replied. *My turn: thx.*

Not necessary, either. Anything for u, he answered.

Be careful.

U too, he replied. *Hope we see each other someday soon.*

I stared at the phone, a hard, sad knot in my chest, and explained it all to Doug, how Tyler and I had pledged to watch each other's backs, and he nodded, saying, "You're sure you can count on him?"

"Yeah, because we're sort of in the same boat in the Outfit."

"Forget boats," Doug said, "I'd be happy with a car."

I wiped away as much blood from my face as possible, tried vainly to do something to my hair so it didn't look as if I'd just scaled a tower wall, and we slid out the door, hurrying but not running to the south lobby. It was nearly deserted, with everyone from security guards to gawkers having rushed to the other side of the building, and—yeah, I could count on Tyler—a black car was gliding to the curb when we pushed outside through the lobby doors. The driver said nothing, only nodded when we jumped in and I told him to head for the Currency Exchange Building. Safely inside the car, Doug took the bullet-dented lighter from his pocket. "I'm going to build a monument to this thing," he said quietly.

I stared out the window thinking of Elzy—how she had had nothing to do with my family's abduction or the Russian mob. I'd always believed in the saying, *Better the devil you know than the devil you don't,* but now I wasn't so sure. After all, I'd known Elzy since I was a kid. As our nanny, she'd nearly lived in our home and—"Holy . . . shit," I whispered.

"What?"

I shook my head as the scales fell from my eyes, seeing how the omnipresent threat of Elzy had blinded me to clues in the past. "She was always listening, always snooping around the house, the bakery," I said more to myself than Doug. "Always pushing Uncle Buddy to . . . what did she used to say? 'To get what you deserve.' I thought she meant from the bakery, but she meant the other family business. And she wanted something for herself, not for him."

Doug said nothing, letting his face ask the question.

"Greta," I said, the name cold on my tongue.

My uncle Buddy's wife, Greta Kushchenko Rispoli. A nice, shy Russian girl who was the exact opposite.

I really had known the devil all along.

24

FROM EARLY WEDNESDAY MORNING UNTIL late at night, in short bursts and deep conversation, Doug and I slid facts into place and filled in the rest with educated guesses.

It had to be Greta.

"Blinders are off," I said, pacing the Bird Cage Club, "it can *only* be Greta."

In the past, knowing the identity of an adversary sparked feelings of bitter disappointment or betrayal or sheer confusion. This was different. As the astonishment wore off, I grew violently angry with Greta for the sustained hell in which she'd kept my family. Electricity pinched my spine. It was as dangerous for me as it was for her.

"How'd she do it?" Doug said, flicking the lighter, staring at the orange flame. "I mean, get hooked up with the Russian mob?"

"Besides the fact that she's Russian," I said, "no clue. Now that I think about it, she just sort of . . . appeared."

It was true: when Uncle Buddy first brought Greta around, she was timid and mousy, whispering back and forth with him but jumping out of her skin when spoken to. If someone asked her a question about herself, Greta blushed and recited the same information every time. Her parents, now dead, had been poor but humble Russian immigrants to Chicago. It was too painful to discuss, as was most of her background.

"Where in Russia did your parents come from?" my mom once asked.

Turning pink, Greta mumbled, "Moscow."

"So what is it you do?" my mom said.

"Hair, sometimes," she said, snuggling close to Uncle Buddy.

"Enough with the third degree," Uncle Buddy said, patting her hand protectively. "Greta's a little shy."

Dead parents. Moscow. Hair sometimes. That was basically it.

And then, as she and Buddy grew closer, Greta began to transform—lips sparkling redder, hair growing blonder, necklines plunging deeper—while her passivity gave way to barely concealed aggression. She snooped around our house and the bakery, opening drawers, inspecting receipts, even nosing through my and Lou's rooms. Worse, she hectored Uncle Buddy every chance she got. He was too lazy, not assertive or ambitious enough, and for heaven's sake—did he really intend to bake *cookies* the rest of his life? A grown *man*? Who *deserved* so much more?

"Weren't your dad and mom suspicious?" Doug asked.

"They were, but they couldn't tell Lou and me why—that their lives were built around hiding the family secret to end all secrets, and now this interloper was rummaging around, berating my uncle," I said. "Instead, my parents told us to be cautious around Greta, just like we were around friends and neighbors, that we were private people—it was how we lived. And my dad made a point that seemed so true."

"What?" Doug asked.

"Everyone loved my uncle to death but he was . . . *hamstrung,* I guess is the word, like, he just couldn't get it together. My dad reminded us that it was Buddy after all, he'd never managed to date anyone for longer than a month or two," I said, "and that Greta would be no different."

"Wrong-o," Doug said.

"After a while, no one in the family cared where she came from. We just wanted her to go," I said.

But Uncle Buddy took her straight to the altar, Vegas style.

After they were married, Doug and I reasoned, she must've squeezed him for as much information as possible about my family and the Outfit before casting him aside. Uncle Buddy redeemed himself before he died, rescuing Lou and me from that vicious psycho Poor Kevin, but no redemption would've been necessary if not for Greta. "She lit a fire under him," I said, "made him resent my grandpa and my dad for excluding him from the Outfit."

"Maybe she urged him to spy on them," Doug said, flicking the lighter.

"Probably," I answered. "He found out about the notebook, that it contained something so powerful that even he, Buddy Rispoli, the one with brown eyes who hadn't inherited cold fury, could take over the Outfit."

"Surely he told his beloved wife about it," Doug said.

"Poor Uncle Buddy." I sighed. "I'm unsure now if he wanted the notebook and ultimate power for himself or for her. Either way, she left him."

"She sounds like a real piece of work," Doug said, lifting Harry into his arms.

"Beyond. She and I were oil and water," I said, "but Lou was more patient with her. Greta even sort of liked him."

"What I don't get," Doug said, cradling the little dog, kissing his nose, "is where she's been all this time. Elzy, Juan Kone, and *poof* . . . he-e-re's Greta."

I thought of Lou again and saw the answer skulking in the shadows. "She's been here all along. On the periphery," I said. "Whatever cosmic joke timed Juan's kidnapping of my family with Elzy's attempt, Greta somehow found out about it."

"Just because she left your uncle doesn't mean she wasn't still watching your house and the bakery," Doug said.

I nodded slowly. "She discovered that Juan had my family, and passed herself off as an ice cream creature. Took Lou to the Ferris wheel to draw me out—"

"Maybe she was going to try to snatch you," he said.

"Maybe. But Poor Kevin got in her way. And then she took my family when Juan's operation failed. And here we are."

"Where?"

"At the place where I'm so pissed off, it's scaring me. I have to stay in control, but I'm not going to Czar Bar unarmed," I said. "I haven't been taking aspirin, Doug. I'm not going to start now."

He shook his head. "Shame on you for lying, but for once, no argument. Just be careful in there," he said. "They'll all be wearing the crimson eyewear," he said. "Greta's tricky, I'll give her that."

"And smart. Smart as hell to have lined up the Russians behind her."

"Smart enough to know you lied about ultimate power?"

"Let's hope not."

"What if she is?"

"Plan B."

"What's plan B?" he asked.

"I was hoping you had one," I said, as Doug's phone chirped.

"That makes ten calls from my mother. More times than she calls me in a year. She heard about yesterday, obviously," he said. "Her messages aren't even complete sentences. She just sputters 'criminal prosecution' and 'reform school.' Do reform schools even exist?"

"She doesn't know about the Bird Cage Club."

"Never asked," he said, tossing the phone aside.

"My high school career ended yesterday. I'm never going back to Fep Prep. But what are you going to do?"

"Focus on the immediate future," he said. "I'm planning nothing other than petting Harry and being your getaway driver."

"Tomorrow night. Eleven thirty."

"Czar Bar. Where only the finest Russian mobsters get loaded."

"First thing in the morning," I said, "we gotta take that seat out of the Ferrari."

It wasn't first thing in the morning.

I slept and slept, Wednesday night into Thursday afternoon, the shock of the Willis Tower incident and anxiety about facing Greta sinking me into a deep, unconscious cocoon.

It also wasn't the Ferrari.

It was an empty space in the subterranean parking garage beneath the Currency Exchange Building where the Ferrari should have been parked.

"Did you hear me?" I asked. "Where is it?"

Doug stood next to me, shoulders in mid-shrug, palms open. "It . . . it was right here last time I saw it."

The Lincoln was either rusting at the bottom of the Chicago River or relegated to a dump (the Vehicle Identification Number had been filed off, leaving it untraceable). There was no way I could rent a car and stealing one was too risky. Trembling with the knowledge that I was in dire need of a getaway car, I said, "It couldn't just disappear. Where are the keys?"

Doug swallowed once, thickly. "Um . . . well, don't you have them?"

"No. You asked me for them last night."

"Right, right," he said, patting himself down, and then deflating with a sigh. "Okay, look. I thought I was doing us a favor," he said. "While you were asleep, I came down here and made sure the car would start, then took it out and filled the tank. So we'd be ready. I must've—"

"Left the keys in the ignition," I said, staring at him. "Doug, it was *stolen*."

"You think so?"

I'd bet on it. Automobile theft was a steady source of income for the Outfit; a valuable model like the Ferrari had either been sold outright or stripped to the chassis by now. The irony was that someone in the Outfit had probably stolen it with no idea who they were stealing it from. "Now what?" I said. "I need a car."

He pursed his lips, thinking. "I know of a Cadillac that's available."

"Cadillac? Wait," I said, "you mean the one at Reebie? Nunzio's?"

"Yeah. It's just sitting there, ready to go."

"It's also from 1929. There are probably fewer cars on the face of the planet that would draw as much attention."

He crossed his arms and put on his logic face. "The pickup at Czar Bar is late at night. It's not like high noon or anything. There won't be many people on the street," he said. "Besides, we know the old car runs. Do you have a better idea?"

I was out of ideas. All I cared about was freeing my mom and Lou, and in the near future, rescuing my dad. Doug and I returned to the Bird Cage Club where we spent the rest of the day trading the lighter back and forth like a good-luck charm, working out the details of the pickup. Doug would drop me off a block from Czar Bar. I'd walk to the meeting and then, as soon as he saw us exit, he'd speed to the curb, gather us up, and roar away. The deal with Greta was in place, but I'd have been a fool to trust her. Once I had my mom and Lou in the car, I intended to get the hell out of there as quickly as possible.

We did nothing else the rest of the evening except rehearse the plan.

At 10:15 p.m., we boarded the elevator, on our way to pick up the Cadillac.

Harry whined as he watched us fall away.

Clark Street was nearly empty outside Reebie Storage, with only a scattering of pedestrians and an occasional taxi floating over the pavement. I pointed past the front entrance, where the twin Ramseses stood guard, and down the alley. "Capone Door, remember?" Doug nodded and we began inspecting the warehouse wall for a tiny *C,* finding only a mosaic of blank red brick.

"Nothing," Doug whispered. "Not a single word or letter."

"Ray Jr. said the Capone Door was in the alley," I murmured, looking up, around, and down. "But 'alley' doesn't necessarily mean a wall." I toed my Chuck Taylor at a manhole cover coated with a veneer of rust, stamped with CHICAGO WATER WORKS. Carefully, I stepped on the *C* in Chicago, and with a pleasing scrape it slid aside revealing a stairway into darkness. "Got your lighter?"

"Are you kidding? I'll never go anywhere without it again," he said, handing it over. I held it like a mini-torch and descended under the pavement to an intersection of two tunnels. A faded sign above the entrance directly ahead read, REEBIE STORAGE—KEY REQUIRED. The other tunnel was pitch-black, emitting a chilly, faraway breeze that was tomb-like and sour with the stench of something long dead. I lifted the lighter to a sign above that entrance; it read, SAL THE BUTCHER. "Why was a guy operating a meat shop way down here?" Doug said.

The senses of smell and taste are intertwined, and I recalled the flavor of that awful scent from the times (too many) when I'd been punched in the face and had licked my own blood. "I don't think he was butchering animals," I said quietly, as we stared at each other. "That's one tunnel I'm never going down."

"Ugh," he said with a shiver. "You got the pharaoh?"

I pulled Ramses II from my pocket. The key did double duty, unlocking a door into the silent hallway lined in green glazed bricks, and then the door leading to the Cadillac. The fluorescent lamps buzzed to life as a set of gaping chrome headlights emerged from the dark, staring at us, until the rest of the automobile took shape behind it.

"What we're about to do is really dangerous. You understand that?" He nodded, and I said, "The Russian mob—they kill easily. They enjoy it."

"Fun." He sighed, climbing onto the running board and into the driver's seat. He wiped sweat from his palms before turning the key. The V-8 engine growled to life and he clunked the gearshift into reverse. With a lurch and a squeal, the Cadillac jumped backward as Doug hit the brakes. He smiled and said, "Five speeds. It's been a while." I opened the garage door and he chugged into the alley. When the stash room was secure, we headed to Wicker Park, where Czar Bar awaited. The old car hummed beneath us as we entered a silent zone, consumed with what lay ahead, until Doug said, "Try the radio."

I turned a button but nothing happened. "Must not work," I said, and twisted the other button. The face of the radio sprang open, revealing a small, dusty pistol.

"Whoa," Doug said slowly. "That's convenient."

I snapped open the chamber, which was filled with bullets, and shut it again. The gun fit snugly into my palm; it would be so easy to fire. I thought of the boxes in the backseat—one holding moth-eaten police uniforms, another filled with blood-smeared cash, the last clinking with old whiskey. I replaced the pistol and closed the radio. "Vlad warned me," I said, "to bring no weapons and no friends. Especially ones that are supposed to be dead."

"I won't make a move until I see you come out."

"Cold fury is useless against these guys. I'll kindle the electricity if I need to."

"As a last resort," he said, rolling down Division Street. "Stick to the plan. Get your mom and Lou, walk to the curb . . ."

"And get the hell out of there," I said, looking at street signs. "Make a left."

Doug turned onto Hoyne Avenue, slowed to a halt, and cut the engine. Czar Bar was a block away; we could see its red neon sign. He cleared his throat and said, "One thing we haven't discussed. If you don't come out—"

"We haven't talked about it because I *am* coming out," I said. "I can't bear to think any other way."

He glanced at his watch. "It's 11:24."

I paused in the open door. "Wish me luck."

"Better than a wish. Take it," he said, handing me the lighter.

I moved from streetlight to streetlight toward Czar Bar, now half a block away. When I glanced back, Doug's gaze was pinned on me. I turned and continued, thinking that even a lucky person needed courage, and a courageous person needed luck.

I rubbed a thumb over the lighter's steel skin, trying to summon both.

25

WICKER PARK IS AN OLD NEIGHBORHOOD MADE from centenarian stone buildings, tarnished copper down-spouts, and mossy brick avenues. Beneath my feet, the gnarled roots of aged trees ruptured the sidewalk; overhead, the moon was a pale wafer, bathing the avenue in milky whiteness.

A beater pickup filled with cast-off metal squeaked past, and disappeared.

I stared across the street at Czar Bar.

Two large windows flanked the entrance with their shades drawn. The only illumination came from the buzzing sign identifying the place, creaking in a slow breeze over the door. I touched the lighter once, took a deep breath, looked both ways, and then coughed it out, seeing a dark ComEd van parked at the curb. It was followed by an empty garbage truck and a school bus. Turning my head, I spotted a squadron of delivery scooters. *Great,* I thought. *No weapons or friends versus half the Russian mob.* I stared at Czar Bar listening to my ragged breath, and then crossed the street.

Thinking of all that my family had suffered, I blinked once, deliberately.

The blue flame flickered and burned in my gut, dancing with each step I took.

It skimmed my veins and tweaked my heart as I paused to crack ten knuckles, and then pushed through the door.

What I saw and heard: dim light unable to penetrate dark corners; the shift and creak of many bodies turning in my direction; a faint, scratchy recording of a woman warbling sadly in Russian. To my left, a row of tables filled with men receded into shadows. The commingled scent of body odor, cheap cologne, and viciousness pervaded the room. To my right sat an old-fashioned booth with panels so high that I was unable to see inside. The only sign that it was occupied came from a ribbon of cigarette smoke curling toward the tin ceiling. Before me, leaning on the corner of a bar that ran the length of the room, Vlad leered with sharp teeth. "Hello, baby," he said, touching the heavy gold chain around his neck, and then self-consciously moving his hand to the bandage covering the damage done by Harry.

"Hey Vlad. What's new?" I said coolly. "Besides the hole in your face."

"I lost a nose." He shrugged. "You lost friend and doggy." The wicked smile remained in place but his eyes taunted me. "The sit-down is scheduled as planned, yes?"

I nodded. Trying to keep the nerves out of my voice, I said, "Where are my mother and brother?"

"Ask the boss," he said, pointing at the booth. I hesitated, and then took a cautious step as three tattooed men wearing goggles filled in behind me, blocking the exit. First I saw the table covered by a white cloth, then a glass ashtray, then a pale finger with a bright red nail lazily tracing its circular contour, and then the bleached-blond harpy once married to my now dead uncle Buddy.

"Greta," I said slowly, suspicion confirmed, anger increasing exponentially.

She smiled with candy apple–colored lips as smoke leaked from her nostrils. With an exaggerated pout, she said, "*Aunt* Greta." Stubbing out the cigarette, she adjusted a tight black leather jacket over a formidable bust. Narrowing her eyes behind crimson lenses, she said, "Surprised?"

"No. Yes," I answered. "I always knew you were up to something, but I never would have guessed it was this." Unable to keep the anger from my voice, I said, "You were part of our family."

"Never a part, only an observer," she said.

"You treated my uncle like a fool."

"*Everyone* did, starting with your father," she said, primping her peroxided locks. "Take a load off. We've got a few minutes."

"Until what?"

"The tearful reunion, of course," she said with a mean little grin.

I sat across from her, staring blankly, and then looked around at the men and the firepower. Despite myself, I blurted, "All of this . . . how—?"

She shrugged and lit a new cigarette. "My Russian parents were dead and I was poor. But Buddy wasn't," she said. "He owned part of a bakery. It wasn't a fortune but it was more than I had, so I married him."

"Seduced him. Lied to him."

"He wuvved his Gweta," she said in the nauseating baby talk she'd used with him, "but was *very* unhappy with your grandfather and father. His confessions to me were like a slow leak . . . first about your family's role in the Outfit, and then about ghiaccio furioso, how unfair it was that he'd been excluded just because he didn't possess it. I stoked those feelings until they were white-hot, urging him to learn more. And he did."

"The notebook," I said.

"He knew there was something in it that was very powerful—ultimate power, as your dad calls it," she said, blowing smoke rings into the air. "How much do you hate me? Can you even describe it?"

I couldn't, and said nothing.

"I don't hate you or your family. Calling Buddy fat and stupid is an insult to fat, stupid people, but I didn't hate him, either. The fact is that I'm ambitious," she said. "As I learned about the Outfit from Buddy, I realized that I could do what it does, and better, with my own organization. So I reached out to a childhood friend with experience in all things criminal to help me. Isn't that right, Vladdy?"

"Right, boss." He grinned, moving closer.

"Things came together after that," she said. "I had men watching your home and the bakery. What a surprise one night, six months ago. So many visitors to the Rispoli household! First Elzy and her brother, and then those little ice cream trucks. Elzy made a hasty retreat. Juan Kone's freaks took your family, my men followed the trucks, and the rest is history." Greta glanced around at the scarred, tattooed mobsters. "In Russia, convicts band together to survive, kill to enforce the rules of survival, and then kill for fun because what the hell else is there to do? They enter prison as men and leave as animals. Chicago is a playground to them."

"How you say . . . easy pickings." Vlad chuckled.

"Elzy kept you on the run while I melted into Juan's organization. Black latex, white makeup, strap-down bra, and saline drops to redden my eyes. My biggest coup was stealing a pair of these from Juan," she said, pointing at her crimson contact lenses. "From then on, the Rispolis had no power over me. Meanwhile, reports of your tenacity got back to Juan's lab. That's when I decided to let you do the rest."

"I got Juan out the way," I said grimly, "so you could take my family."

"I have them, and this. A mess but legible." In a swift movement, she threw the notebook onto the table, its formerly waterlogged pages dried to a fine, yellowed crisp.

"Now?" Vlad said.

Greta nodded, and he lifted a metal bucket onto the table. Slowly, enjoying himself, he tore off the notebook's cover, ripped out its pages, dropped it all into the bucket and used a small can of lighter fluid to coat the debris. Greta slid him a pack of matches. Vlad lit one with a flourish and dropped it into the bucket, too. The fire worked quickly, chewing up the old paper, emitting a swirling cloud of gassy vapor and ash.

"There go your family secrets, up in smoke," Greta said.

"Whatever help they provided is now gone. Frankly, they're useless to me, frivolities at best. What matters is that I have you."

I watched the notebook burn, the sense of security it had provided me burning away with it, and then looked at Greta. "We have a deal."

"Correction. I hold every card and you have nothing, not even that scary electricity. One crackle, and you'll catch a hundred bullets to the heart before you take a step." With an amused smile, she said, "Wake up, child. There's no deal."

"But we agreed," I said, with a chill of unease, like being scratched by a cat's frozen claws. "I'm going to name you boss of the Outfit."

"Yeah, of course. But I still want ultimate power."

"I told you—"

"Please. Buddy was the fool, not me," she said calmly, drawing a pinkie over her lips, fixing a smear. "Personally, I'm completely without nuance when it comes to the life I've chosen. I want what I want because I want it, just like every man in this room." She leaned forward, gazed over her shoulder, and back at me. "Do you think they would follow me if I didn't pay them well?"

"Loyalty," I said, the word sounding idiotic on my tongue.

"Nonsense." Greta snorted, sitting back and crossing her arms. "I don't know specifically what ultimate power is, but I know one thing—it's most certainly money in some form, because there's nothing in the world as powerful. It's the singular driving force behind the Outfit, my organization, *every* organization, criminal or civilian. This is real life. Whoever has the most money rules the world, whatever world she occupies."

It was so quiet that the creaking sign outside the door provided the only noise.

"Do you deny it?" she asked politely.

I'd been in too many crisis situations not to understand the dire consequences of telling anything but the truth. "No," I said, "ultimate power is—"

Greta lifted a hand, silencing me. "When we're alone. If I'm satisfied, we'll attend the sit-down where you'll name me boss, and then you'll hand it over. Afterward, you can have your parents. They're useless to me now."

"Parents," I said. "What about Lou?"

"Lou stays with me," she smiled. "Juan had quite a collection of drugs in his lab. The psychotropics were the most useful. At the right dosage, they alter a person's behavior and conception of reality. The drugs had to be combined with torture, of course . . . Vlad's specialty."

He winked at me with a pointed smile.

"But what a difference they burned into Lou's brain. Your brother despises you, his failed *savior*," she said.

That word, scrawled in blood by Lou, cut me like a razor.

"He's devoted to his aunt Greta. He's become quite a soldier, although that's not why he's staying," she said. "Lou is my permanent hostage. He'll die in front of your eyes unless you serve me as counselor. After I merge the Outfit and the Russian mob, it'll be comprised of violent men who've been at war, who hate each other to death. Your first job will be to command the Outfit to fall into line behind me."

Suspicion rising sickly, I said, "What about my dad?"

She raised a plucked and penciled eyebrow. "What about him?"

"Why not use him to get the Outfit to fall into line?"

"Good question," she said, nodding at Vlad.

He called out a command in Russian and a shuffle sounded from the back of the room. Vlad met the noise halfway, dismissed a pair of men, and dragged a bent form onto a barstool. I rose in slow motion from my seat in the booth, seeing first a torso in a stained white shirt and then an unmistakable Roman profile, even though he was slumped toward the bar. As if in a slow nightmare, heart in my throat, I whispered, "Dad?"

"Sara Jane . . . ," he said in a faraway voice, here but somewhere else, as he lifted his head and turned it searchingly. I saw that his right eye was gone.

"Oh god . . . *Daddy!*" I cried, going to him, gripping his shoulders. He came forward, head lolling on his neck, a thick scar sunk inward and empty over a socket that once held cold blue power flecked with gold.

"I knew you'd find us," he said, smiling weakly. "My smart girl."

26

THE MAN IN MY ARMS WAS MY DAD, BUT HE wasn't.

Years and years had been piled onto him. Confinement, vile experimentation, and torture had aged my poor father long before his time.

His other eye, clouded, searching, found me. He tried to speak again, mouth opening and closing like a suffocating fish, breath fetid, cheeks covered with ashen whiskers, and I kissed him, kissed his cracked lips and rough chin, kissed his scarred brow that used to be smooth, kissed his head that once was covered in hair that was black, lustrous, and wavy, but was now thin, brittle, and white, kissed his sallow skin and pulled him close until ever so slowly his hand spread over my back, feeling me there, that I was real.

I stared at the scar running from his forehead to his cheekbone as the cold blue flame danced in my gut. Turning to Greta, I said, "Why? For *what* reason?"

She shook her head. "It wasn't me. Juan Kone was a genius

and a fool in one disgusting package," she said. "When he was unable to extract enough enzyme GF from your father's blood, he cut out his eye, hoping to mine the last precious ounces required to build his army. He failed, and came after you." She sighed ruefully. "That lost eye . . . cold fury is weak to point of uselessness without both of them. That's why I needed you as badly as the notebook."

I looked down at my dad again, how crushed he was, and said, "You have me. I'll serve. But only if you give me my mom and brother, too, right now."

"Your mommy." Vlad chuckled. "We broke her like glass."

"Juan did a number on her, but I have to say, it was fun washing the rest of the curiosity from her brain," Greta said, stubbing out the cigarette. "She's a lot less . . . inquisitive these days."

I was vibrating now, the dam between cold fury and the deadly voltage beginning to weaken. "My mom, dad, and Lou," I said, biting back the rage, "now."

"Or what?" she snorted.

When I moved my gaze to hers, the flame was jumping so high and furiously that a cobalt glow washed across her face. "Or I'd rather die," I said, feeling the charged electrons soldiering up my spine, along my shoulders, into my fingertips. "If my family can't be together, intact, you can't have me, or cold fury." I was crackling like a live wire, and stood away from my dad.

"Sara Jane," he whispered, "be careful . . ."

"She's bluffing." Vlad chortled. "Go to hell, bitch."

"You first," I said, lunging at the gold chain around his

259

neck as a ferocious bolt of electricity shot through my body, more powerful than I'd ever experienced. It infiltrated my bones, my veins, racing into my hands, and then a blue wave of energy exploded outward from me, through Czar Bar, blowing mobsters off their feet, out of their chairs, overturning tables—followed by a deafening sonic *boom!*, as if lightning had struck the building. I was on the floor, my dad crumpled next to me. Voltage surged though my body, burning me from the inside out, biting at my intestines. I spit bile and rose with a painful effort, as if I were a hundred years old.

My fingers tingled with heat and I looked into my hand at Vlad's gold chain, burned black and stuck with strips of his flesh.

Vlad's head was on the floor staring past me into eternity.

The rest of him, burned away from the neck down, was still smoldering.

I dropped the chain and weakly tried to lift my dad, stumbling to my knees, my hands red and painful, hearing the metallic *click* of a hundred guns. Greta had been thrown from the booth and across the room, but was on her feet. Dazed and enraged, she pointed a red fingernail and croaked, "Take her alive! But kill *him*!"

And then a high-pitched whine was followed by the roar of eight angry cylinders.

The chrome face of the Cadillac exploded through the front window in a cacophony of shattering glass, twisting steel, and erupting brick.

There was a moment of collective shock, a short one, in which I mustered every ounce of strength to drag my dad to the passenger door, shove him inside, and leap in afterward. A hail of bullets rained down on the old car as Doug grinded into reverse, and we roared onto the street. The tires bit asphalt as we sped down Hoyne Avenue in a cloud of gassy smoke.

"Plan B!" Doug screamed. "I saw the blue flash and— what's plan C?!"

I pushed my dad in back, onto the floor, and leaped on the backseat watching a wave of men scrambling into vehicles. "Just go!" I shrieked. "As fast as you can!"

"This old thing's got power!" he said, glancing into the rearview mirror, "but *Jesus*! They have an entire army!"

"The guns," my dad said.

"This one?" Doug said, pointing at the radio.

"No," he said, clawing his way beside me, pushing at a decorative button sewn into the upholstery, "these." A section of backseat slid away revealing two tommy guns. Facing me, throat clogged, he said, "Sara Jane, don't give up until the gun is empty." His words were smothered by bullets battering the Cadillac, punching into metal, and shattering the back window. I grabbed a gun and peeked out at a dozen scooters bearing down, each manned by a goggle-wearing assassin. Close behind, the careening garbage truck led a ComEd van followed by a packed school bus. Another barrage of ammo hit the car as the scooters split, six buzzing along each side of the Cadillac.

"It's too many guys!" I shouted. "They'll rip this old car to pieces!"

"Maybe not," my dad said, grasping a tommy gun. "It's armor-plated." He closed his eye, took a deep breath, and when he opened it, said, "You take one side. I'll take the other. All you have to do is aim and squeeze." He leaned out the side window. "Ready?"

I was always in a state of readiness, but not for this—seeing my dad as I'd never seen him before. He knew how to handle the gun, that was a surprise, but what shocked me even more was his calmness, as if he'd done this a thousand times. Maybe he had.

"Sara Jane!" he said. "Now!"

I came back to myself, squinting down the barrel, and letting off a round of bullets, understanding immediately how the guns got their nickname—Chicago typewriters—as I was deafened by a resounding *tack-a-tack-a-tack-a-tack-a-tack!* First one scooter collapsed, and then another and another, some with slumped bodies still attached, others flinging riders into the air.

"Hang on!" Doug said, squealing onto North Avenue. The garbage truck barreled through the intersection behind us, hurtling toward the Cadillac's bumper.

"It's going to—!" I said, as the huge vehicle rammed the back of the car so hard that it threw me to the floor. Doug swerved maniacally, trying to shake the relentless truck. When it hit us a second time, I felt the Cadillac lose its bearings like a dizzy ice skater. "One more shot like that and we'll tip!" I cried.

My dad was huddled next to me. "You have to take out the driver . . . my eye . . . I can't aim well enough."

"What!"

"Kill him, sweetheart," he said.

I pulled myself onto the backseat and peered out at the truck gathering speed, coming closer, so near that I could see the nose ring of the thug in the passenger seat holding an AK-47. I glanced from him to the rigid face of the driver. In one motion, I stuck the barrel out the window, ducked down, and squeezed. The report of bullets was followed by splintering glass and an emphatic groan, like a giant that had stumbled over its own feet. I looked out at the steel beast sliding on its side, skidding and sparking, the bloody driver hanging lifelessly from his seat belt, the passenger screaming, seeing his fate coming as they plowed into a building with crushing force.

The ComEd van hurtled past the wreckage and I leaned out to shoot, hearing a dull *click* from the empty ammo magazine.

"Dad!" I yelled, and he used both hands to throw his tommy gun at me. I snagged it and heard a short *crack!* from the van, felt a sharp, cutting sting, and rolled inside with pain and moisture soaking my shoulder. "I think . . . I'm shot," I said stupidly.

My dad pushed his thumb into the wound, making me scream. Then I saw something I thought I'd never see again— my dad smiling, though only briefly, there and gone—and he said, "It's a graze. No bullet," and lifted the tommy gun. "Kid, whatever your name is," he said to Doug. "Slow down, and when I tell you, swerve into them."

"Yessir, Mister Rispoli!"

"Wait . . . wait . . . *now*!"

Doug cranked the wheel, slammed into the van, and it bounced away. In that instant, my dad seemed to gather every last shred of power left in his body. He kicked open the passenger door, held on to the inside of the car with one hand, stepped onto the running board, and said, "You shot my daughter," as he sprayed the van with ammunition. There was ripping metal and splintering glass, a screech of brakes, and then everyone inside was killed for a second time when the school bus hit the van, spun it, left it for dead, and bore down on us.

There was a guy in every seat gripping an automatic weapon that put the tommy gun to shame; armor-plated or not, there was no way the Cadillac, or we, would survive.

My dad flopped inside, sucking air, and threw the rifle on the ground. "Empty," was all he could manage to say. Doug's eyes met mine in the rearview mirror as everything went eerily quiet, the only sound a rolling *clink* of bootleg whiskey bottles.

"Whiskey . . . whiskey!" I said, groping for the wooden crate.

"What the hell? A farewell drink?" Doug yelped.

"Not for us. For them," I said, pulling out bottles, pushing them aside, and opening the box containing the cop uniforms. I yanked at a sleeve, the old wool peeling away in strips. "They're Russian. Maybe they'd like a Molotov cocktail."

Doug's eyes widened. "Chapter six . . . 'Methods'! 'How to Build an Incendiary Device'!" he said. "Please tell me you've still got the lighter?"

"I'd never leave home without it," I said.

When my dad saw what I was doing, he began quickly

shredding the uniform. We worked at hyperspeed, splashing whiskey over pieces of cloth and jamming the soaked strips into bottles, leaving an inch hanging out as a fuse. It took thirty seconds to make three sloshing alcohol bombs and another thirty seconds for the nose of the bus to reach our bumper; the onslaught of bullets would begin at any second. I flicked the lighter but wind rushing in the open window snuffed it, did it again, same thing. I said, "Quick, anything that will take a spark . . . anything that burns. I need a flame."

My dad fell to the floor, ripped open the Rispoli & Sons Fancy Pastries box, and pulled out a sheaf of blood-spattered cash. "I never knew why I kept this," he said, "but now I do. Light it." I flicked the lighter, a spark bit the crispy greenbacks, and then my dad was holding a ten-thousand-dollar torch to the Molotov cocktail. The fuse smoked and caught, filling the car with the stench of burning molasses. "Give it a second . . . wait . . . now, throw it!" he yelled.

I side-armed the bottle and it skittered over the bus's hood, rolled, and exploded in a burst of flame. The bus swerved crazily but no real damage was done, and it sped after us without pause.

My dad said, "Kid, you ever see *The Godfather*?"

"Are you kidding?" Doug called out. "I've seen *everything! Twice!*"

"When the Turk is taking Michael Corleone to the sit-down in Brooklyn and he thinks they're being followed? Remember what he does? Can you do it?"

"I—I don't know. Maybe!" Doug said.

"Good enough. Sara Jane, switch sides with me, and get ready," my dad said as I rolled to his side of the car and grabbed a Molotov cocktail. "Both of them," he said. "This is our last chance," and I picked up the other one, too. He lit the first, got it smoking. "Now, kid!" my dad said, as Doug cranked the wheel, and spun the Cadillac into a stuttering U-turn.

"Like that?" Doug said.

"Perfect. Okay, sweetheart, one after another!" my dad said, as we sped straight for the bus, engaged in a deadly game of chicken. We roared up to the big yellow vehicle, Doug swerved, and I threw a cocktail, watching it shatter against the bus's windshield before it could detonate. I heaved the other a split second later—a bull's-eye that sailed through an open window. A pair of guys leaped from the rear door, but Doug couldn't hit the brakes fast enough, nailing one of them as we passed by, crushing him beneath the Cadillac with a body-shattering *thump!* We skidded to a halt and looked back. The bus had stopped, too—maybe the rest of the Russians inside were scrambling to get rid of the bomb? And then the cocktail made a muted, burping nose, blowing up the bus like a firebomb from hell. It rocked on its wheels, consumed in white flames.

"Drive, kid," my dad said weakly, slumping onto the seat.

"Huh? Oh," Doug said, peeling his eyes off the conflagration from which no one emerged, and speeding away. We were turning onto Ashland Avenue when I heard a *scrape-thunk* and turned to see the other Russian who'd made it off the bus. He stood on the running board leering with a mouth full of gray teeth, pulled a handgun, and shot wildly into the backseat. I drove my fist into the Orthodox cross tattooed on his face, but he held on, swinging the gun, clipping me in the mouth. I tumbled backward as he yanked open the door and pushed inside. The car skidded to a stop.

Calmly, Doug said, "Don't touch my friend—"

The guy turned to the radio pistol, muttered in Russian, and Doug shot him in the arm, saying, "Ever," blasting him once more, this time in the kneecap. The guy screamed, slumped, and I kicked him in the face, into the street, as we screeched away, barreling toward the Currency Exchange Building.

"Doug," I gasped. "You're not shaking. You didn't panic."

His eyes flicked to mine in the rearview mirror. "You didn't flinch," I said, and he nodded with a tight smile. I sat back, staring at my dad, thinking of how he'd swung onto the running board and gunned down the van with ease, even grace, cold and composed. It seemed wrong to be impressed, but I was. He'd done it because he had to, but more so, for me. "Dad?" I said.

"What, sweetheart?"

"The last time I saw you, I . . . was so mean to you," I said. "I wasn't sure—I never really knew if we'd ever see each other again, and, anyway, I'm sorry."

He sat up, licking dry lips. "Sara Jane. It's me . . . I owe you a lifetime of apologies."

"Are you okay?"

"Tired, darling," he said, reaching out to squeeze my hand. "So tired . . ." And he lay back again.

We made it to the Bird Cage Club, where he wrapped up

in a warm blanket and collapsed on my mattress, battered and scarred but free.

I treated my bullet graze and then slept next to him, holding his hand.

It wasn't until early the next morning when he woke me, groaning, that I realized he'd bled all night.

27

WHEN I WAS LITTLE, MY DAD WOULD SOME-
times glance out the window of our house on Balmoral
Avenue, see dark feathery clouds massing in the sky, and rush
us all to Hollywood Avenue beach. He loved living by Lake
Michigan, that large inland sea, and loved it best when it was
raining. The hurried race to watch a storm roll in became a
family ritual. By the time we arrived, the lake would be a pane
of green glass engulfed by the sound of nothingness, as if the
interim between the world being a dry place and a wet one
required a moment of silence. There was an old park bench
on the boardwalk, a front-row seat to lightning over the lake.
We'd jam onto it, the four of us, and wait, smelling the rain
before it arrived. And then the heavens would crack open and
we'd sprint for the car, trying to get ahead of something that
was faster than we were.

It was raining lightly now, the drops feeling like the touch
of soft fingertips.

My dad and I sat side by side on the park bench. He was hunched over, wrapped in the same blanket.

He'd woken me that morning as the sun rose, looming over the mattress like a specter. His scarred eye socket was purple against sallow flesh. "Let's go," he said.

"Where?" I asked groggily.

"I want to see the lake."

"Now?"

He nodded, coughing from deep in his lungs, and said, "Yes, sweetheart. Now. It's important."

"I'll wake Doug."

"No," he said, stifling another cough. "Just the two of us."

We took a cab to Hollywood Avenue, crossed the cold, deserted boardwalk, and sat on the bench. It was six forty-five in the morning, with a dome of fog rising over the chilly lake water. My dad seemed to have fallen asleep sitting up and I spoke his name softly.

He lifted his head, and said, "I'm going to die in a few minutes, Sara Jane. Maybe ten minutes . . . maybe less . . ."

My body and brain turned to ice. I didn't laugh with incredulity or cry out in horror; I was incapable of either. Skin is the ultimate indicator of a failing body, its temperature and tone. I took his icy, gray hands in mine, watching a red line stream from his nose.

Later, I would see only a few red spots on the mattress.

The Russian who fired into the Cadillac had hit him, the bullet staying in his body, tearing through vital organs. All the bleeding, the damage, was on the inside.

"I didn't feel it," he said. "Something Juan Kone did . . ."

my nervous system, brain. Pain barely registers anymore. But I'm dying, Sara Jane. The bullet was too much."

He was such a diminished human being—beaten, malnourished, experimented upon for too long. If there had been a remote chance of survival, we'd slept through it.

"This is crazy. We need a doctor," I said, mind reeling, looking around the boardwalk.

"Wouldn't help me now . . ."

"But how do you know?"

"Because I've murdered men, and watched them die," he said. "I know what it looks like . . . how fast it happens."

I stared at him, the heaving chest, the whites of his eyes gone yellow, and knew he was correct. "I have, too," I said. "Murdered people."

"I know," he said quietly, looking away. "I never wanted that . . . all of this, for you. When you were born with blue eyes, I thought maybe, because you were a girl, ghiaccio furioso would skip you, but that was silly . . . delusional . . ."

"Why didn't you take us away from Chicago?" I said.

He scared me with a bark of laughter. "I asked my father the same thing when I was about your age, when he told me about being counselor-at-large and what I possessed. He said that we were trapped by our responsibility, there was only one way out . . ."

"Ultimate power," I said.

"You found it?"

I nodded, as a chilled wave of wind blew across us.

"It's a trap, too—of wishful thinking. My dad, my grandfather, they clung to it, thinking that if life in the Outfit ever got too bad . . . but it was always *too* bad and the worst things happen *too* fast . . . no time to plan. I tried though, Sara Jane. I tried . . ."

"What? What did you try? Dad?"

I squeezed his hands and he shuddered, his breath ragged, breaking up his words. "Removing those bricks . . . turning it into money without drawing attention . . . it's impossible. But one at a time . . . even two," he said. "We'd been planning for so long, to make an escape, your mom and me . . . almost five years . . ."

"Five years?" I said.

"*Never* the right time. The Feds made an offer but . . . too dangerous . . . so . . ."

"What?"

He glanced away, staring across the water. "Lake Michigan isn't really a lake. It's a sea, like the Sea of Cortez . . . bought a villa . . . going to run . . . but Juan Kone . . . ," he said, voice fading, head sinking between his shoulders.

"Dad! Dad, can you hear me?!" I said, shaking him harder and harder until he faced me. When he did, his eye was clear and focused, as if he were seeing me for the first time.

"He helped you, didn't he, Sara Jane?" he asked.

"Who, Dad?" I whispered.

"Buddy, at the Ferris wheel. Lou told me . . ."

My teeth chattered with the effort not to cry, to remain as strong as he was not, and I told the truth. "Yeah, Uncle Buddy helped me. You can be proud of him."

"I always was. Buddy . . . Benito, my little brother," he said, and straightened with an insistence that startled me.

"*Your* brother, Lou. Sara Jane, your *mother* . . . what you did for me . . . do for *them*. There's not much time left . . ."

"But how? Greta—"

"Give her . . . ultimate power. Give her that . . . golden trap," he said.

It was my only chance left—to hope that she'd be so overwhelmed by the glittering prospect of its value that she'd make a deal to release my mom and Lou without considering how she'd ever actually cash it in. Doubtless, she'd still demand that I serve as counselor. If she freed Lou from being a hostage, though, I would. "Okay, Dad. Okay."

"Last night . . . the Russians we killed . . . ," he said.

I nodded, remembering the carnage we'd left behind.

"You've been forced to do terrible things, I know. But there's still time for you, sweetheart . . . choices you can make . . . so you don't become like me," he said, blood bubbling at the corner of his lips. "Remember . . ."

"Please, Dad. Let's go back, find a doctor . . ."

"There's a line," he said. "There's *always* a line."

I was quiet as he turned, staring at me, searching my face.

"Don't cross it, Sara Jane. You'll leave . . . too much behind. Understand?"

"Yeah. I think I do."

He smiled a little as a tear rolled down his cheek, wrapped his feeble arms around me, mouth so close I could smell warm blood, and whispered, "I should have told you everything . . . my smart girl . . ."

"Daddy." I breathed into his shoulder. "I thought this would be the end."

It was.

I knew from the way his arms stayed in place and the sudden heaviness of his body. Was my heart broken, and did I cry out, sending a howl of grief echoing across the lake? Maybe. That's what a normal human being would've done. All I know for sure was that I didn't move for a while, just held on to him as tightly as I could.

There was so much to say, but all that mattered was, "I love you, Dad."

Lightning creased the sky above, followed by a distant boom. Rain began to fall in harder, colder droplets.

And then I did my duty as the daughter of Anthony Rispoli.

Just like the civilian world has 911, the Outfit has an emergency number of its own. I dialed, identified myself to the faceless entity who answered, and asked to be connected to the Department of Funeral Operations; I'd once read about it in chapter 7 of the notebook, *Procedimenti*—Procedures." Even at that early hour, the phone was answered on the first ring. I explained who I was, where I was, and who had died, while the deep voice answered with three terse *mm-hm*s, and said he was on his way.

Twenty minutes later, an unmarked van pulled up near the boardwalk.

A pair of bald, mournful-looking thugs, a young and an old version of the same character in black suit and sunglasses, gently but quickly lifted my father onto a stretcher.

"When do you want the service, counselor?" the younger one asked.

"Soon. I'll let you know." I stared into my dad's face,

absorbing its look of peaceful escape, kissed him once, and said, "You can take him now."

"Condolences," the older one said, and they hustled him away.

I stood on the boardwalk, watching as the van curved onto Lake Shore Drive, accelerated, and disappeared.

All the things my father never told me went with him.

28

I SAT ON THE COUCH AT THE BIRD CAGE CLUB across from Doug, who was still holding the bottle from which he'd tapped an aspirin into my hand. Harry was curled in my lap, trying to comfort me with his warmth. It wasn't until returning from the lake that I fully realized how badly I'd hurt myself at Czar Bar the previous evening. My hands were red and blistered from fingertips to elbows and the air in my lungs was fiery when I breathed. I'd come close to doing something irreversible to myself. I would never do it again.

I swallowed the pill with a quick sip of water, nullifying the electricity.

It was just past noon, five terrible hours since I'd said goodbye to my dad.

"Are you okay?" Doug said.

"I don't know," I said honestly. "I feel like I failed him."

"Don't think that way."

"I lost him."

"No," Doug said, "you saved him. Your dad didn't die a

prisoner." He rose, lifted my phone from the control center, and handed it to me. "It rang a couple of times while you were gone. Might be important."

I had two voice-mail messages and listened to the first. In a tone both officious and groveling, Knuckles reminded me that the Outfit-wide sit-down was today, and then plugged himself as boss, saying how experience and muscle always trumped youth.

The next message was from youth himself.

Tyler's voice mail was urgent and alarming.

"No, I haven't left Chicago yet. I'm in trouble, Sara Jane," he said quietly, trying and failing to steady his voice. "I can't . . . it's not safe for me to talk, but . . ."

My hand holding the phone began to tremble

"I need your help. Meet me at Calo Ristorante, on Clark Street, at one thirty p.m., in the kitchen. Please, Sara Jane. Shawshank."

The message ended and I recited it word for word to Doug. My mind was racing faster than my heart.

"What the hell happened?" he asked.

I shrugged, biting a thumbnail. "I don't know, unless," I said, my gut curdling, "someone in the Outfit found out he was about to run. Maybe they think he's a rat."

"Shit. You have to help him," Doug said.

"I know, I know, but time's running out between now and the sit-down. I've got to make a decision, what I'm going to do about Greta." The queasiness of uncertainty spread through me; I'd experienced it infinite times during the past six months, asking myself what would happen to my family if ——. (Fill in the awful blank.) So many ifs, so many disappointments, so much violence. I folded my thumb around my fist, knowing that the time had come to accept my fate. My existence would be one of servitude, but at least my mother and brother would be alive and free.

I'd worried so much about crossing a line; now I had to draw one in the sand.

Without a word, I dialed the number.

Greta answered at Czar Bar and called me a vile name.

In response, I told her everything about Al Capone's vault made of gold bricks except where it was located. She was quiet for a second, breathing on the other end, and then she said, "How much all together?"

"My estimate is four billion, give or take a million."

She was quiet again. "How do I know you're not lying?"

"I have one of the bricks. I'll give it to you," I said, and then spoke the plainer truth. "There's nothing for me to lie about anymore, Greta. You won."

"You'll serve me or Lou dies."

"I'll serve you but Lou walks away free with my mom. If not, you can kill us all," I said. "And then what'll you have? No counselor. No gold."

"Vlad was right about you," she said. I expected her to tell me that I was the mother of a dog, but instead she said, "You're committed. All business. We'll work well together." When the agreement was in place, she instructed me to meet her at the bakery at three p.m. and to bring someone to take my mom and brother away. "The friend of yours, the one with the old car. Tell him that I owe him one for what he did to Czar Bar—"

"I'm sure he's sorry," I said.

"And that I always pay my debts," she said coldly. "After the bakery, you'll lead me and two of my men to ultimate power. When I'm satisfied, we'll proceed to the sit-down where you'll name me boss."

Simple and airtight in the deadliest of ways; there was no wiggle room. Greta hung up on me and I told it all to Doug.

His ruddy face was pale, all the way to the freckles. "Jesus, Sara Jane, you just gave yourself to her. She'll own you."

I shook my head. "She'll own part of me, the Outfit part. The other part, the one that loves my family and my friend, will be locked away inside of me," I said. "I guess it's what Rispolis do."

He watched me, unblinking. "Clock's ticking," he said quietly.

"Has been since the minute my family disappeared," I said, rising to meet Tyler. "Will you do me a favor? While I'm gone, make sure the Cadillac still runs?"

He nodded. "Let's hope. It looked shot to pieces when we got back here last night."

I went to my room and changed into a Cubs T-shirt, faded jeans, and Chuck Taylors. I twisted my hair into a ponytail while pointedly not looking at the mattress where my dad had slept. Doug was waiting by the elevator, and as I climbed on, he offered me the lighter. I shook my head. "Not this time. Good luck and I aren't on speaking terms."

"Don't take it for luck," he said, folding it into my hand. "Take it because you never know when you'll need to set something on fire."

I rode the Brown Line north, transferred once, and was soon walking up Clark Street in the Andersonville neighborhood; my house on Balmoral Avenue was only blocks away. I'd grown up on this street, buying back-to-school footwear at old-timey Alamo Shoes, feasting on ice cream at George's, eating dinner with my family at Calo Ristorante; what I hadn't known until I'd read the notebook was the restaurant's status as a reliable sit-down location for the Outfit. I passed beneath the striped canopy at 1:29 p.m. and pushed through the door. The place was empty except for a scattering of employees prepping for the dinner crowd. The bartender stood peeling a lemon, a shock of white hair bent over his work as he carved the rind into yellow curlicues. "Help you?" he drawled.

"The kitchen . . . ?"

He looked up and his face changed. "Oh, counselor. Straight back, no detours," he said, quickly returning to his task.

I passed waiters polishing glasses and folding linen napkins until I reached a set of double doors. When I pushed through, the restaurant's owner—thick, bald, imposing—glanced at me and clapped his hands. Without a word, line cooks and dishwashers walked silently from sudsy sinks, boiling pots, and sizzling grills. Everything in the large room was stainless steel—refrigerators, freezers, prep tables—except for the tiled walls. The owner smiled nervously, saying, "It's all yours," and shut the doors carefully behind him.

"Hey," Tyler said, stepping around a corner, handsome as always, opening his arms for a hug. Despite the urgency of the meeting, his embrace calmed me. "I was scared you wouldn't make it," he said over my shoulder.

I stood back, facing him. "You should be gone by now."

He nodded. "I know, but listen, I own a couple of cops. For a few hundred bucks a month they pass me information so, you know, I always have a leg up."

"Go on."

"Seems they were called to North Avenue last night and found a bunch of dead Russian mobsters all over the street. Well, not all dead," he said. "One was still alive, barely, when the police arrived. He was babbling about the Outfit, and you."

My face was blank but my guts were churning. "So?" was all I could muster.

"So I had the cops bring him to me. Guy suddenly clammed up, refused to talk. But with a Russian translator and some sodium Pentothal . . ."

"Sodium Pentothal?"

"I learned everything," he said slyly, green eyes gleaming. "From Juan Kone to Greta Kushchenko."

Now I was unable to muster anything, not a word, feeling my blood freeze.

"What a story! Your dad was taken by a bunch of anorexic *freaks* with red eyes? So an evil genius could infiltrate his *brain*?" he cried, crossing his arms. "It sounded like bullshit to me, and I know it's true!"

"You said—you needed my help," I mumbled, confused.

"I do. But just in case you refuse," he said, turning, rummaging in his pocket, and spinning around with a thousand-watt smile. "Ta-da!"

"Oh . . . my god," I whispered at the pair of crimson goggles he'd strapped to his face.

And then I saw the snub-nosed .38 aimed at me.

"I know, right?" he said smugly, tapping the gun to the goggles. "The Russian told me all about these babies. So yeah, you're going to name me boss."

It was like listening to someone I knew and had never met, both at once. My mouth was dry when I said, "You told me you wished the Outfit didn't exist. That in a perfect world you'd walk away from it. We—you hate it."

"Yeah," he replied. "That's why I'm taking this opportunity to screw it over, just like it did to my dad. To survive, you have to use hatred like fuel." His smile turned condescending, as if he pitied me. "How many times have I said it? Perfect or not, this is the world we live in. We may as well take it for all it's worth."

The facts faced me now with perfect teeth and a killer grin—he was tall, handsome, and as rotten to the core as any pimp or drug dealer. His title didn't make him better than the rank and file; it only elevated him to where the mud couldn't spatter his imported Italian shoes. On the one hand it was like being angry at a shark for following its nature. But on the other—the one that had once held mine while he told me how it felt to lose his parents in an airplane accident—it was pure betrayal.

"Helping each other take the Outfit for all it's worth," I

said. "That's what you meant about watching each other's backs."

"Hey, neither of us is going to make a dime if someone sticks a knife in yours *or* mine," he said. "I'm your Whispering Smith, and you helped me with the smash-and-grab guy. Thanks for that, by the way. I fenced the gems and made a tidy little profit."

"Profit? You mean you sold that stuff and settled his operating tax with the money, right?" I said, thinking of how I'd used cold fury to make the guy stand aside while Tyler took a small fortune from his stash house, designated for Outfit coffers.

"Some of it." He shrugged. "The guy had more than he needed, so I helped myself. You know the rule. Money is money. You take it where you can get it, always."

I saw then what a fool I'd been.

He'd used me to pull a cruddy little robbery.

That I could've trusted him about—anything—was suddenly ludicrous.

"Look, that heist was small-time," Tyler said. "When I'm in charge, new Outfit rule, enforced through cold fury, the boss gets twenty-five, no, *fifty* percent of revenue generated by the rank and file. You and I will clean up!"

"You and *I*?"

"Well, yeah. Business comes first, but you know I like you, Sara Jane. More than like," he said. "Face it, we belong together."

All I could do was stare, disbelief and rage coursing through me. "So I'm going to be, what, your combination girlfriend and counselor-at-large? Like the prom king and queen of organized crime?"

"In time, you'll see that I did this for both of us," he nearly purred in his charming way that now seemed creepy. "I need you, and even more, you need me."

"I'm about to say something you probably don't hear from women too often," I said, gritting my teeth. "No."

"No *what*?" he said, stepping closer without lowering the gun.

"No to *all* of it. If I don't name Greta boss, something terrible will happen to my mom and brother. You probably know that."

"She has them." He shrugged. "But you did so much damage to the Russians, I can wipe out them *and* her, and free your family. Don't you see how perfect this is? It's like my dad said, once I'm boss, you really can neutralize all of my—our—enemies inside the Outfit, too! Trust me."

I smirked once myself. "I'm not naming you boss, Tyler. What are you going to do? Shoot me? Where would that leave you?"

He laughed then, loud and in my face. "*Me?* Where would it leave *you?*" he brayed. "In a landfill, for starters. My guys will bundle your dead ass out of here and I'll show up at the sit-down but hey, where's the counselor-at-large? Maybe she defected, like her dad, or—no, much better! She turned rat, went to the Feds!" He moved toward me again, so close I could smell his lemony cologne. "I'll sell it like a pro, have my cops fake documentation proving you're a turncoat, whatever. A boss will still have to be chosen, whether or not the counselor is there to do it. Now let me think, if it's between crusty old Muscle and fresh young Money, I wonder who the rank and file will choose?"

There was nothing for me to say. Money trumped everything.

"One pair of goggles and the world turns toward me. Cold fury is good for one thing only—settling disputes so the rank and file can keep earning." He chuckled. "It sure didn't help you save your family."

He's right, I thought.

Tyler said, "From now until the sit-down . . ."

Neither did the electricity.

"You're going to stay here with me."

Even ultimate power was useless, so . . .

"It's only a couple hours," he said, glancing at his watch.

Time froze as I watched his head turn toward his wrist, taking his eyes from me, and I thought, *All that remains is a left hook.*

Time restarted. Tyler said, "We have to—" and his words were lost to my fist cracking into his perfectly formed jaw. He fell against a prep table and I punched him again, hard against the other side of his head as he reeled but didn't fall, didn't drop the gun, so I grabbed his wrist and hit it once, twice, three times on a counter until the .38 clattered away. I reached for the goggles but he staggered upright, pushed me back, and threw a wild roundhouse that grazed my shoulder, another that missed by a mile, and lost his balance. I yanked him into a choking headlock, ripped the goggles free, crushed them underfoot, and dragged him over to the red-hot grill.

Holding his head inches above it, I said, "You've got a choice, handsome. Stop fighting or start wearing a bag over your head."

"Fug-oo . . . bish!" he gasped.

"Have it your way," I said, pushing him closer, his sweat and tears popping and sputtering on the grill.

"O-a, o-a! Please!" he said, high-pitched and desperate.

I let him go and grabbed a knife from a cutting board in one motion, and when he turned, I put the tip of the blade to his throat. Blinking once, I said, "Look at me," and saw his deepest fear.

Tyler gasped, biting his lips, unable to look away.

I'd used cold fury on him once before, to make him turn our jet to Rome back to Chicago, and then—just for an instant— I'd seen him watching from the ground as his parents died in a fiery plane crash. I didn't understand at the time that it was a terrible memory rather than a fear, but I'd blinked it away so quickly. Now, watching further into the scene, I saw young Tyler's eyes widen as the plane exploded, and felt what he felt—first shock and then, slowly, a rising, secret pleasure— as his lips curled into a smile. Quietly, in a whisper, he said, "Tyler Strozzini, VP of Money."

He caught himself then, wiping away the vile grin, and his true fear became clear—he was mortally terrified that someone would realize how delighted he was that his parents were dead, and that he would soon ascend to his father's position in the Outfit.

"Sick son of a bitch," I said quietly.

"Please . . . please . . . ," he whimpered, as I stared even harder into his eyes.

"Get this straight," I said. "You won't tell anyone what you know about my family. It goes with you to your grave, which will happen sooner than you think if you ever threaten me again, with words or a weapon."

"Yes, oh god, yes!" he cried.

"Every pair of goggles, every pair of contact lenses, you'll personally destroy them. Crush and torch every single one until there's not a crimson sliver left."

"I promise," he whimpered. "Just please *stop!*"

"Finally, you'll be present at the sit-down tonight and you'll abide by my decision. In fact, you'll be my most loyal supporter," I said. "Whatever happens to you after I name Greta boss, you brought it on yourself."

Tyler wagged his head in assent, mewling like a tortured kitten, and I blinked once, setting him free. He leaned against a table, nose leaking blood, and slid to the floor.

It was two o'clock when I left the kitchen—an hour until I had to be at the bakery.

The bartender had finished with the lemon and was stuffing olives with blue cheese. As I passed by, he said politely, "Have a nice day, counselor."

According to Ms. Ishikawa, there are 229,000 words in the English language.

I couldn't think of one that applied less to this day than *nice.*

29

FIFTEEN MINUTES LATER I WAS ON AN EL TRAIN, and thirty minutes after that, standing half a block from Rispoli & Sons Fancy Pastries on Taylor Street. This time Coffinetto's Funeral Home had a new sign in its window, reading NOW MANAGED BY R.I.P. CO. It seemed like there were fewer Italian grandmothers monitoring the street from behind lace curtains and more slim hipsters and baby strollers. I could've been mistaken. My mind wasn't really on the neighborhood.

It was on the bakery, where I could see the glowing neon sign.

The place had been locked up and dark for a month. The buzzing pink light was a signal—Greta was inside, waiting for me.

A tap on my shoulder made me jump. Doug said, "Easy. It's just me. I'm also a little early. Too nervous to wait." He was dressed in jeans and his Blackhawks jersey, baggy over his slim frame. "So what did you learn from Tyler?" I explained quickly as Doug listened, shaking his head. "It's always the good-looking ones," he said. "Think they can get away with anything."

"He thought wrong," I said. "Where's the Cadillac?"

"On a side street, where it won't draw so much attention. A vintage car is one thing. A vintage car that looks like it drove through a firing range is another."

"But it runs . . ."

"It's a monster," he said, looking at the bakery.

"You have the gold brick?"

"In here," he said, handing me the backpack. "Where do you want me to wait?"

"I don't. I want you to come with me."

"You sure?"

"Yeah. I need you to walk my mom and Lou out of there, quickly. But you should know, Greta threatened you. The damage you did to Czar Bar."

"Plan B," he said, looking across the street. "Scared?"

"Suspicious."

"You have every right," he said.

"This is the big one, Doug, which means it's the most dangerous. Greta wants to be boss, and wants ultimate power even more. Only I can give them to her," I said. "My mom, Lou, you, you're all disposable. Understand?"

"Yeah," he said gravely.

"If you don't want to go in there—I mean, it's dangerous, you know?"

He shook his head. "I'm all in. You know that."

Here I was again, putting Doug into another precarious situation. I felt guilty and selfish at the same time, but selfishness won. I needed him, and besides, I knew he wouldn't turn back. "Let's do it," I said, and led him across Taylor Street. The bakery door was unlocked and I pushed through, jingling the bell. Murmuring voices died in the front room. The pinkish glow from the Rispoli & Sons sign gave off enough light to see Greta perched on the counter, ankles crossed, smoking a cigarette. She wore a shoulder holster filled with a handgun. One of her guys loomed beside her. He was tall, dark, and ugly, eyes covered by goggles, sawed-off shotgun on his shoulder. He grunted in Russian, sneering at me, and Greta chuckled through her nose. "Hope you don't mind that I let myself in," she said. "I kept Buddy's keys, just in case."

"Where's my mom and my brother?"

"In the kitchen," she said. "Where's the gold?"

I handed her the backpack. She opened it and removed the yellow bar, inspecting its engraving, feeling its heft. "It's right here, in my hands," she said, "and I still don't trust you. You're taking me to where you got this."

"I know," I said.

She narrowed her eyes at Doug, blowing smoke through sticky red lips. "You did a lot of damage, you little shit." She nodded at Ugly and he marched across the room, patted me down, and then threw Doug against the wall, slapping at his arms and legs.

"They're clean," he grunted, sounding like *deer klen.*

Greta slid from the counter, smoothed her jacket, and aimed her crimson eyes at me. "The deal has changed. Wait . . . it's the *same* as it was originally. You can have your mother, there's not much left of her anyway. But Lou stays with me after all."

"No," I said, moving toward her until Ugly stopped me with the shotgun.

"Maybe you'll serve me willingly if I free him. Maybe you won't," she said. "I once asked Buddy why his father, who could control any man with ghiaccio furioso, would take orders from the boss. Why wouldn't the counselor use cold fury to defy the boss and enrich himself? Do you know what his answer was?"

"Fear."

Greta nodded. "If you used those blue eyes on him, how would he use the tentacles of the Outfit to hurt you? But Enzo's fear was larger and less selfish. He was terrified of what the Outfit would do to his family. Something you didn't have to worry about," she said, "until they reappeared."

"I won't use it on you," I said. "You have the lenses. I can't."

"But I need you to feel the fear, every day, that Lou could die at any moment. Call it an incentive to do your job properly," she said, crushing the cigarette under a stiletto heel. "I wouldn't have brought him today, but I wanted you to feel for yourself how much he hates you."

"I don't believe it."

"Let's see," she said. "Bring them out!"

The kitchen door swung open. The first person through was another of Greta's men—short, thick, and red-faced, a goggled fireplug in need of a shave, carrying a shotgun. His gaze flicked from me to Greta. She nodded, dipping her peroxided head.

A ghost drifted into the room.

It was as if someone had taken an eraser to my mother, fading the silken blackness from her hair, the olive tone from her smooth skin, the life from her eyes. She was barely past forty but, like my dad, now appeared so much older—body bent and shrunken, moving with a shuffle. The beautiful hands that had stroked my hair were bony fists, held out before her in steel cuffs; the jagged red scar where her index finger had been sliced off by Juan Kone was sickly visible. She was dressed in a pair of stained pants and an oversized sweater with gaping holes—Dumpster-wear for an expendable person.

"Teresa. *Teresa!*" Greta barked. My mom shuddered, lifting her head guardedly, scared of what she'd see. "Say hello to your daughter."

My mom turned toward me, her face twisted in confusion until, slowly, her eyes widened. "Sara Jane?" she mumbled. "My . . . daughter. Darling . . ."

"Mom," I said hoarsely, flooded with half a year's worth of terror and love. I pushed past Ugly's shotgun and went to her, folding my arms around the frail, broken apparition. No cold fury coursed through me, no flickering flame; only pervasive sorrow, and regret at how terribly I'd failed her, too. Her bluish lips grazed mine, she touched my forehead with hers, and then she tried clumsily to reach me with her bound hands.

"Take off the cuffs," Greta said. "She couldn't harm a flea."

Fireplug unlocked her wrists and my mother pulled me into a weak embrace. When our heads were together, she whispered, "Lou . . . isn't . . . what . . ."

"That's enough," Greta said. Fireplug yanked us apart and

gripped my mom's arm tightly. Greta grinned at me and said, *"Louis!"*

The door swung open and my brother strode out, or at least a version of him did. This Lou was rangier than the thirteen-year-old I'd last seen at the Ferris wheel, now in the process of taking on the long tallness of a Rispoli. His head was shaved so that only a black five o'clock shadow dusted his skull. A wave of shock rolled through me at the Soviet red star earring, hammer-and-sickle ink on his neck, crosses tattooed across the knuckles that gripped a .44 Magnum pistol—and worse, the crimson eyes trained on me. It was a piercing look that could cut diamonds. He moved toward me with a cockiness I'd seen in the most seasoned of enforcers, muttering, "Sara Jane . . ."

"Lou," was all I could say before he spit in my face. It oozed down my face but I stood still, transfixed by horror.

"Our *savior*," he crowed, and Greta laughed with him. "Our *failure* is more like it. The needles, the knives. Juan Kone ripped us to *pieces*! And what did you do? Betrayed us! Kept yourself *safe* by serving as *counselor-at-large*!"

"That's not true. You don't understand —"

"We were his lab rats while you *hid* inside the Outfit! You were supposed to hate it, like I did!"

"Lou, don't," my mom whispered.

He moved so close I could feel him vibrating. "You left us for dead, *counselor,* and we would've been if it wasn't for her," he said, turning his head abruptly toward Greta.

"No, I was there, at the lab . . ."

"Our *true* savior." He turned an absent gaze on our mother.

"You want her. Take her," he said, facing me again. "My life is with Aunt Greta."

Finding the voice of the older sister who protected and never lied to him, I said, "You're a hostage to her and nothing else. It's the drugs—psychotropics, Lou—strong, deadly drugs. She brainwashed you to hate me and to make you dependent on *her*. Look at your arms." His eyes quivered, flicking down to the needle marks and bruised veins lining his skin. "Why does she give you drugs? Think . . ."

"He knows the reason," Greta said. "The damage done by Juan Kone has to be repaired, isn't that right, Louis? It's for your own good. Without it, you'd die."

"I'd die," he repeated, teeth clenched.

"*Think!* Use that big brain! I would *never* leave you for dead! You know me. I would *never* have served as counselor unless I was forced to!"

"Except you did," Greta said. "His place is with me now, with us."

"They killed your dog."

The room turned as one to Doug. I was about to tell him to be quiet for his own safety but I swallowed my words, understanding his lie. He was trying to drill down to the part of my brother that hadn't been manipulated by Greta—that still felt something stronger than the drugs.

"Harry?" Doug said nervously, beginning to shake. "Remember?"

A tremor crossed Lou's shoulders and he moved his head oddly, as if a fly was pestering his ear. "My dog . . . what the hell do *you* know about Harry?"

"I know bravery and love. I know what it meant to have him as a friend."

"Louis, that bastard drove into Czar Bar," Greta said. "Let's do it Russian style. Cut him."

Lou pulled a knife from his belt and crossed the room in three steps. "Where?"

"Start with his nose," Greta said, "in memory of Vlad."

In that split second, I saw my friend's eyes change and I heard the confidence he injected into the lie as he said, "He's the one—Vlad. He killed Harry. Held him underwater and drowned him, left his body at the bottom of the Chicago River. You knew Vlad. He'd do that to a dog, wouldn't he? He loved to torture."

Without lowering the knife, Lou aimed his eyes at me. They were distant but the pinpoints had expanded, drawing in light.

"It's true. Every word," I said, and his gaze lingered, inspecting me.

"Vlad laughed about it, didn't he, Sara Jane?" Doug said, glancing from the knife pointed in his face to me. "They all had a big laugh about it. I bet Aunt Greta laughed the loudest."

"I don't have time for this," she said, bored. "I've changed my mind. Shoot him."

Lou put the knife away and lifted the .44. I lunged, but Ugly did, too, ramming the shotgun deep into my stomach. I gasped, struggling to remain on my feet, and then the same shotgun was aimed at my head. Lou moved the pistol to Doug's forehead, saying, "Harry is *my* friend. You didn't even *know* him."

"Knew him and loved him," Doug said, in a tone that was flooded with the truth. "He's dead. Our friend is dead. All that's left of him . . ."

"Do it, Louis," Greta said, lighting a cigarette. "Now."

"Is this," Doug said, pulling back his sleeve.

Lou's brow furrowed, seeing the dog collar with *Harry* etched in bronze resting on Doug's wrist. For a second, he looked like my little brother again, the one who was uncertain to the point of fear about walking into the first day of pre-school. His gun hand began to tremble.

"Louis," Greta said, almost a sigh, "it was just a damn dog."

"We're Rispolis, Lou," I said. "We stick together—"

"Even when we're not together," he said quietly, turning, eyes pinned to mine.

"Filthy little dog." Fireplug chuckled. "Who *cares* if it's dead?"

"I do," Lou said, and he turned and fired twice into Fireplug's chest, knocking him off his feet, the Russian dead before he hit the floor. And then the room was a contained whirlwind as Ugly shot at Lou, ripping a hole in his arm, and Greta put her gun on me while another explosion echoed through the bakery. And then all was still and quiet.

Lou bicycled on the floor, writhing in pain.

Doug stood against the wall, face ashen, chest heaving.

My mom held Fireplug's shotgun, both barrels smoking. Ugly examined the hole in his stomach and said, "I'm . . . dead," before collapsing in a pile.

With a clatter, my mom dropped the rifle. "He shot Lou," she whispered.

"I'll shoot your daughter if anyone—!" Greta screamed, grabbing me by the hair, reminding me of Elzy, and I hammered my skull into her mouth. She stumbled toward the window as the back of her head crunched into the neon sign.

What followed was disgusting and riveting, anchoring me to the floor.

First came the *pop* of glass tubing breaking and then the *hiss* of scalding neon, and then Greta's otherworldly shriek as her hair smoked and her skin sizzled like bacon in a hot pan. She lunged away from the window, retaining the presence of mind to point the gun at me, her other hand pressed to her head. "My beautiful . . . *hair*," she rasped. Her shaking fingers uncurled and I gasped, seeing the reflection in the window—a screaming Rispoli *R* seared into her flesh. She flung herself at me, punching the gun barrel into my cheek, screaming, "Dead. You're *all dead*!"

"You'll never find ultimate power," I said. "It will die with me." The stench of melted skin and hair assaulted my nose, my guts, but didn't make me half as sick as the unhinged look she flung at my mom, Lou, and Doug. "Kill them and you'll have to kill me, too," I said. "The only thing that will get me out of this bakery is a coroner."

She jerked me in Doug's direction and said, "Follow us. I *dare* you."

"Doug," I grunted, as Greta yanked me by the hair, "go." He looked at her and back at me, nodding. "Lou's arm—get the drugs out of him . . . both of them."

"Turn. Walk," she said, and I did, gun in my spine, out the door and down the sidewalk. She shoved me across the seat of a cargo van, into the driver's side. "Steer this thing anywhere other than directly to ultimate power and I will blow your brains out," she said, cradling the back of her head. I dared a glance, saw moisture in her eyes, and she screamed, "Watch the road!" To herself, as if I wasn't there, she mumbled, "Damn you Rispolis all the way to hell."

Cursing us wasn't necessary.

I sped toward the Green Mill thinking of my parents, Lou, poor Uncle Buddy.

We'd all been in hell for a long, long time.

30

WHEN IT COMES TO A BUSINESS, ESPECIALLY A bar, owners tend to lock the back door in a way that could withstand military invasion. No one ever really thinks that a break-in will occur in the front, in broad daylight, where anyone could witness it.

It was four o'clock on a normal Friday afternoon.

I had to be at the Gray Line subway stop in precisely one hour and three minutes.

Greta and I stood outside the Green Mill, which didn't open until six.

People milled around on the sidewalk doing what they do in every big city in the world, smoking and spitting, waiting for the bus, pointedly minding their own business. I still had the bent metal clip I'd used in the Willis Tower and I worked quickly, jimmying the lock. No one looked twice. We stepped inside the empty club. A thin wire over the door led to an alarm box, where a tiny red signal was flashing. I knew (from the notebook, of course) that I had only seconds to disable it before a signal was sent to the security company. A quick flick of Doug's lighter burned the wire in two and the signal went dead. I slid it back into my pocket, thanking it for being the luckiest little gadget in the world.

"Hurry," Greta said, gun between my shoulders. I led her behind the bar, looked around, and picked up a small paring knife. Immediately the gun was in my face as she said, "What the hell are you doing?"

"We're going to need it."

"Give it to me," she said, plucking it from my hand.

I slid back the mat and pulled open the trapdoor. The rickety stairway yawned before us, exhaling the mustiness of deep earth. "Watch your step. The stairs are dangerous. Wouldn't want you to fall."

"Shut up," she said, and then we were descending, Greta close behind as I felt my way along the cool wall. We reached the bottom and moved through a short tunnel, the weak glow of the overhead lights I'd left burning visible at the end. Seconds later we entered the enormous room with the igloo-like vault in the middle of the floor. "Is that it?" she asked. I nodded and she pushed me forward. I turned the knob on the heavy brass door and it clicked loudly. As we stepped inside, half a dozen rats skittered in with us. I had time to think, *Antonio and Cleopatra?* before Greta said, "Filthy rodents," and pushed the door shut with an audible click. The rats skulked around the edge of the room as she glanced at the headless corpse of Al Capone, and then at me, eyes tapering to slits. "Where is it?" she said suspiciously.

"Right here." I waved a hand at the white bricks. "Everywhere."

"What do you mean? Where the *hell* is it!"

"Give me the knife and I'll show you."

She paused, and lifted it slowly. "Don't be stupid."

"Been there, done that," I said, and went to the nearest wall. I chipped at it, the paint falling like dry white snow until a coppery yellowness broke through. Greta approached, inspecting it, as I crossed to the opposite wall and did it again. She followed, running her hand over the smooth, cold metal. "The whole thing," I said. "Thousands and thousands of gold bricks. Al Capone's fortune."

Licking her lips, she said, "More. More." I scraped another brick, and another, ten more, thirty more, as Greta stood back, looking up and around the domed room. "My god," she whispered, awestruck, a joker's grin spreading over her face. "*My god!* This is it! Ultimate power!"

"Four billion dollars' worth."

"It's all mine, the biggest score ever," she said, as if she'd just been handed the deed to planet Earth, and turned to me, eyes shining. "I can do anything, go anywhere. I don't need the Outfit, the Russian mob . . . I don't need anyone . . ."

Including me.

A blazing moment of clarity told me how stupid it was to have brought her here. Greta didn't care about revenge, or my servitude, or controlling Chicago—those things were means to an end. Like the purest of criminals, she cared only about money. With ultimate power, she didn't need me any longer.

My second thought—how much better it would've been to die with my family and my best friend. I would never see sunlight again because I was defenseless. Cold fury had no effect on her and the aspirin nullified my internal electricity. I could attack her, but in the enclosed space, she would shoot me down before I threw a punch.

And then I remembered what my old boxing trainer, Willy Williams, had taught me.

Sometimes running from a deadly opponent is the best defense.

Greta was distracted as she scraped at bricks, lost in a golden haze. My final move would not be cold fury or a left hook—it would be a mad dash for the tunnel to the Green Mill. I might not get far, might catch a bullet in the back, but at least I wouldn't die just standing here, waiting for it. Stealthily, I moved toward the door, and with my back against it, found the doorknob.

Except there was no doorknob, only a small handle.

I pulled it, and then once more, with as much strength as I could muster.

It was locked tight.

When Doug and I discovered the vault, the door opened without need of a key since there was no keyhole; we'd turned the knob and it had opened with a *click* that echoed through the subterranean chamber. We entered and left the door ajar, mindful of the need for a hasty escape. When we exited, I closed it, tried it again, and it opened. We couldn't figure out why Al Capone hadn't simply walked out, and why Great-Grandpa Nunzio had taken such care to place the U.N.B 001 key in the notebook, and—

I felt around the cool brass, finding a deeply engraved indentation.

There was no doorknob, just a small handle—but there was a keyhole.

It was a classic Outfit touch, courtesy of Joe Little—a door that unlocked from the outside with a simple twist of the knob, but that locked on the inside when the door was shut. Anyone could enter the vault, but no one could exit, ever, without the key. It was a wickedly ingenious design. If anyone ever found the vault, he'd enter looking for what lay inside, closing the door behind him so as not to be discovered, not realizing until too late that ultimate power was—and my dad's words echoed from a park bench near Lake Michigan, chilling my spine—*a golden trap.* He must've assumed I knew how the lock worked. I didn't then, but I did now.

"So have you figured it out?"

My head snapped up and I saw Greta, red lips parted, moving toward me while twirling the gun on a manicured finger. "What?" I said, swallowing thickly.

"Your fate," she said with a smile, "the one you'll share with your mother and Louis, and that friend." When I didn't answer, she said, "Let me demonstrate," and turned and fired once. The report of the gun was cut by the shrill cry of a gut-shot rat. Its compatriots shrieked in a terror that became rage, skittering protectively around the body, shielding one of their own. Greta blew on the barrel theatrically and swaggered to the middle of the room, lifting her arms like a goddess in her realm. "Screw the Outfit!" she said, turning in a slow, celebratory circle.

As soon as her back was toward me, I fumbled the key from around my neck.

I spun and pushed it into the keyhole but it didn't work. I flipped it over, tried again, and it fit snugly.

I turned quickly, hands behind my back, fingers gripping the key.

"And screw Chicago!" she crowed, turning. She looked at me with a raised eyebrow and nodded peroxided locks at the withered corpse. "Al Capone?"

"Yeah."

She walked toward him, hands on her hips. "Thanks, Alphonse, you dead son of a bitch. You and the rest of your organization underestimated *real* ultimate power—a determined woman. Then again, some of us broads have it and some of us don't," she said. She swiveled her head at me and said, "I guess you learned that the hard way."

"I guess so," I said, turning the key with a cautious thumb and forefinger.

Greta looked back at the dry bones and webby flesh, showing the raw, red *R* burned into her skull. "Hey Al," she said, "let a master criminal tell you what she's going to do with four billion dollars . . ." and in that split second I pushed open the door, slid outside, and jerked it shut behind me, hearing a loud, lovely *click!*

And then it was as silent as a tomb.

Muted behind the heavy door, a small, confused voice said, "Sara Jane?"

There were footsteps, a useless yank on the inside handle, and then the yanking became furious, desperate—and stopped. An Outfit instinct kicked in, and I stepped away just as the firing began, bullets punching heavy brass, causing little metallic bumps to rise on the outside but doing no real damage. When the gun was empty and the ringing faded, Greta said quietly, "What do you want?"

"You can't give it to me. No one can," I spoke to the door. "It disappeared the night my family was taken."

"I'll give you anything," she pleaded. "You can have half . . . no, *all.* You can have *all of the gold*!"

"Say please."

"Please! Please!"

"No thanks. You wanted ultimate power. Now you've got it," I said, slipping the key back around my neck. "Forever."

"Let me out! We were family! *Sara Jane!*" she screeched, as I turned and entered the tunnel. I climbed toward the Green Mill quickly, and had just stepped on the platform and pushed open the trapdoor when the stairway groaned beneath me, followed by a loud splitting of old wood. I scrambled into the Green Mill just as the stairway collapsed, and then the platform did, too, clattering to pieces into the tunnel below. On all fours, staring into the hole, I heard Greta's final, distant words drift up like eddies of graveyard dust.

"You can't leave me here . . . *all alone!*"

I shut the trapdoor and slid the mat into place, knowing that I hadn't.

The term *rat* is used unfairly.

In reality, a rat is a loyal and courageous beast that will do what's necessary to protect its family, always making sure they're safe, cared for, and, especially, well fed.

31

FOR SOMEONE WHO'D SPENT THE DAY BEING assaulted, had nearly been shot several times, was reunited with her lost mother and brother, and had sealed away her worst enemy in middle earth, I was, not surprisingly, running a little late.

It was 5:01 p.m. when I locked the front door of the Green Mill behind me.

The Lawrence Avenue El station, where I'd ride the Gray Line subway to the sit-down, was just across the street. I hurried over the concrete knowing that ultimate power and its occupants lay beneath my feet. Greta and Al Capone—roommates for eternity.

As I crossed the boulevard, a flash of light caught my eye.

A rainstorm was looming, making it darker than usual for that time of day. I reached the sidewalk, looked up, and spotted a beam of light. It had come from the south, sweeping dark clouds as if sending a signal, just like—

"A beacon," I whispered.

There was no other proof than the assurance of my gut that it had come from Doug, shining it from the Bird Cage Club. What was he trying to tell me—that he'd gotten my mom and Lou there safely, to be careful and find my way home? I looked up at it once more before rushing into the station. My instructions had been clear—locate the Capone Door that led to a secret platform and be waiting there on the dot at 5:03 p.m. I had two minutes. Reverse commuters, people arriving back on the North Side early from work, were already pushing through the turnstiles. I looked around the station, eyeing the Chicago Transit Authority logo—CTA—emblazoned on a wall. It was large and visible, in the middle of everything, but that *C* had to be the Capone Door. I went to it, casually leaned against it, and—nothing. I tried again, this time turning and pushing on it, not caring if anyone was watching. Same result, nothing. I glanced at the cashier, who was watching me. She shook her head in a bored, just-another-crazy-at-the-train-station way and went back to work.

A digital clock suspended from the ceiling clicked to 5:02.

I looked around anxiously, stalking through the station, elbowing people in a hurry, and glanced into a dark corner. Squatting in a shadow like a small, abandoned house was a crusty, flyspecked soda machine. I moved toward it, reading its name—FizzyCola—a weird brand that I'd never heard of. A person would have to be as thirsty as if he'd crossed the Sahara barefooted to buy a FizzyCola, and I carefully pressed the raised *C*. The face of the machine opened and I stepped inside to a stairway so narrow my shoulders brushed the walls. I descended as quickly as possible, hearing the whistle of an approaching train. The wooden platform was there, I could see it, and I leaped the last few steps, landing like Spider-Man on my feet and fingertips as the single steel subway car shuddered to a stop. It was empty, not even a conductor. The doors slid open. I brushed myself off and stepped aboard, and it barreled away before I sat down. The train took fast corners, dipping and falling. I tried to orient myself, deciding finally that I was traveling east, which gave me pause. Like all great cities, Chicago is a water town. The Chicago River cuts through the metropolis, snaking north, south, and west, all the way to suburbia.

The only thing east of the city was Lake Michigan.

How could I be traveling toward that great inland sea?

There was no one to answer the question and nothing to do but wait.

Thinking of the golden vault, I touched the key around my neck; I'd never know how Great-Grandpa Nunzio acquired it. Did he use cold fury to make Capone give it up, and then order the gangster to sit inside forever? Had he somehow lifted it from Capone and snuck out, closing the door behind him, like me? Either way, the letter he'd left for Grandpa Enzo beneath the notebook's back cover made it clear—he'd hidden the key for future Rispolis, suspecting that history might repeat itself. Another psychopath would come along, wreaking havoc while seeking the power of a magnificent fortune. When it happened, Nunzio wanted his family to be prepared.

Fortunately, in those last crucial seconds, I was.

What I was wholly unprepared to do was name a new boss.

My deal with Greta had been entombed with her.

The rules called for me to name either VP of Money or Muscle, of course, but I'd effectively erased Tyler's chance of ever holding the position, and Knuckles—if I named him boss, I was sure he'd never again meet me face-to-face without someone, or a bank of closed-circuit cameras, watching. I'd used cold fury on him in the past. The devious old killer would not allow it to happen once he was boss. I thought of the beacon, yearning to follow it safely home, but it was a fantasy, no help to me now. With a sigh, I stared at my reflection in the train window and reviewed my options.

I could name someone boss, anyone, and offer him four billion dollars in exchange for allowing my family and me to go free.

But I'd tried that with Greta, who was as untrustworthy as any thug in the Outfit, and I had no doubt it would restart the entire tragic cycle. Plus, the stairs had collapsed; it would be nearly impossible to reach the vault. Even if the new boss believed it existed, even if he was patient enough for me to lead him there, he'd take the gold, break the deal, and shackle me to my duty. It was also possible Greta would still be alive. That would be a little tough to explain.

We could run for it. I'd name a boss, shake his hand with a promise of loyalty, go back to the Bird Cage Club, and pack up.

Another fantasy. Lou and my mom were broken, physically and mentally. Making an escape required time, planning, and a significant amount of money. I'd been paid as counselor-at-large, but not nearly enough to disappear without a trace. Besides, it still wouldn't assure our freedom. Lucky had it said it plainly—no one walks away. I knew from my tenure as counselor that even when someone tried, the Outfit was unusually talented at tracking down defectors and their families and making sure they never walked anywhere again.

The train began to rise quickly from the tunnel. Watching beads of water stutter along the cool windowpane, I thought of the three generations of Rispoli men, willing participants in the organization, and how their involvement had infected our lives.

I was the opposite of a willing participant.

"I'm a prisoner," I said aloud, the words making me feel as lonely as I'd ever felt.

With no other thought than hearing his voice, I dialed Max's number.

Two short rings and he said, "Hello?"

The normalcy of the question, the clear, steady tone of his voice, made my heart swell with remorse, love, and loss. I pictured him in the bright L.A. sunshine, curly brown hair flopping over an eye, holding the phone in one hand while Vampire Girl held the other. I didn't care. I just wanted him to say hello once more before I hung up.

Instead, he said, "I know it's you."

I froze, mouth open, silent.

"Sara Jane," he said. "Come on. Those calls . . . I could feel it was you."

Whatever wall I'd built between us came tumbling down. "Max." I sighed.

"There you are," he said, and I could hear the smile in his words.

For a few minutes we talked about nothing. *Where was he?* Between classes. *Where was I?* On the train. *How's school?* He had three weeks until holiday break, but I'd finished early (actually, forever). *Are you seeing anyone?* He was, but not seriously, she was too clingy. *And me?* I'd gone on one date but it didn't work out—I'd turned around and headed home.

"I can't believe it's only been a month," he said.

"It seems like longer," I said, and then, "Max. It—the way it ended up between us. What you said in your letter. There are so many things I should've told you."

"Yeah, you should've. Why didn't you?" he asked.

"Because," I said. "I just couldn't, okay?"

"No, not okay. It was answers like that one that broke us up."

"I know. You were so patient," I said.

"That was my mistake. But the rest is on you," Max said, and then he was silent. He wasn't angry or accusatory; he was just speaking the truth, and I bit my lip, unsure how to answer. "By the way," he said, the smile back in his voice, "I'm a totally impatient asshole now. So thanks for that."

"You're welcome," I said.

"Can you tell me those things?"

"I'm about to get off the train," I said, feeling it slow down. "I have this really important meeting. But I want to tell you, Max. I will tell you, someday."

"Someday . . . ," he said.

"I promise," I said, as the train shuddered to a stop.

"Okay, sure," he said quietly. "Call me someday."

I stepped from the train onto a slick stone platform. The subway tunnel was empty and quiet, cut by the sound of the dripping ceiling. A painted hand pointed up a flight of stairs that clung to a brick wall. A sign affixed to the wall read MEMBERS ONLY—NO EXCEPTIONS.

Smoothing and retwisting my hair into a ponytail, wiping the grime and sweat of the terrible day from my face, I started up the stairs. Through the wall along which I climbed, in the guts of the building, a muted exhalation sounded, over and over again, of water being pulled in and pushed out. The stairs ended at an outdoor walkway where I could smell the clean, fishy scent of the lake. I stepped outside, peering across glassy water at the faraway city. Looking around at the enormous round brick structure upon which I stood, and which squatted miles from shore in Lake Michigan, I knew exactly where I was: Water Intake Island, the largest pumping station and one of the most isolated spots in Chicago. The train had carried me beneath the vast inland sea.

"Counselor Rispoli," a voice rumbled, sounding like *Rizbooli*. I turned to the stern, gray presence who'd been the gateway to Lucky at the Algren Hotel. He shifted an AK-47, and said, "This way." We climbed another set of stairs to the large, circular lighthouse sitting atop the pumping station like the second layer of a wedding cake. Pausing outside double doors, he appraised me coolly and then pushed them open, followed me inside, and bolted them behind us.

We entered a high-ceilinged room, also built of brick.

Hundreds of rank-and-file members crammed the space, some sitting, some milling about, others in murmuring groups beneath hovering clouds of cigarette smoke. They consisted of young and old men of every body shape and size. The only common themes among them were being armed (they trusted no one) and anonymity. They were dressed to blend in with the general population, looking like a quiet neighbor, a reliable mechanic, or a friendly plumber, since that's what they were on the surface. In reality they were enforcers and hit men, drug dealers, pimps, counterfeiters, and thieves, one life a façade, the other operating in the underworld. There was not a man present who would not slit a throat for a dime. They were evil wrapped in skin and hair, two legs, two arms, and a head, and all of them were staring at me now.

A dais stood in the middle of the room.

I climbed it with the stern gray presence behind me, and stared back.

The rank and file crowded forward like the audience at a concert. Tyler and Knuckles occupied opposite ends of the front row where everyone could see them. I scanned the room, spotting no crimson lenses or goggles. Tyler had done as ordered, bruised and bandaged but with chin held high— my most ardent supporter. Knuckles sat in his wheelchair, hat off, thin hair combed greasily across his skull. Now and then, one of his men would lean in and whisper, and the old killer would grin confidently, striving to look like a leader of men. My decision would be announced, and then enforced with cold fury.

The answer came to me then in the blink of an eye.

When I blinked mine, I would have the entire Outfit under my control.

They would stare at me because it was the rule—because they wanted to be led.

I'd killed human beings to survive and protect my family. If it was justified, what was the difference between two or three, or a thousand? I could command them to stand still, not make a move as I went man to man, using their own weapons. Or even better, I could order them to kill themselves. Blood would flow on Water Intake Island. It would swirl and mix into Lake Michigan and my family's greatest sin, its greatest threat, would wash away forever.

Looking at the rapt crowd, I heard my dad's voice speaking to me again: *There's a line. There's always a line . . .*

This was it—mass murder that would lead me across an abyss.

I'd be free of the Outfit but lose myself forever. I could already feel it. Alive on the outside but dead on the inside, smothered beneath a thousand souls.

Other words came back to me, Peek-a-Boo Schwartz in a glass dome whispering that the only way to destroy the Outfit was: *Like cancer . . . from the inside out.*

A sudden realization stretched before me, filled with six months of fear that the Outfit would discover my dad was missing and assume he'd gone to the Feds as a rat. In that moment—feeling the danger, tasting the peril—I knew exactly who should be boss.

Someone who would betray the rank and file.

Conspire with the Feds to kill the Outfit from the inside out.

Become the queen of all rats.

"The new boss of the Outfit," I said, as the flame flickered and burned, lighting the room with a cold, blue glow," . . . is me."

EPILOGUE

MY NAME IS SARA JANE RISPOLI.

I've kept a journal since I was a freshman in high school. From the night my family disappeared, it has had little to do with my life as a student.

That's okay. I don't attend school anymore.

Instead I wake early in the morning, before the sun has risen over the large body of water right outside my windows. With the tile floor cool on my feet, I walk silently first to one room, and then to another.

My mother talks in her sleep.

Sometimes she begs unseen phantoms for mercy. Other times she speaks to my dad, comforting him—reassuring him that I'll save them all. If her dreams are too intense, I'll rouse her gently. She'll blink into the shadows, seeing me, remembering that she's safe. I will ask her if she's okay and she'll touch my cheek. Better every day, she'll say, and *finchè c'è vita c'è speranza.*

Where there's life there's hope.

I adjust her blankets, stroke her soft hair that's now gone gray, and leave her in peace.

Lou does not talk.

He sleeps so quietly, so deeply buried in his mind, that I lean close to make sure he's breathing. His chest rises and falls without pause. The drugs have nearly cleared his body. The gunshot wound to his arm has healed well. My little brother grows stronger each day, finding more and more of his lost identity.

A day doesn't begin or end until I'm sure they're okay. Even though we're all together, I think about them—worry about them—constantly.

Old habits die hard.

Forming new ones is harder.

There are times, sitting on the white beach, listening to nothing but the crash of waves, when I don't know what to do with myself. No one's chasing me. There's no one to chase. Indolence is the best feeling in the world. I hope I can get used to it.

I'm trying to get used to not living in Chicago, too.

We traded it three months ago, my mom, Lou, and me, for an island.

Isla Ángel de la Guarda—Guardian Angel Island—on the Sea of Cortez.

My parents bought the villa when they were planning our escape. I think about my dad whenever I look at the cool, blue water—how proud he would be of the deal that I made, and how relieved that my term as boss was the shortest in Outfit history.

It never would've happened without Doug.

Days after I assumed the role, he accompanied me to Bal-moral Avenue to help prepare for my mom and my brother's return. We checked lights and locks, and descended to the basement to inspect the furnace. It was there that he noticed bricks in the wall that did not quite match the rest—ten in all—painted an odd shade of red. He chipped at the wall, revealing white paint, scraped more, and a faint yellow glow winked out at us.

My dad had been cautious during those five years of plan-ning our escape.

He'd removed nearly ten million dollars' worth of gold, two bricks at a time, more than enough for us to flee Chicago.

Not nearly enough bricks to ever allow Greta to flee the vault.

Soon after, I called my first sit-down as boss. Peek-a-Boo arrived early, looking around Club Molasses, saying how she'd danced there in the old days.

My pitch was simple.

I would name her boss.

She would allow us to leave Chicago and never hunt us down. She would open Outfit coffers—full to the brim since the elimination of the Russian mob—and give me cash for the gold bricks, no questions asked. I ended by assuring her that even without a counselor-at-large and cold fury, the Outfit would fall in line behind her. After I'd gone, it would exist under her command. Peek-a-Boo nodded with hard eyes that understood. Even now, I'm unsure if I needed to use cold fury to make her agree, but I did. Her worst fear was one I understood well—a woman at the mercy of brutal men who wanted to kill her for who she was and what she knew. My hope in naming her boss was that she'd use her newfound power to punish those same men, Outfit style, every chance she got.

My second sit-down was my last.

Outfit members reconvened on Water Intake Island. They stared at me obediently as I made Peek-a-Boo their leader with a blink of my eyes, and not a single enforcer, pimp, or pickpocket objected. I informed them that the office of counselor-at-large was now defunct, never to be restored, but that they would obey Peek-a-Boo's judgment in every dispute without question—they would obey her every *order* without question.

I wasn't blinded by gender.

I knew I'd handed over the Outfit to a person who would pursue its insatiable appetite for money in just as brutal a fashion as Lucky had. With a woman in charge, it might not be business as usual—Peek-a-Boo might indeed punish some of those men who had threatened her—but it would be close.

I didn't care.

Outfit business had never been mine. I was in the business of saving my family. As far as being queen rat, if it was a choice between that and freedom, it was no choice at all. After I named Peek-a-Boo boss, I left without a look back.

I didn't want to waste a single minute killing the Outfit from the inside out.

I'd done enough killing.

I wanted to live.

Now I'm on the beach, nearly finished writing for today. I have other things to do. First on the list is to make an overdue phone call. I have a lot of things to tell Max.

Today is someday.

Second is to pick up Doug at the airport.

In the beginning, he stayed for a week, maybe longer, and then returned to Chicago, but this time he's staying for good. He knows that at some point his mom will finally notice he's gone, but he doesn't care. We lost my dad, he's irreplaceable, but we gained Doug. We're friends and partners, and now he's joined a family that loves him.

He's going to get his GED and then pursue film school. As he said recently, he has a great idea for a movie about a girl, organized crime, and Chicago.

I have no doubt that when my family is accustomed to our new life, my mom will insist that Lou and I resume our education, as well. That sort of normalcy, the continuity of things left undone—I crave it. And now here she comes with my brother, Lou holding her arm, both walking slowly but steadily. The olive hue of my mom's skin has returned under the warm Mexican sun. My brother is becoming his inquisitive self again, consuming a steady stream of books as the days pass.

Harry's following behind them, dancing in the sand.

I just flipped through the journal, skimming the secrets I recorded from the notebook. I considered throwing it into the Sea of Cortez when it's full—to exorcise it, like I'm trying to do with the past half year of my life—and watch it float away.

Except.

Those secrets, old and new, saved my life, and Lou's and my mom's.

The Outfit taught me to prepare for every bad situation and to think through every wicked scenario. So I'll record my last thought for now, scratching the pen across paper:

I'll keep the journal, just in case . . .

ACKNOWLEDGMENTS

I OWE A DEBT OF GRATITUDE TO THE CITY OF Chicago for its mythology, the filthy yet fascinating story of the Outfit; the smart, resilient women who inspired Sara Jane Rispoli (there have been many), and family and friends who have been a constant source of encouragement. Sincere thanks to Jason Anthony at LMQ, agent extraordinaire, and to Stacey Barney, an editor who knows a good story when she reads it. And, finally, never last and far from least, Laura, always my first and best audience of one.